RODEOLA

THE WINTER COWBOY'S INDIAN SUMMER

Don Manning

"Rodeola" by Don Manning. First published in 2008 as "The Indian Summer of Bronco Billy."

ISBN 978-1-947532-20-5 (softcover); 978-1-947532-21-2 (hardcover).

Published 2015, 2017, 2024 Virtualbookworm Publishing P.O. Box 9949, College Station, TX, 77842, US.

TABLE OF CONTENTS

PART ONE

At precisely six a.m., the radio alarm sprang to life, filling the air with the sounds of George Strait singing "Amarillo by Morning." The bulky form lying prone in the king-size bed stirred heavily under the covers; and then, with what appeared to be great effort, slowly rose to a sitting position. The man remained motionless for a moment, holding his head in his hands, when he heard a knock at the door.

"Billy?" a female voice called from the hallway. "Get decent...I'm comin' in." Immediately thereupon a squat, elderly woman entered and walked directly across the room to open the heavy light-blocking drapes that covered a bank of windows lined against the far wall. A gentle golden glow flooded through the windows, illuminating the face of the large man sitting upright on the bed. It was a strong face that radiated a quality of fierce character, a face that was, even at his advanced age, still reminiscent of the handsome young man he once had been. "Rise and shine, darlin'," the pudgy little woman said with a good-natured smile. "You got a really big day ahead of you today."

"Maggie, I'm gettin' too old for this."

1

"Nonsense," she said, making a scornful gesture. "You're just gettin' better and better." The woman went to the closet and picked out some clothes, which she draped over a large chair near the windows. "Now, here's your uniform of the day, and you'd best be movin' along. I'll have breakfast on the table in about an hour."

"What time is that reporter supposed to be here?"

"You told him to be here at eight sharp because you're goin' over to the research center to meet with Dr. Keeler at nine."

"Oh, yeah. Okay. I'll be along soon."

Maggie's face took on a more somber appearance. "And I guess I'd better go ahead and tell you...Jenny's decided to leave us and go back to her husband. She's gonna help me with the mornin' chores, and he's s'posed to pick her up around noon."

The old man looked perplexed. "You've gotta be kiddin' me."

"No," she said, shaking her head. "She's already packed 'er bags."

Billy ran his fingers through his thick gray hair in a gesture of frustration. "Crazy girl." He gave a large sigh. "Okay. Let me get cleaned up, and I'll be down. Maybe I can talk some sense into her."

Maggie took her leave, and the old man forced himself to his feet. With painful effort, he stood up and shuffled uncertainly toward the bathroom. Suddenly his body made a convulsive seizure and he clutched at his chest, softly moaning, "Oh, God, help me...help me, Lord" ... The old man braced himself on the large chair beside the window until the pain subsided, and then he proceeded unsteadily into the bathroom. Holding on to the edge of the sink, he stared at his ashen-gray face in the mirror with an expression of sadness, shaking his head in a gesture of hopeless resignation. In the background, the radio announcer droned on in a homey Texas drawl:

... *"and our local weather continues to be unseasonably warm. Today's high is expected to reach ninety degrees by three p.m., with overnight lows in the mid-seventies. Whoo-ee! This Indian Summer weather pattern is really some'n else ain't it? And here's the good news, all you podnuhs out there in Braddock country— the weatherman says this balmy pattern shows no signs of abating any time soon. So enjoy it while you can, friends—winter will be here soon enough. But in the meantime, let's play some good ol' country music to go with this great weather we're havin'. Here's the late, great Buck Owens"*
...

"Indian Summer," Billy muttered aloud at the image in the mirror. "If only it could be" ...

When he had completed his morning preparations, the old man came out of the bathroom, standing tall and erect, his broad athletic shoulders square, apparently having fully recovered from his seizure. He stepped out of his large bedroom and walked down a long carpeted hallway, then went down a spacious staircase that descended gracefully to the floor below. Walking briskly through a large dining room, he followed another short hallway to a large kitchen area at the back of the house. As he entered the room, a young woman who was working at the sink turned to greet him.

"Good morning, Reverend Braddock," she said with a smile. "We're just waitin' for the biscuits to get done."

Braddock walked across the kitchen and hugged her. "Jenny, Jenny, Jenny—only the angels themselves should have the right to be so beautiful this early in the morning. When I get out of bed in the morning and see that radiant smile of yours, I always think of diamonds sparklin' in the sunlight." He planted a fatherly kiss on her forehead. "Where's Maggie?"

"Oh...she just stepped out. She'll be right back."

"I know you don't normally like to eat breakfast, Jenny, but today I want you to set an extra place here at the kitchen table with Maggie and me. I understand today's a special day for you, and I want you to have a good meal before you leave us."

Jenny blushed slightly and averted her crystal-blue eyes. "She told you."

"She did," he answered.

There was an uncomfortable moment of silence, and she said, "I know you don't think it's the right thing to do, Brother Braddock, but he's my husband...I mean, he really needs me. And I know he's sorry for what he did. Really, he is. You know...it's like...I'm so grateful for everything you've done for me, but" ...

"Jenny"—he began with a scolding glance, then thought better of what he was about to say. "Well, I don't want to lecture you. It's not my place to come between a man and his wife. It's just that I'm concerned for your safety."

"I know," she said, touching his arm in a gentle gesture of reassurance. "But I feel sure he's learned his lesson."

"I pray to God he has. But always remember you can call me, day or night, if you need me. Nobody in this town has more influence with the law-enforcement community than I do. If he hurts you again" ...

"He won't," she interrupted. "I'm sure of it."

The oven alarm went off just as Maggie re-entered the room. She opened the oven door and slid the pan out. "Okay," she said. "Looks like the biscuits are done to a turn. Breakfast is served."

The silver van roared down the two-lane asphalt highway that unraveled like an ugly childish scrawl across the desert terrain. Inside the van, the heavy-set man in the passenger seat squinted toward the horizon and complained, "Two days of this—scrub brush and sand...and when you need a break in the monotony, you can try sand and scrub brush. And it goes on forever and ever." He raised his eyes toward Heaven. "How long, O Lord? How long?"

"It's just over that rise in the distance," the driver replied. "I figure we'll be at the church-house door just about right on time—assuming, of course, we don't find a way to get lost in Braddock, Texas."

"I doubt that'll happen unless we run across a beer joint between here and there," the passenger replied with a grin. "What's the population—about fourteen?"

"It's a small town, but there's a lot of money there. I figure it's fairly good size."

"Be honest, Steve—you think we're on a wild goose chase? I heard this Braddock guy told the BBC to get lost when they tried to interview him a few years back. The BBC!"

"That's true. But this guy's an odd duck. They say he's a really humble guy—no-shit dedicated to his mission. And not too fond of publicity. That's why he told the BBC to take a hike. He's kinda like Howard Hughes, but not quite as rich or quite as crazy. And I know for a fact he doesn't need any publicity to hustle contributions for his church—he's already richer than God. I'm just hopin' we can figure out an angle he'll buy into, so he'll go along with us. If we can persuade 'im to cooperate, this won't be just another documentary—I guarantee you we'll find someone to back us on a national theatrical release. I'm talkin' Michael Moore-style success here. None of that small-time PBS, gospel-channel crap—we're goin' *big time!*"

"I like the sound of that," the passenger agreed.

The driver shrugged. "Well...this Reverend William Braddock ain't necessarily the greatest story ever told, but he's definitely up there in the rankings. You were too drunk last night, so I didn't tell you I talked to Artie while you were out."

"Really? What'd he have to say?"

"He said they're findin' a lot of rare footage in various archives," Steve replied. "Some of the film has the original Bill Braddock—the preacher's daddy—bringin' in his first gusher back in the Twenties. Can you believe that?"

"He had someone *filmin'* it?" Bobby asked in a tone of disbelief.

"Apparently so, strange as it seems."

"Man, he musta been *real* confident he was gonna strike oil."

"I guess so," Steve replied. "Plus, they've found quite a bit of stuff on the preacher himself, back when he was playin' a lotta sports. Artie said it's some killer stuff. He's all excited." As they neared the top of the rise, Steve said, "By the way, Bobby—get the camera ready. We're gonna wanta film our approach as we come into town."

Bobby immediately complied, crawling to the back of the van to retrieve his equipment. He hurried back to the front seat, making a preliminary check to be sure all systems were go, and held his camera at the ready in his lap. When they topped the hill, the City of Braddock lay in full view below them, a waffle-iron grid of square blocks and straight streets bounded on the south and west by oil refineries that loomed like steel cliffs around the edge of town, punctuated by several blazing flare-stack burnoff towers that continuously spewed forth the Eternal Flame of Big Oil Making Big Money. Beyond the refineries, away from the town, white storage tanks dotted the landscape like giant aspirin tablets haphazardly spilled across the desert floor. Besides the oil refineries and a few small multi-story buildings in what was obviously the downtown area, only one other dominant structure was discernible in the distance.

"Look, Bobby—in the foreground to the left—see that big building with the steeple? The green grass all around? See it?"

"I see it," Bobby answered.

"I got money that says that's the Church of the Living God right there. Start rollin' tape."

Bobby focused his camera and began to shoot as they descended the hill. When they reached the outskirts of town, they saw a sign that read:

CITY LIMITS
Braddock, TX
Pop. 32,481

The cameraman focused on the sign as they drove by, but Steve suddenly stopped the van and started turning around. "What are you doing?" Bobby asked, with a startled expression.

"Let's don't miss the forest for the trees. Look at that billboard." A few yards beyond the city limits marker stood a large billboard. The image was old and faded, but it was clearly a rather crude portrait of a football player in full gear, running at full stride. The caption read, "*Welcome to Braddock, Texas!*

*Home of Bronco Billy Braddock! Braddock's First All-
American College Football Player!"* At the bottom of
the billboard were dozens of tumbleweeds piled one
on the other, an accumulation of years, which made
the sign look even more shoddy than the erosion of
time had already achieved. "Yeah," Steve said, with
a look of smug satisfaction, "I'm gonna back up, and
I want you to focus on the city limits sign and then
kinda pan beyond and linger on that billboard.
There's somethin' metaphorical here."

"Like what?"

"Like...I dunno...something like...faded glory,"
Steve thoughtfully intoned as he gazed toward the
timeworn painted image of the young Billy Braddock.

"Can't we do this afterwards?" Bobby asked.
"We've got the rest of the day to prowl around town
and shoot footage."

"I just wanta capture a few first impressions,
okay? That billboard's talkin' to me."

Bobby followed instructions, and then they
continued on their way. Not far inside the city limits,
they came to Glory Road. There was a large sign on
the corner where Glory Road intersected with the
main highway into town:

CHURCH OF THE LIVING GOD
William Davidson Braddock, Pastor
Come, And Be Welcome

An arrow pointing to the left indicated the
direction to follow to find the Church of the Living
God. "Hmm," Steve muttered, "this must be the
place." The driver turned onto Glory Road and
headed toward the church, which towered
majestically seven long blocks away at the end of the
street. All along the avenue, up to where the church
property began, were stately mansions with neatly-
trimmed hedges and lush green lawns that nestled

8

below ancient oaks and graceful old willows. With only the chirping of birds and the steady hum of insects to be heard, a serene, almost ethereal, calm seemed to permeate the entire neighborhood. The two men looked with interest as the van slowly rolled down the tree-lined thoroughfare.

"Wow!" Bobby breathed aloud. "So this is Paradise."

"I smell Old Money," Steve said. "When you think that we were in the middle of a desolate wilderness only a few minutes ago...either this is Paradise, or it's a living testament to the power of God or Money."

"Or a combination of both," Bobby added: "The Almighty Dollar."

When they got to the end of the street, they followed a circular driveway to the front steps of the church, where they saw a big policeman standing beside his cruiser. Steve and Bobby got out of the van, and the officer gave them a cordial greeting:

"Howdy, boys," he said with a welcoming smile. The officer extended his hand. "I'm Police Chief John Wilkins. Are you the reporters?"

"We are. I'm Steve Jackson. This is my cameraman, Bobby Pardo. We're here to interview Reverend Braddock."

"Okay," the police chief nodded. "We just gotta get a few ground rules laid out first."

"Ground rules?" Steve asked with a suspicious glance.

"Right," the police chief nodded. "First of all, you can leave that camera in the van for now."

"But we're doing a documentary here. We need our camera," Steve protested.

Chief Wilkins squared his shoulders. "Well, here's the way I understand it, boys—Reverend Braddock agreed to talk to you first. That's all—just talk. Whether or not you get to do anything at all around here is gonna depend on what the Reverend decides after he talks to you."

"Yeah, but"—Steve tried to object.

The policeman dismissed their objections with a peremptory gesture. "Okay, here's the deal: You can do it your way...which means you and your camera can vacate the premises immediately. Or, you can do it my way...which means you'll forget the camera for now and give yourself a fightin' chance to enlist Reverend Braddock's cooperation. And I'll tell you for your own good—my way is better...that is, if whatever it is you're tryin' to accomplish means anything at all to you."

The two filmmakers exchanged glances, and then looked back at Chief Wilkins, whose firm-set jaw and steely stare convinced them that the demand was non-negotiable. Steve relented with a shrug. "Okay, Chief...we'll do it your way."

"Fine," Wilkins said with a grin. "And you boys will also please empty everything out of your pockets and put it all in the van, and then I'm gonna pat you down, just to make sure you ain't wearin' no wires. If you pass muster, we'll proceed to Reverend Braddock's office." Reluctantly, the two men complied with the order, after which the Chief patted them down thoroughly. Satisfied they were wearing no hidden recording equipment, he said, "I guess that's good enough. Normally, I'd make you bend over and spread your cheeks, but after seein' your faces, I don't think I could handle lookin' at your asses. Besides, I just had breakfast, and I'm just not in the mood to inspect any hippie buttholes this mornin'." He laughed at his own joke, and then motioned for them to get in the police car. "Reverend Braddock's private residence is out behind the church. Hop in."

The Chief drove out of the circular driveway and turned onto a paved road that ran along the edge of the church property. They followed the road a short distance and came to a wrought-iron gate supported by two stone pillars that opened on a large fenced property. Beyond the gate, a panorama of verdant splendor appeared: A lush, green, professionally-landscaped property covered with all sorts of trees, ornamental hedges, bushes and carefully-tended flower beds that made the lawns on Glory Road seem sparse by comparison.

"Now, *this* is Paradise," Steve said, looking at Bobby in the back seat.

"God, I've never seen anything so beautiful," Bobby exclaimed. "There must be a million dollars' worth of landscaping here."

"More than that, I guarantee you," Chief Wilkins said, looking at Bobby in the rearview mirror. "The water for all this plant life comes from a pipeline that was laid by the preacher's daddy at his own expense back in the late Twenties. To this very day, that pipeline brings water to our little town directly from the Rio Grande. That's why you have this beautiful oasis in the middle of the desert. Every time I come here, I tell myself the Garden of Eden itself couldn't-a been much better than this. It's really somethin', ain't it?"

Reverend Braddock's residence was no less impressive. The house was a sprawling two-story Spanish villa, standing in the middle of the ten-acre plot that was William Braddock's private estate. The two reporters, trained by experience to look at everything with a cynic's eye, were visibly impressed.

"Who, in the name of God, woulda thought we'd find something like this out here in the middle of this godforsaken wilderness? It's incredible!" Bobby enthusiastically declared.

"You're right, Chief," Steve agreed. "This really is somethin' else."

Chief Wilkins drove the car around to the back of the house, and stopped in front of a small Spanish-style bungalow that was an appendage to the larger structure. "This is it, boys. Let's go meet the preacher."

The Chief led the way onto the porch and knocked on the door. Presently a large, tall man with a shock of gray hair answered the summons. As the door opened, Chief Wilkins said, "Reverend Braddock, your guests have arrived." The preacher greeted them warmly, invited the group inside, and shook hands as introductions were made all around. Once the preliminaries were completed, the policeman said, "Reverend...if it's okay with you, I'll take my leave now. I got things to do at the office. I mean...I'll stay, if you want me to, but I really need to be gettin' on."

"No, John—that won't be necessary. I'll have Jenny drive 'em back when we're done here."

John Wilkins nodded and took his leave. William Braddock invited the men to sit down, and he took a seat behind the desk. "Okay, gentlemen...so what do we have in mind today?"

"Well, Reverend...like we discussed on the phone...we'd like to do a documentary about your life in general, and your missionary work in particular. We think it's the kind of story that'll interest a broad spectrum of the population in this country and around the world."

"How so?" the preacher asked.

"I mean...well, to illustrate my point, I've gathered a few facts that are all in the public record. May I just mention a few?"

Braddock nodded. "Go ahead."

Steve reached for the notepad he normally carried in his shirt pocket, then apologized, "Uh...I'm sorry, Reverend Braddock. Chief Wilkins made us leave everything back at the van, so I can't mention everything I had written down. But some of the things I remember are...for instance...you're President and CEO of Braddock Oil Company, which is arguably the largest independent oil company in the United States. That's one thing. People are always fascinated by the lifestyles of the rich and famous."

The preacher gave out a scornful snort. "I suspect your prospective audience will find my rich and famous lifestyle something less than fascinating. And I can assure you that I deserve no credit for being rich. That's all my daddy's doing. He was a wildcatter in the days when wildcat oilmen could really strike it rich. William Edward Braddock—everybody called him *Wild Bill*—he was the one who built Braddock Oil—the drilling operations, the refineries, all the subsidiary companies controlled by the corporation...that's all my dad's handiwork. The only credit I deserve is that, after Dad died, I hired competent people to keep the company intact and viable and growing in these ever-changing times. When you start out with the kind of money I inherited, that's really not much of an achievement. The only credit I can claim is that I hired some really smart guys to run the company for me."

"Well, that seems overly modest to me, Reverend," Steve said.

"Not really," he demurred. "Everything I have in this world is due to the efforts of others, startin' with Wild Bill Braddock. I will admit that I have made a few personal decisions I feel pretty good about—but, even then, it all goes back to my daddy's Irish luck and his innate business-savvy."

"Like...what personal decisions are you talking about...that you feel good about?" Steve Jackson inquired.

"Well, for instance, right here in little ol' Braddock, Texas, we have a world-class medical research facility that's run by Dr. Charles Keeler, who—as you probably know—won a Nobel Prize a few years ago for his work in genetic research." The guests nodded their acknowledgment, and he continued, "I'm the one who made the decision to build and fund the center and to hire Dr. Keeler. We have a team of top scientists who are workin' on everything from cures for cancer and Parkinson's and Alzheimer's disease, all the way up to findin' a way to reverse the aging process itself. We're gainin' ground every day on cures for many of the ills that beset mankind. I *will* have to admit I do take some pride in that." He smiled, then added, "I hope not a sinful pride. But if you wanted to talk about the Braddock Institute for Medical Research, I wouldn't have any objections. I'd prob'ly even help you with it."

"I think that's something you *should* be proud of," Steve said reassuringly. "And that's one of the things we're especially hoping to cover in our film."

"I might go along with that," the preacher replied with a nod.

"And, you know, Reverend"—

"Billy," the preacher corrected. "Just call me Billy."

"Well...Billy—I was just going to say that when we were coming into town, we saw a billboard that talked about Bronco Billy Braddock being the town's first All-American football player" ...

Braddock smiled. "That was my daddy's doing—the sign, I mean. He commissioned a local artist to paint it right after I made the Football All-America Team. He was real proud of that. That doggone sign always embarrassed me, but it made my daddy happy, so I didn't complain about it. I've been meaning to have that eyesore torn down, but I just haven't got around to it. Only time I think about it is when I'm drivin' into town from the main highway. Thank God that's the only one he put up."

"Well, from all I've read, you were a really big sports hero back in the day, weren't you? I mean, not just football—you excelled in all kinds of sports."

"Hero? There's only one hero to me—our Lord Jesus Christ. I was only an exceptional physical specimen who inherited the size, speed and skill to excel on the athletic field. That was God's doin', not mine. All I did was put the gifts God gave me to good use—and even at that, with all the blessings I had, not to full use. I was young and arrogant and undisciplined, so a lot of the athletic potential I had was never realized. I'll admit I was pretty good, but I coulda been a lot better if I hadn't been so stupid. As the Scriptures say, 'Foolishness is tied up in the heart of a boy.' And I was the walkin' fulfillment of that scripture. But however good I was, or might have been, I was no hero...not by any stretch of the imagination."

"Even so, there's a whole world of sports fans out there who'd enjoy hearing about it. It's a ready-made market—a *huge* market."

"Mmm-hmm," Braddock intoned in agreement. He got out of the chair. "I wanta show you fellas something. You might get a kick out of this." He walked over to the far wall of the office and pressed a button that opened a series of large cabinets that covered the entire wall. Flipping a switch, he illuminated the glittering contents inside the glass cases that were hidden behind the cabinet doors. There was shelf after shelf of trophies that had been awarded to Billy Braddock for excellence in a wide variety of sports. Included in the collection were an assortment of loving cups and golden statuettes of golfers, batters, basketball players, bowlers and tennis players. In one glass case were silver and gold belt buckles awarded for rodeo events ranging from bull-riding to calf-roping. On other shelves were dozens of trophies and championship belts for achievements in the boxing ring. All in all, it was a truly impressive display, and the light reflecting off the gleaming trophies gave the impression that the entire room was filled with a glittery golden light.

The two reporters involuntarily stood up and walked over to look at the incredible collection. "Wow! It looks like King Tut's tomb!" Bobby Pardo said. "I've never seen anything like this in my life! They've got *whole teams* that don't win this many trophies. Check it out, Steve—All-District, All-Regional,   All-State...baseball,   football, basketball...man, you musta really been somethin', Reverend Braddock."

"Well, like I say...I was pretty good. And because my daddy was rich, I had all the time in the world to pursue any sport I wanted to pursue. For sports like golf and tennis—since I wasn't as naturally gifted in those sports as I was in others—my daddy hired world-class tour pros to teach me. I was good enough to compete in golf and tennis at the high-school level, but they prob'ly woulda smoked me like cheap bacon in the Southwest Conference. But by the time I reached the college level, golf and tennis were off the table as anything but recreational sports for me. I was always best in contact sports, so over time football, basketball and boxing became my major sports activities in college. Plus, I found time to rodeo in the summer months, so baseball kinda fell by the wayside, too. But no matter what sport I chose to try, my daddy made sure I got the best instruction money could buy. In fact, when I got big enough to fight as a heavyweight in the Golden Gloves, Dad paid Joe Louis himself to come to Braddock and teach me the finer points of the sport."

Bobby Pardo gave him an incredulous look. "Joe Louis—the Brown Bomber? *That* Joe Louis?"

Braddock nodded. "That Joe Louis."

"That's incredible! Did you spar with 'im?"

"Yeah, some, but we never went at it full tilt. I can tell you, though—even well past his prime, Joe could throw some heavy leather. I've always wondered what it woulda been like to fight 'im when he was at the top of his game. Even though by the time I met 'im, he was just a shadow of the fighter who knocked out Max Schmeling back in the Thirties, I could still see glimpses of the great champion he once was. I had nothin' but respect for 'im." There was a thoughtful pause, and then he added with a wry grin, "Even so, though...that didn't stop me from thinkin' I woulda beat 'im if I coulda fought 'im in his prime."

"Man!" Bobby exclaimed. "I just can't imagine it—gettin' a chance to spar with Joe Louis! That's one of those memories that last a lifetime."

Braddock nodded in agreement. "Sometimes when I think about the life I've lived, it all seems like a dream." Just for a moment, the old man had a faraway look in his eyes, as if he were gazing across the years to a world gone by. It appeared that he was about to add some poignant thought to his reminiscence; but he paused for a moment, seemed to think better of it, and then abruptly returned to the conversation at hand. "I'll admit that I did have the talent to make all that special tutoring pay off, but Daddy's money made it all possible. If I'd-a been a poor boy, I mighta been forced to go to work while I was still in high school, and there wouldn't be a single trophy in this room. This room—this house— even this town—prob'ly wouldn't be here if it hadn't been for Wild Bill Braddock and his wildcat oil company." He made an affirmative nod, then added, "Yes, boys...I was born under a lucky star, and I remind myself of that fact every day to keep things in the proper perspective. All that I am, or ever was—

17

or ever will be—I owe to my daddy's luck and the grace of God. And all of this stuff"—he gestured toward the trophy case— "it's just stuff. I know that. I keep it for the memories. And there were some great memories." There was a wistful quality in his voice as he repeated, "Great memories." Then he added with a shrug, "And there's also some memories I'm not too proud of—bad memories. In the end, I guess it was the bad memories...the shameful memories... that finally drove me to seek my salvation with God."

"Why'd they call you Bronco Billy?" Steve Jackson inquired, trying to keep Braddock's thoughts focused on his sports career.

The old man smiled. "The local high-school football team is called the Braddock Broncos. I made All-State fullback the year we won the State Championship. The local paper started callin' me that, and the name followed me to SMU, where I was All-Southwest Conference two years in a row, and then I was First Team All-American my Senior year...and after that I was stuck with it. To this day, people still call me that sometimes."

"Well, look here, Reverend"—Steve began, then corrected himself— "I mean...Billy—I don't have my notes with me, but I know there's a lot more here that would be really interesting to the general public. Didn't you win some kinda professional rodeo championship one year?"

Billy Braddock nodded. "Yeah. I was out of college by then, and rodeo was the only sports activity I was pursuing. So I had all the time in the world to stay focused and get really good. And that year, I won the title of World Champion All-Around Cowboy. That was a great moment in my life, it really was. Of all the things I ever did, I think that made my daddy the proudest. He was just about as Texas as you can get, but he wasn't much of a cowboy— never had the time. When I won that title, it was kinda like the cowboy genes he always knew he had in his blood were proven out by his son. There's an old saying among breeders: 'Blood will tell.' So when I won that title, I think that convinced my daddy he coulda been a champion rodeo rider himself, if he'd only had the time."

"Hey, look, Steve"—Bobby Pardo suddenly interjected, as he stood looking into the trophy cases— "National Golden Gloves Heavyweight Champion!"

Braddock smiled. "I worked harder for that trophy than I did any of the others. Knowin' what I had to go through to win it, I guess it's my favorite. Dad was proud of that, too, but the rodeo championship I won later on was the biggest thing to him."

Steve Jackson shook his head in awe. "Man, it just gets better and better! This is such a *great story*. I just wish you'd let us be the ones to tell it."

The preacher seemed to tire of the conversation. "Let's get to the point, fellas. I have to be somewhere at nine. What, exactly, is your proposal?"

"Well, here's what we have in mind: We wanta show people a portrait of a man...a gifted athlete, the son of a rich oil baron, a man who had all the temptations of the world laid out at his feet"—

"Kinda like Jesus bein' offered all the kingdoms of the world by the Devil," Braddock helpfully suggested.

"Exactly," Jackson enthusiastically agreed. "And, like Jesus, you rejected the Devil and all his worldly temptations. You chose the path of righteousness and service to God and fellow-man. I mean...don't you see—that's a great story! This could be inspirational to millions of people around the world. That's the kinda story we wanta tell— something that will inform and inspire."

Braddock directed a sardonic smile at Steve Jackson. "So you'd paint me as a cross between Jesus Junior and Mother Teresa...something like that? Maybe throw in a little Mahatma Gandhi for good measure?"

Jackson shook his head. "Oh, no, Reverend...Billy...I didn't mean it like that."

The preacher made a dismissive gesture. "I'm just kidding." He pondered for a moment, then shook his head. "No. That wouldn't be a true story. And I'm not the least bit interested in self-glorification, anyway. The truth is, I *did* wallow in the ways of the World, the Flesh, and the Devil. In my youth, I was rotten in just about every sense of the word. That's why I wasn't as good an athlete as I coulda been. I was a party boy, a drunk, a pothead, a liar, a cheat, a skirt-chaser...the works. If it was bad, I probably tried it. It was only later in life that I realized the error of my ways—much later. And not until I had piled up a whole mountain of sin that I still feel a need to atone for."

"That's so much the better," Steve exclaimed. Then, realizing what he'd said, he added, "I mean...not that that's *good*, but it's *better*, in the sense that it makes for a great tale of Sin and Redemption, how the Love of God overcame the Temptations of the Devil in the life of one man who had every reason and excuse for doin' just the opposite. You know...it gives the whole story that dramatic tension that makes for the best stories of any kind—not to mention that it offers hope of salvation for all sinners, no matter what their station in life. You know what I mean?"

Braddock nodded. "I do. But I'm not sure I wanta go into all that stuff. A lot of the local people know about my crazy past—and they've mostly forgiven me my sins—but I'm not sure I'd like to air my dirty laundry for all the world to see."

"We don't have to go into sleazy detail, or anything like that. It's just one of those things we'd mention in passing as we go on to the bigger story—the research center, the ministry, the good works you do for others. That's the real story. I swear, Reverend—I mean, Billy—there's an epic tale here. We just wanta be the ones to tell it. And if you'll agree to help us, we'll see to it the story's told the way you want it told."

Billy Braddock stared thoughtfully toward the ceiling, gently drumming his fingertips together. At length, he said, "You know, I would have become a public figure with or without all the sports, and with or without having built this church. Bein' born the son of Wild Bill Braddock guaranteed I'd come into the public eye once I inherited the family fortune. After my days in the sports world, I did become a much more private person for awhile. Then Dad died suddenly of a heart attack, and I was back on the public radar screen. Now I can't get away from it. But this church I started—it wasn't for personal recognition. I've got more of that than I want. I paid out of my own pocket to build this church for the glory of God, to do my part in spreading the good news of salvation to all who would listen. I've focused my efforts here, in this community, because the people of Braddock are like my family. If I wanted to, I have the money to launch fifty satellites into orbit and broadcast simultaneously all over the world, twenty-four hours a day. But that's not for me. I don't trust Big Religion. From what I've seen, it seems like Big Religion leads to Big Money, leads to Big Politics, leads to False Religion." He shrugged. "That's my opinion, anyway. I believe gettin' your money, your politics and your religion all mixed up into a Devil's stew can have serious and lasting consequences. I try to avoid that."

There was an expectant hush, and then Steve Jackson said, "*Wow*, Billy. You're the first preacher I ever heard say *that*."

Braddock nodded in agreement. "Well, that's not just my personal opinion. That comes straight out of the Bible. In the Book of James—Chapter Four, Verse Four, if you wanta read it yourself—it states very clearly that friendship with the world is enmity with God." He paused a moment to let that thought sink in, then continued, "Of course, there's a lot of politically involved preachers who would vehemently disagree with me on that—and they certainly have the right to their opinion, no matter how wrong they are. But, in any case, I have no desire to become a political wolf in religious sheep's-clothing. Nor do I wanta be a household name. To the extent that I can be a private man, I am. I'm content to serve as Christ's earthly surrogate to shepherd the little flock of believers who attend my church right here in Braddock, Texas. I've been happy doing that for the past twenty years. For me, that's as noble a calling as I could ever seek in this life."

Fearing that Braddock was about to talk himself out of cooperating with them, Steve's face took on a look of anxiety. "But, listen, Reverend"—

The preacher silenced him with an imperious gesture. "Let me finish. Certain circumstances in my life have persuaded me at least to consider the idea of entertaining your proposal. That's why I allowed you to stop by this morning—I'm willing to consider the idea. Are you boys gonna be in town for a few days?"

"Well, yeah. We were gonna shoot some footage, maybe do some interviews," Jackson replied.

"So you're gonna do your film, with or without me," the preacher said in a tone of disapproval.

Steve smiled sheepishly. "Well, like I say...Billy...we'd rather do it with you. But Bobby and I are just the hired help. The bosses in Houston make the final decisions on what gets done, and what doesn't get done."

"And if I decide not to participate—what? You figure they'll wanna work up a hatchet job? That always sells tickets."

"No, I swear," Steve protested, raising his hands in a placating gesture. "That's the absolute furthest thing from our mind. It won't be like that, with or without your cooperation. We don't wanta tear you down, Billy. We're big fans of yours—me, Bobby, everybody at company headquarters in Houston—we're *all* fans. You've done so many great things—*any one* of which would have provided a lifetime of bragging rights for most people. But you—you've got a *whole long list* of incredible accomplishments to your credit. We respect that. And anything we do will be a whole lot better if you'll help us. Plus, it'll give you some personal input into the direction of the overall production, so we can put the proper emphasis on the things you want to highlight. You know what I mean? Having you to help us develop the project would be beneficial for all of us."

An expectant hush fell over the room as Billy Braddock took a moment to weigh his options. At length he said, "I'll tell you what, boys—give me some time to contemplate this matter, and get back to me."

"Like...how much time?"

"I have to be in Houston for a company board meeting next week, so call my secretary here at the church on Saturday morning. Maybe I'll have a definitive answer for you by then."

"Oh, thanks, Billy," Steve said with a sigh of relief. "I swear we'll do you justice. Our intentions are only the best."

Braddock raised a warning finger. "I didn't say I'll do it. I said I'll think about it." He pushed a button on his phone. "Maggie?"

A voice responded, "Yes?"

"Send Jenny to my office. I need her to give these gentlemen a ride back to their car."

"She'll be right there."

The old man leaned back in his chair. "I wanta thank you for comin' by. If you're still in town Sunday morning, I hope you'll attend our service. We're non-denominational and totally egalitarian. Our congregation includes some of the richest citizens in Braddock, and some of the poorest, and some of everything in between. Come, and be welcome—that's our motto."

"We just might do that," Steve Jackson said with a nod.

About that time, a beautiful young woman with a thick mane of flame-red hair entered the room. Upon being confronted by this vision of beauty, both men sat bolt upright in their chairs. "Ah, Jenny," the preacher said with a smile, "this is Steve and Bobby. They're reporters. Gentlemen...meet Jenny. She's one of our congregation." The two visitors nodded greetings as Jenny trained her sparkling blue eyes on them. "She's been helping us around the church the past few weeks." He turned back toward the young woman. "Will you give these fellas a ride back to their car? Take the van. The keys are in the ignition."

"I'd be happy to," she replied with a smile.

The two visitors stood up, thanked Braddock for his time, and assured him that they would be calling back on Saturday. They exchanged goodbyes, and Jenny escorted the men out the door. Braddock walked over to the window, staring thoughtfully after them, as Jenny led the men toward the garage. He then returned to the trophy cases and, closing the cabinets, made ready to leave for the research center.

Inside the animal research laboratory of the Braddock Institute, Dr. Charles Keeler was completing the examination of his star subject, a chimpanzee named Kimba. Listening to the chimp's heartbeat, he smiled with satisfaction and gave the animal a warm hug. "You're doing great, old boy. A miracle of modern science." He nodded to his assistant. "That'll be all for now. You can take Kimba back to his apartment." Then, he added, "No—on second thought, just put him in one of these lab cages for now. I want Billy Braddock to have a look at him." Removing his rubber gloves and throwing them in the waste dispenser, Dr. Keeler left the lab and went to his office, where he closed the door and sat down at his desk. He pushed a button on the intercom and said, "Suellen, let me know as soon as Reverend Braddock arrives."

"I think I see his car comin' now," came the response.

"Fine. Show 'im directly to my office."

Dr. Keeler rose from the chair and opened a file cabinet. Sorting through the files, he removed some manila folders and returned to his desk. Adjusting his spectacles, he thumbed through the folders, opening them to certain pages and spreading them out across the desktop. As he was in the process of this activity, there came a light knock at the door, and Billy Braddock strode into the room. Dr. Keeler rose from the chair and walked over to greet him with a handshake.

"Billy...so good to see you again."

"I hope you don't mean that sarcastically, Charles—but even if you do, it's okay. I know I've been a thorn in your side lately."

"I'm always glad to see you, Billy," Keeler responded.

Without waiting for an invitation, Braddock sat down in the large lounge chair that stood in front of the desk. "We need to talk."

"Certainly," the doctor nodded, returning to his chair. "I assume it's about the state of our progress."

"That's right. I have urgent reasons to wanna know where you are at this point."

"Is your health getting worse, Billy?"

Braddock dismissed the question with a wave of his hand. "I'm not here to talk about me. I'm here to find out how far you've gotten on that genetic regeneration stuff you've been doin'."

"Well, I've laid out some files here, if you'd like to read them—or I can print out some copies of the pertinent information for you to read at your leisure."

The big man shook his head. "I don't wanna read. I probably wouldn't understand it, anyway. Just cut to the chase and tell me what you've got."

The doctor nodded. "Let's go to the lab. A picture is worth a thousand words." Leading the way, Dr. Keeler took Braddock back to the animal laboratory, where Kimba waited in his cage. Upon entering the room, Dr. Keeler pointed to the chimp. "This little guy here represents the pinnacle of our achievement so far. Say hello to your benefactor, Kimba."

The chimp grinned and stuck his fingers through the cage toward Billy Braddock. "Hey, boy," Braddock said, touching fingers with the chimp. He smiled toward Keeler. "Cute little fella."

"How old do you think he might be?" asked the doctor.

Braddock shrugged. "I wouldn't have a clue."

"You don't wanna guess?"

"I don't know anything about apes, Charles."

The doctor smiled. "He's fifty-five years old."

"Fifty-five!" Braddock exclaimed. "Good Lord! I didn't know they lived that long."

"Oh, they live longer than that. But it's not his chronological age that makes him so important—it's how old he is at the cellular level, since we tried our formula on him, that makes him so special. Physiologically, he's about ten or twelve years old. We injected our serum into his bloodstream about six months ago, and in that short time, he's made a remarkable transformation. Kimba had a number of physical problems associated with the aging process when we decided to use him as a test subject. Some of those problems were induced over a period of time by our own scientists, to approximate the sorts of problems humans develop from bad dietary habits and other things, like smoking and drinking."

"Whadda ya mean?"

"I mean Kimba was a two-pack-a day smoker and a hopeless drunk."

Braddock looked doubtful. "You're kiddin'." He grinned. "Did 'e cuss, too?"

"That, I can't say for sure, but he did get on a mean drunk every now and then. But, several years ago, we taught 'im to smoke and drink, and we fed him all the worst kinds of food—burgers, fries, sugary foods, trans-fats, saturated fats...all that really bad stuff people put in their bodies."

"What are you guys doin' here—practicin' animal cruelty?"

"It was necessary for our research," Dr. Keeler said with a serious look. "We had to do it. But the thing is that by the time we decided to use the formula on him, he was in really bad shape. He had everything from arthritis to cardiovascular disease. His prognosis was that he would likely be dead within a year or two, give or take. You can never say for sure. But now, in an incredibly short time, his heart is ticking like a Swiss watch, the plaque in his arteries is gone, his skin tone has improved, the arthritis is completely cured, he's leaner and more muscular...he's even regained his sexual potency. Even his gray hair has changed color."

"Unbelievable," Braddock said.

Keeler nodded in agreement. "You know, as a scientist, I'm loath to use the word *miracle,* but this is as close to a miracle as I ever thought I would see in my lifetime. I feel honored to have worked with such a team of scientists as we have here. I don't want to inspire any false hope, but we may be getting very near to finally discovering the real Fountain of Youth."

"Yeah, but it's for monkeys, right? A fountain of youth for monkeys."

"No, it's more than that," Keeler disagreed. "We've tried this same formula on mice, rats, dogs, cats—even pigs and horses. We've had some level of success on every species we've experimented with, and we've never had to adjust the formula to make it specific to any species. All it takes is a single injection of the serum, and that sets some internal genetic process into motion that seems to reverse the aging process...at least to some extent. We don't know what the mechanism is, or how it works, but we're working every day to try to understand it."

"Why do you have to know *how* it works, as long as it works?" Braddock asked.

"Well...a lot of reasons. One is that our having an understanding of what's going on inside the body might enable us to assess the risks for human application—which, of course, is what we ultimately hope to achieve."

"I can understand that."

"And we may be much closer to human application than even we suspect at this point."

"Why do you say that?"

"Because, amongst the many peculiar things about this serum is that, the higher we go up the evolutionary chain, the better the results we've been getting—whether it's a mouse, a dog, a pig, a horse—it doesn't matter—the serum works...at least to some extent. Of course, some results have been better than others. In our experiments with the mice, they changed very quickly, but the changes lasted only a month or so, then they went back to their former state, and ultimately they died about the time they would have died, anyway. Some of the other animals are still physiologically younger than their chronological age, but they're deteriorating back into old age—some species faster than others. There's a lot of uncertainty involved here." He returned his gaze to the chimpanzee. "But Kimba here...he's exceeded all of our expectations by quantum factors. Since we're just in the early stages of this particular experiment, we don't have any idea how long the effects of the drug will last, but considering the magnitude of the changes he's undergone in such a short period of time...it's just mind-boggling, Billy."

"*His flesh shall be fresher than a child's. He shall return to the days of his youth,*" Braddock uttered in a low tone.

"What's that?"

"It's a scripture—Job, Chapter Thirty-Three." The preacher looked thoughtful. "You said you're gettin' better results the higher you go up on the evolutionary chain. So when are you gonna go to the top of the ladder—try it on a human being?"

"There's a lot more research to be done before we can even think about trying this on a human subject. Conservatively, I would say maybe ten or fifteen years, at best. We have to understand what's happening, and what the potential negative ramifications of the treatment might be, before we start trying this out on people."

"I haven't got ten or fifteen years left, Doc."

"I understand that. But this isn't a Saturday-night crapshoot, Billy. We have to approach this very carefully."

"Lemme look at that serum."

"What for?" the doctor asked.

"I just wanna see it."

Dr. Keeler went to a large refrigerator at the back of the laboratory. The door was locked, and he used his key to gain entry. Reaching into the refrigerator, he took out a small vial labeled *FYX-14*. He handed the vial to Billy Braddock.

"What's this *FYX-14* stand for?"

"Just a name we gave it—Fountain of Youth Experiment, fourteenth version of the formula. We tried several earlier variations before we discovered this particular combination of ingredients."

The preacher eyed the vial. "Just looks like clear water to me."

"Well, trust me—you wouldn't want to drink this stuff to quench your thirst. It might make you sick to your stomach." The doctor retrieved the vial and replaced it in the refrigerator, carefully taking the time to lock the door. "Believe me, Billy...I know you want immediate results, but that's not how the scientific process works. Just take my word for it that we're light-years ahead of any studies of this kind that have ever been done. If we eventually succeed"—he paused, measuring his words— "I can't even contemplate the possibilities of what it might mean to the future of mankind."

"That's all well and good," Braddock replied. "But in the meantime, I'm dying *now*. Suppose I were to volunteer to be your guinea pig?"

Dr. Keeler shook his head firmly. "No. Absolutely not. It's too early in the experiment, and much too dangerous to your personal safety. I wouldn't even consider it."

A look of suppressed anger was creeping into Braddock's face. "Dr. Keeler, I'm paying you a million dollars a year to run this clinic...not to mention an unlimited expense account and all the other perks that come with this job. And you can't do this for me?"

The doctor made a gesture of supplication. "Billy, if I could, you know I would. But I'm not doing you any favor by killin' you."

"You don't know if it'd kill me or not." Braddock protested.

"That's right—I don't. But the odds are good that it would, and it's a chance I'm not willing to take." The doctor placed a hand on Braddock's large shoulder. "Billy, it's more than ethical considerations, more than the potential legal ramifications for me if I were to go along with you and the serum were to kill you. It's *you*, Billy. You're a great asset to so many people—myself included. You're not just an employer to me—I consider you to be a friend, and I'd rather have my friend sick and alive than cold and dead. That's the bottom line, as far as I'm concerned. I just won't do it."

The subtle hint of anger in Billy Braddock's eyes faded. "I understand, Charles. It's just that I know, the way things are going, I won't make it much further down the road. The signs are all there."

"Well, Billy, why don't you slow down a little? Delegate some responsibility to that assistant pastor, Joe"—Keeler paused, unable to remember the name.

"Lindsey," Braddock said. "Joe Lindsey."

"Yeah—Joe Lindsey. He seems like a really fine young man, Billy. Why don't you let him carry more of the load for you? I know you love your work, but you're actually hastening your demise by doing so many things that you could delegate. You do it in your secular business—why not your church, too?"

"I...I guess it's because the church means so much to me. I've done so many things in my life, but for me...this church is my true life's work. All the rest is nothing compared to that. It's just hard to delegate such an important task to anyone. I know Joe is as fine a man as you could find anywhere. That's why I chose 'im. About the only gift I have left is that I can size up a man extremely well. That's why you're running this institute—you were the best man for the job."

"Well, that's very nice of you to say."

The old man shook his head. "No, it's not nice. It's just true. But it's really hard for a shepherd to allow someone else to watch his flock."

Sensing the anguish in the old man, and hoping to reassure him, Keeler said, "Look, Billy—we may have some kind of breakthrough tomorrow that'll change everything. I promise you...I'll keep you posted on everything of any significance that we find. In the meantime, why don't you take a little time for yourself, let Joe earn his keep around there—maybe even take a little vacation?"

"There's just so much" ... Braddock didn't complete the thought. Abruptly, he extended his hand. "Thanks for your time, Charles." He turned and walked out of the office, heading toward the exit. Charles Keeler called after him:

"Think about what I said, Billy! Take some time for yourself!"

Braddock offered no reply. Keeler noted that the form silhouetted in the hallway against the bright sunlight beyond the glass doors seemed stooped, not as square and erect as it had been when the preacher had arrived. He felt sad for the old man.

"I wish I could help you, Billy," he muttered to himself. "I really do" ...

When he returned to the house, Billy Braddock was obviously out of sorts. As soon as he walked through the door, Maggie recognized the look. She laid down the dust-cloth she was using to polish the furniture and walked over to meet him as he passed through the living room. Placing her hand gently on his forearm, she asked, "What's wrong, Billy?"

"There's nothin' wrong, Maggie. Nothin' at all," he answered.

"Billy, we've known each other too long for that. Did somethin' happen at the Institute?"

He paused. "I don't wanta talk about it right now," he said with a scowl. "Is Jenny still here?"

"She's vacuuming upstairs, I think."

"Ask her to come to my office. I'm gonna try one more time to see if I can talk some sense into her. The last thing in the world she needs is to go back to that wife-beatin' slob of a husband."

"I'll go get her."

Returning to his office, Braddock picked up the phone and placed a call. After a few rings, he heard a voice on the other end of the line: "Good morning. This is Pastor Lindsey."

"Joe! How are you today?"

"I'm fine, Billy. How 'bout yourself?"

"As good as can be expected, I guess. Listen, Joe...I hate to put you on the spot, but I need you to do me a favor."

"Sure, anything."

"I'm supposed to attend a Lions Club luncheon at eleven today, and I can't make it. Could you fill in for me?"

"You mean, just go somewhere and eat? Yeah, I can do that real good. I'll do you proud."

Braddock gave a small chuckle. "Actually, it's a little more than that. I'm s'posed to give a little speech afterwards, somethin' along the lines of leadership and service to others—you know...throw in a few scriptures to underscore the point and wrap it up with some sort of exhortation to keep up the good work. You can handle that, can't you?"

Lindsey's voice sounded doubtful. "This is pretty short notice, Billy. I don't know if I can really do that good a job on just a few minutes' notice."

"I have faith in you, Joe. You'll do just fine. But you'd better start scribbling notes right now. You need to be there by eleven a.m."

"Okay, Billy. I'll try."

"Oh, before I let you go—we need to have a little talk real soon. I've got some ideas about expanding your ministerial duties."

"I'd like that," Joe said.

"Well, for now, get over to the Lions Club and inspire the crowd. I'll see you later."

The old man rested his elbows on the desktop and covered his face with his hands. He remained that way for a few moments, then raised his head and stared toward the window. Alone, with no one present, there was a quality of weariness in his face that he usually managed to hide when others were around. He picked up the Bible he always kept on the desktop and opened it to Psalms:

> *"As for man, his days are as grass: as a flower of the field, so he flourisheth. For the wind passeth over it, and it is gone; and the place thereof shall know it no more. But the mercy of the Lord is from everlasting to everlasting"* ...

Braddock laid the open Bible down on the desk. "All is vanity," he muttered. About that time, Jenny entered the office from the side door. He turned around in his chair and smiled. "Jenny. Come in. Have a seat over there on the couch."

"I'm sorry I took so long. Shooter called me on the cell phone to tell me he's comin' by early. They're havin' a big biker convention near Austin this weekend, and he wants to get started early."

Braddock walked over to sit beside her on the couch. "Actually, it's Shooter I wanted to talk to you about."

"I know what you're gonna say, Reverend Braddock."

"No," he said, holding up his hands, "hear me out." He paused a moment, collecting his thoughts, and continued: "Jenny...it's not just your safety that concerns me, although that's my biggest concern. But even if he never beats you again...you've gotta think about the choice you're making. He's been in jail...God knows how many times...for everything from burglary to drug possession. All of his friends are just like him—dope-fiends, rapists, robbers, pimps, thieves...I'm sure some murderers, too. That's not the kind of environment you need to be in. Don't you see that? It's like the Apostle Paul said: '*Bad associations spoil useful habits.*' That's in First Corinthians, Chapter Fifteen, if you'd like to look it up."

"No, that's okay. I know what you're saying, but"—

"Please—just let me finish," Braddock interposed. "I mean this for your own good." He paused, and then continued, "It's just a matter of time till his evil influence affects you, too. You can't wallow with the hogs and not get dirty. I tried it when I was younger, and I couldn't do it. Nobody can. To

35

be decent and *stay* decent, you need to have decent influences around you."

"But he swears he's changed."

"And to celebrate his change, he's goin' to a bikers' convention? Does that sound like a changed man?" She shook her head in response, and Braddock went on: "He can no more change what he is than a leopard can change his spots." The preacher paused thoughtfully, then amended his statement: "Maybe I'm being too harsh in my assessment. Actually, I should say he *could* change, but a person has to really want to change before that change can ever begin to happen. And I have no reason to believe he has the slightest desire to be any way other than what he's always been—and you know what that is better than I do." Realizing from her expression that his words were to no avail, he tried another tactic. "Look, Jenny—you're...how old?"

"Twenty-one."

"Twenty-one," Braddock repeated. "Did you graduate from high-school?"

"No. I dropped out in the tenth grade."

The preacher laid his big paw on the girl's tiny hand. "Look here—what if I were to tell you that I'll see to it you get a high-school diploma or a GED, and then I'll pay your way to college, so you'll have an education that'll allow you to live a good life the rest of your life, without having to rely on some wife-beatin' criminal to help you survive? I'll even see to it that you get some kind of good-paying job at one of the companies owned by the Braddock Corporation. All you have to do is stay here long enough for me to help you get on your feet."

"You'd do that for me?" she asked in surprise.

"Of course I would," he declared. "Do you remember that first day I saw you at our church shelter for battered women?"

"Yes," she said with a smile. "I thought you were the kindest man I had ever met in my life."

"Really?" he said, in mild surprise. "That's interesting, because I thought you were the prettiest girl I'd ever seen in *my* life. And when I saw that beautiful face, and how that animal had blacked your eye and busted your lips, all those bruises on your neck and arms...I'll tell you—it made my blood boil. And I told myself right then and there that if I never did any good for anybody else the rest of my life, I was goin' to help you get out of that situation. And I meant that. And I mean it now." He threw up his hands. "That's why it baffles me that you'd even consider going back into that sinkhole of darkness. I'm offerin' you a chance you may never have again."

Her eyes welled with tears. "That's so nice of you."

Billy Braddock put his arm around her. "Listen, I know what kind of upbringing you had. It's a testimony to your strength of character that you're not a dopehead street prostitute by now. I didn't know your daddy that well, but I knew *his* daddy *all too well*. Did you know I once beat your grandpa to a bloody pulp in a beer joint one Saturday night?"

She laughed. "You? I just can't see you as a barroom brawler."

"Well, I was, at one time. And that loudmouth bully Wes Fairfield deserved every punch I laid on his no-good head that night. And you know what started it all?"

"What?"

"He was slappin' your grandmother around because she'd caught him with another woman in the bar that night. He started beatin' her right there in front of everybody, and it made me mad, so I dragged him out to the parkin' lot and beat the hell out of 'im."

"He was a mean old man," she agreed.

"And this is a small town, so everybody knows somethin' about everybody else, and I knew just enough about your daddy to know that he was just like his old man—sorry. And your mother...well, I think we both know what she was."

"Oh, yeah," she said with a knowing look. "I knew how she made her money when my daddy wasn't around. It was a really bad time. That's why I married Shooter in tenth grade—I just had to get away from all that craziness."

"Yeah, but you *didn't*," Braddock remonstrated. "You married Shooter Dobbins, and went right back into the situation you tried to run away from."

Jenny nodded. "You're right. It's just that" ... Her voice trailed off.

"What?" the old man persisted.

"I know I messed up by gettin' involved with Shooter. But I still have feelings. I mean, even if I wanted to get away from him, you just don't know how crazy he is. If I don't go with him, he's liable to do anything. He might burn down the church, or even kill you and Maggie. I wouldn't want that. I'd never forgive myself if somethin' like that happened because of me."

"Jenny"—

At that moment, Jenny's cell phone rang. She checked the caller ID and said, "It's Shooter." Answering the call, she said, "Hello. Yes, I'm ready. No, don't do that. Just wait right there. I'll just be a few minutes. I have to get my bags, Shooter. Okay...I'll be there as quick as I can." Returning the phone to her purse, she said, "He's parked on the highway, by Glory Road. He sounds like he's high."

"Changed man, huh? This is what you're goin' back to?" the preacher said with a look of disgust. "Jenny, I beg you—don't do this."

She stood up. "I have to."

"Then let me drive you to the highway, at least."

"That's okay...Maggie said she'd do it."

"I wanta do it," Braddock insisted.

She paused thoughtfully. "Well, if you want to." She shrugged, then added, "But I need to tell you— if he's high, he might try t' start somethin' with you. He says it was you that had him put in jail for beatin' me."

"It *was* me," Braddock said. "And I'll do it again, if he starts any trouble."

She seemed to calculate for a moment. "He's crazy, but I don't think he's that crazy. He knows how much pull you have with the police department." She gestured toward the garage. "My suitcases are already sittin' out by the van."

Once they were in the garage, Billy Braddock loaded Jenny's two small suitcases into the van, and then he got behind the wheel and pulled out of the driveway. Driving across the estate at a leisurely pace, he said, "We're sure gonna miss you around here, Jenny. You've really brightened the place up since you arrived."

"I'll miss you, too," she replied. "This is such a wonderful place, and you guys are all such wonderful people. Except for the stress I've been goin' through because of my situation with Shooter, it's been one of the best times I've ever had."

"Well, as long as I'm still alive and kickin', just know you're welcome back if this thing doesn't work out."

"You're too nice," she said, patting his arm.

As they got to the end of Glory Road, they could see Shooter's van sitting beside the highway. Braddock made a sharp turn and parked the church van head-to-head with the other vehicle. "I'll get your bags for you," he said.

"That's okay. I'll do it."

"No, I insist."

Jenny gave him an anxious look. "Well...could you wait here, just a minute?" Seeing Braddock's hesitant expression, she gently pleaded, "Please?"

He nodded his assent. "Sure. Go ahead."

Getting out of the van, she walked over to the driver's side of Shooter's vehicle. He was tilting back a quart-bottle of beer when she got to the window. "Shooter, Reverend Braddock's gonna bring my suitcases to the van, so don't start any trouble, okay?"

"You tell that old snitchin' sonofabitch to keep his ass away from my van. You bring the bags yourself."

"Shooter, please"—

He angrily interrupted, "Just get the goddamn bags, bitch! And hurry up—we gotta drive all the way to Austin. There's a big party already started, and we're missin' it. Go get the fuckin' bags, and hurry up about it!"

"You've been smokin' crack, haven't you?" she protested. "Look at your eyes—I know good and well you're cracked up! You told me you've changed!"

"Now, look—I don't need this goddamn shit. Get your stuff, and come on."

Her eyes were sparkling with rage. "You know what, Shooter? Just go to hell. I'm not goin' with you. You'll be beatin' on me again before we get twenty miles down the road, and I'm not goin' through this again."

"All right, that's it"—

Shooter Dobbins set the beer bottle down in the floorboard and got out of the van. At almost the same moment, Billy Braddock opened the door of the church van, moving as quickly as his old body would allow. Jenny turned to run away, but she only managed a few steps before Shooter caught her by the hair.

"Shooter, don't!" she screamed.

He pulled her head back, spun her around and slapped her with the back of his meaty hand, applying the full force of his two-hundred-and-forty-pound bulk. She fell to the ground like a stone, blood trickling out the corner of her mouth.

"You dirty coward!" Braddock roared as he charged toward his bulky opponent. "I'll tear your head off!"

The long-haired biker laughed. "Yeah, sure you will."

The old man tried to hit the burly biker in the face, but the punch was so slow that Shooter easily sidestepped out of harm's way. Laughing wildly, and realizing that his antagonist was helpless to do him any harm, Shooter started dancing around in an old-fashioned bare-knuckles posture, taunting his adversary: "C'mon, old man—hit me! Tear my head off! I dare you!" Doing his best to oblige, Braddock aimed a mighty blow at Shooter's chin, but the younger man easily dodged again, laughing as the old man stumbled forward of his own momentum. "Aw, you can do better than that, can't you? I heard you was a big bad football player back in the day." He pointed to his chin. "C'mon—put one right here on my chin. Right here." Again the old man made a futile attempt to land a punch on the bully, and Shooter again laughed in derision. "You crazy old fool—you gotta be kiddin' me." Then, having grown tired of the sport, the biker's face turned serious. "Okay, you old sonofabitch—the fun's over. It's time for you to pay for your sins. Court's in session, and *here come da judge.*"

The fat biker aimed a roundhouse right at Braddock's chin, sending the old man's false teeth flying out of his mouth and leveling him to the ground. Dazed, Billy Braddock rolled side to side in the dirt on the shoulder of the road, instinctively trying to regain his feet, aware of little more than the excruciating pain that followed as Shooter kicked him several times in the ribs and kidneys. For a few moments, the old man lapsed into a state of semi-consciousness, and then he opened his eyes again. As if looking through a fog, the last thing Braddock saw before he completely lost consciousness was Shooter dragging Jenny to her feet by the hair and throwing her into the van. Raising one arm toward the vehicle as it roared away, he moaned, "Jenny...don't go...Jenny" ... Suddenly there was a pain in his chest as if he were being squeezed in a giant vise, and then the sunlight faded to black.

"Hey—check out the bank," Bobby Pardo said as they drove past a six-story building covered with black marble and decorated with a metallic trim that glittered like real gold. "Braddock Bank and Trust—you think that's *our* Braddock, or is that just the geographical Braddock, Texas?"

"You see the symbolism? Black marble with gold trim? Black gold...Texas tea? I'll lay odds he's the main shareholder in this bank," Steve Jackson answered. "Just in case, I'm gonna drive back around. I want you to get some really good shots of that building. That's one expensive piece of work right there, and it's got Billy Braddock written all over it."

"You wanna go inside?"

"No. Let's just do exteriors for now. I don't wanna torpedo the whole deal by gettin' obtrusive. We go in there with a camera, and if he *is* affiliated with this bank, he'll hear about it within ten minutes, I guarantee you—and that might spook 'im. We have to play our cards right, or he's gonna back out."

"How do you figure 'im?" Bobby asked as he squinted through the camera lens. "Is he some kinda tinhorn dictator in a small town, or is he a repentant sinner turned livin' saint?"

Jackson shook his head. "I dunno. He doesn't fit any mold I'm aware of. He built that beautiful church with his own money, but he hasn't really tried to capitalize and go national or global, like those money-hungry televangelists do. The way he was talkin', he hates preachers who grab for political influence, like some of those guys who turn their so-called religious platform into an advertisement for their favorite political parties. He said he doesn't trust Big Religion—how many times are you gonna hear *any* preacher say that?"

"Prob'ly once."

"That's just it—I'm tellin' myself I gotta keep an open mind on this subject. I mean, I don't trust people with money—period. Maybe it's my proletarian upbringing, but, in my personal experience, they're all a buncha sorry bastards. I never met one of the wealthy bastards I thought was worth a plug nickel. But this guy...I dunno...he seems different somehow. I came here prepared to hate 'im, but the journalist in me is sayin' to give the guy a chance."

"Well, all that football and basketball and boxin' and rodeoin' he did—that wasn't powder-puff heroics with Biff and Chip and Buzzy on the Ivy League circuit. That was Southwest Conference, and Golden Gloves, and professional rodeo cowboys. That's blue collar, and ghetto, and dirt-poor until you hit the big money—if you ever do. And that's what makes it even tougher—poor people fightin' each other for the money and the glory. The way I see it, this guy was born with a silver spoon in 'is ass, but his interest in sports put him up close and personal with a lot of people who didn't have a pot to piss in. That's bound to change your perspective, don't you think?"

"You'd think," Steve agreed with a nod of the head.

"Maybe he learned somethin' that a guy like...oh, say for instance...George Bush Junior...never had the slightest desire to find out," Bobby Pardo suggested.

"How so?" Jackson asked.

"Well, you heard that Bush Junior was a boy cheerleader when he was goin' to school, right?"

Jackson grinned and nodded. "So they say."

"So maybe for Bush and guys like him, it was enough to shake that ass and wave pom-poms with the girls, instead of gettin' down and dirty with all them poor boys with their hairy armpits and sweaty old jockey-straps out there on the football field. The smell mighta curled his pretty nose-hair, or somethin' like that, you know? Plus, he mighta got 'is tender ass kicked real bad. Everybody knows we can't be havin' no shit like that goin' on amongst the hoity-toity class."

"Nah...you're overstatin' the case, Bobby—I think Bush Junior at least played some baseball in high school. Maybe some kinda kickball, too." Jackson suggested. "And I know for sure he plays golf real regular at the country club."

"Well, woo-hoo to you, too, sailor-boy," Bobby replied with a limp-wristed gesture. "Do you think that's really in the same league as fightin' in the Golden Gloves?"

Jackson laughed. "Oh, come on, Bobby—you're just goin' on like that 'cause you don't like the Bush family. But I think I see what you're gettin' at. Maybe there's two classes of rich people—you got your sons-a-riches and then you got your *dirty* sons-a-riches. It's just a matter of siftin' through the bullshit to figure out who's who."

"And that's a *whole lotta bullshit* to sift through," Bobby said, grinning. "But I'll tell you something"— Bobby turned off his camera— "I fought in the Golden Gloves when I was in high-school, and I was up against some really low-level competition. But even at that level, I damn near got beat to death a coupla times. And these guys I was fightin' were *chumps*! So do you know how good you have to be to win a *national title*?"

"I can't even imagine," Steve said as he maneuvered his way out of the downtown area. "I spent my whole sports career ridin' the pine. But I *was* injured once durin' a game when I was slidin' down the bench and got a splinter in my ass."

Bobby chuckled. "I don't doubt that. But seriously—you gotta be a *whole lot* damn good to win a national title in the Golden Gloves. And tough— *real* damn tough. Just seein' that championship belt in that trophy case gave me a lot o' respect for the guy. That's a big deal, no shit."

Noticing that Bobby had put his camera in his lap, Steve asked, "Are you done shootin'?"

"Yeah, man. I been hung over all day. Let's go find the hair-o'-the-dog somewhere."

"I saw a pretty decent-lookin' bar at the edge of town, over by refinery row."

"Yeah, I saw that, too," Bobby said. "Let's check it out."

Steve Jackson drove toward the outskirts of town, following the road that went by all the refineries and chemical plants that ringed two sides of the city. Arriving at their destination, Steve said to Bobby, "Hmm—they call this place 'The Country Club.' I tell you what—bring your camera inside with you, okay?"

"What for?" Bobby asked.

"You know how these redneck bars are. If there's a tush-hog in there looking for trouble, he might try t' start shit, just because we're strangers in town. But if he sees our camera, the odds are he'll think twice before he gets 'is back up and starts fuckin' with us. We might be important people. That'll slow the bastard down."

"Sounds like you know your redneck bars," Bobby grinned.

"I do. I got my ass kicked in a dump like this one night in Amarillo. But also I want you to keep the camera running—be discreet about it—but keep it running, just in case we dig up a few useful little chestnuts of gossip about Reverend Braddock from somebody we might meet in here. It's a small town, and tongues do wag. You never know what somebody might tell you."

"Gotcha," Pardo cheerfully replied. Shouldering his camera, Bobby followed Steve into the establishment. They headed toward the bar, where a pretty blonde was sitting near the cash register. "Hi," Steve said. "We're with DocuTex—an independent film company outta Houston? We're doin' a piece on Braddock, Texas. Do you mind if we take a few pictures?"

The woman was hesitant. "Uh—I'm not sure. I need to call the owner."

"What's your name?" Steve asked.

"Well...it's Sherry. But I need to call the owner, just to be sure it's okay. Could you turn the camera off for just a minute?"

Steve turned to Bobby. "Kill the camera, Bobby. Let Sherry call her boss first. We don't wanna upset these nice people." Bobby set the camera on the bar and pretended to shut if off; but he was careful to keep it running and casually pointed toward the barmaid. Steve said, "While we're waitin'...could we get a coupla whisky rocks?"

"What kind?"

"Whatever," Steve said with a careless motion. "Give us the best you got. We're on an expense account."

The barmaid brought their drinks, then got on the phone to call the owner of the club. She mumbled into the phone for a few seconds, then hung up and walked back over to the reporters. "The boss doesn't want y'all takin' any pictures inside the club. He never heard of your company. But he said he'll be down later and talk to you about it, if you're still here." She smiled apologetically. "It's a privacy thing...you know, the customers, and all."

"Oh, sure," Steve said. "Doesn't look like anybody's here, anyway."

She nodded her agreement. "It's been slow today. But they're about to have the shift change, and then it's gonna get real busy."

Steve looked at Bobby. "Hey, man—I left the credit card in the glove compartment. Could you go get it right quick?"

"Be right back," Bobby said with a cheerful grin.

When Pardo walked away from the bar, Jackson extended his hand toward the barmaid. "I'm Steve Jackson."

"Nice t' meet you," the young woman said with a friendly smile.

"You lived here long, Sherry?"

"All my life."

"Well, could you point us the right direction...you know, kinda let us know some local points of interest?"

She shook her head. "There's not much of anything here. We've got the oil refineries. That's about it. And there's some kind of medical research thing over on the other side of town, but I don't know anything about it, except that it's s'posed t' be a really big deal. Other than that, I don't think you're gonna find much of a story to tell in Braddock, unless you wanta do a piece on who's sleepin' with who when who ain't lookin'. Drinkin', fightin' and fuckin'—that's Braddock, Texas, in a nutshell."

Steve laughed. "Sounds like my kinda town."

Returning from the van, Bobby sat down at the bar and handed Steve the credit card. "Here you go. Drinks on me."

"Thanks," Jackson said, taking the card from Bobby and putting it in his wallet.

"Do you wanna pay as you go, or run a tab?" Sherry asked.

"We'll just run a tab. We're gonna be here awhile."

"By the way," Bobby intoned in a low voice— "there's a cop car buzzin' the parkin' lot like he's trollin' for somethin'. He sure was givin' me the eye."

"We haven't done anything. Don't worry about it."

Bobby shook his head. "I dunno, man—he was really eyeballin' me. I think he was checkin' out our license plate."

"They do that all the time," Sherry said. "It's no big deal."

About that time, a big policeman came through the door. Removing his sunglasses, he strode directly to the bar and stood beside Steve Jackson. Sherry forced a smile and said, "Hello, Bob. Can I get you somethin'?"

"No. I'm on duty. I'm lookin' for Shooter Dobbins. Has he been in here today?"

"He hasn't been here in over a month. The owner permanently barred him from the club after he started that big fight awhile back."

The cop nodded thoughtfully. "Well, if he does come in here, you call the department immediately and tell us, okay?"

"I sure will. What's he done this time?"

"We just wanta talk to 'im." The officer looked directly at the reporters. "You guys new in town?"

"Yeah. We're just doin' some background for a documentary we're plannin' to do. We met Chief Wilkins first thing this mornin', over at the Church of the Living God."

"Oh, yeah. I know who you are." He eyed them closely for a moment, then said, "Well, you boys enjoy your stay." Putting his sunglasses back on, he gave Sherry a parting glance. "You be sure and call us if Shooter shows up."

"I'll do that," she said. The policeman exited the club, and Sherry muttered after him, "Prick."

"I take it you don't like him much," Bobby said.

"I don't like any of these local cops. A buncha assholes. The only thing worse than them is the local slimeballs like that guy he was askin' about, Shooter Dobbins."

"Is he one of the local bad guys?" Jackson asked.

"He thinks he is. He'll end up in the pen someday, if he doesn't get outta town pretty quick. They've got 'im in their sights, and they don't kid around. It's just a matter of time till he draws the short straw—and so much the better, if you ask me. I hate that bastard." She picked up a rag and started wiping the bar. "Did you say you were over at the church today?"

"Yeah. We had an interview with Reverend Braddock."

"You mighta seen Shooter's wife—a cute little redhead named Jenny?"

"Yeah, we did see her," Steve nodded. "She gave us a ride back to our van."

She nodded. "Well...that's Shooter's wife. She's been stayin' over at the church ever since Shooter beat 'er up real bad awhile back."

"Now that's a hottie," Bobby said with a leer.

"She's real sweet," Sherry said. "I just can't understand why she won't divorce that piece of crud and find herself a good man. She could have any man in this town, if she wanted to, but she just stays with that worthless bastard Shooter, no matter how bad he treats 'er. It's a shame."

"And Reverend Braddock just gave her shelter out of the goodness of his heart?"

She gave a little laugh. "I guess so. He's too old to be doin' it out of the lust in his heart."

"Does he do stuff like that all the time?"

"Well...I don't go to church, or anything like that, but he does do a lot of good in this town. He does a lot of charity work."

"Such as?" Jackson asked.

"Well, such as...one Christmas, after my sister's no-good husband ran off and left her, Billy's church people brought clothes and toys for her and the kids, and a turkey dinner with all the trimmings." Tears unexpectedly welled in her eyes, and she wiped them away with a bar napkin. "It was really strange. The church people just showed up all of a sudden. Nobody knows how they found out about the situation she was in, but my sister and her kids were in a really tough spot that year. Me and my mama tried to help out a little, but there wasn't much we could do. And then, all of a sudden, there's Billy Braddock with toys and clothes and food for Christmas like they never had before in their lives." Again she picked up a bar napkin and daubed away the tears that filled her eyes. "That was really sweet."

"That *is* nice," Jackson agreed.

She continued, "Plus—he helped her get a full-time job as a cashier at the drugstore down on Main Street and paid her rent for several months till she could get back on her feet. Never asked for anything in return, and refused to let my sister pay 'im back. And my sister didn't even ask 'im for any help. That was the weird thing about it—she didn't even know 'im. The church people just showed up on Christmas mornin' and started unloadin' presents and groceries. That's how it started. After that, my sister started goin' to Reverend Braddock's church with the kids, and now she never misses a Sunday. Before that, she'd hardly ever been to church in 'er life. So, yeah...Billy Braddock does a lotta good things for this town. I think he's a fine man."

About that time, two of the club regulars came through the door and sat down near the pool tables. "Set 'em up, bartender!" one of them yelled.

"Hey, boys...the usual?"

"Yeah."

Sherry opened a couple of bottles and carried them over to the table. In her absence, Jackson whispered to his cameraman, "Did you get the footage of her tellin' that story?"

"I did," Bobby answered. "If I've got 'er framed up right—and I'm pretty sure I do—it's a gem. That story's sure to make the final cut."

"Great," Steve said, giving his friend a thumbs-up gesture.

Over at the table, Sherry said, "How you guys doin' today?"

"Real good. They ran out of material at the job site, so we got to knock off early—with pay."

"If I'd-a known you guys were comin' early, I'd-a called Jake's Wholesale and told 'em to bring a rush order of extra beer."

The man chuckled appreciatively, then asked, "Did you hear about Billy Braddock?"

"Billy Braddock? We were just talkin' about him. What about 'im?"

"They found 'im lyin' unconscious on the side of the highway awhile ago. My wife works over at the hospital, and she said they got 'im in intensive care."

51

"What happened?" Steve Jackson called to the stranger.

"I don't think they know," came the reply. "Since he was lyin' beside the highway, they think maybe a car hit 'im. That's what my wife said."

Steve and Bobby exchanged urgent looks. Jackson threw a twenty-dollar bill on the counter. "Here you go, Sherry," he said. "Keep the change. And thanks for the memories." He motioned to Bobby, who was draining his glass at a gulp. "Let's go."

Joe Lindsey found Maggie all alone in a private waiting area near the intensive care unit of Braddock Memorial Hospital. As soon as she saw him, she stood up and came toward the door to meet him. She appeared very distraught, and it was obvious that she had been crying. He walked over to her and hugged her. "Maggie! I came as soon as I heard."

"Oh, thank you, Joe," she said, grasping him in a clinging hug. "I'm so glad you're here."

"Have they told you anything?"

She shook her head. "Just that he hasn't regained consciousness. They won't tell me anything else."

"Is he on life support?" Lindsey asked with a concerned expression.

"They didn't say that. They just said they're monitoring him closely."

Lindsey gently guided her back to the chair she had been sitting in. "Let me grab some Kleenex here." He handed her the tissue and sat down beside her. "Use this." He waited as she wiped her eyes and blew her nose. "Do you know what happened?"

"No. The last thing I knew was that he wanted to talk to Jenny Dobbins because she was goin' back to that no-good husband of hers today. He was gonna try to talk her out of it. Jenny went to his office, and I got busy in the kitchen, and that's the last I knew till Chief Wilkins rang the doorbell and told me Billy had been rushed to the hospital."

"Who's the doctor?"

"David Mendelson—he's the chief resident, and the best doctor in town."

"And what about Jenny?"

"She's gone. I guess she's gone off with that husband of hers. I just *know* he had somethin' to do with this. Billy's the one who had him arrested after he beat Jenny up so bad she ran away to the shelter."

"I know."

"Jenny's a sweet girl and all that, but I warned Billy she was gonna bring trouble along with 'er, if he moved 'er into the house."

"What are the police doing?"

"I don't know. I called the police station about an hour ago, and Chief Wilkins told me he'd be here soon."

Pastor Lindsey shook his head. "This is just...awful." He clasped his hands. "Dear God, please be merciful unto your faithful servant Billy Braddock. Please—let not these works of the Devil prevail. We ask in Jesus' name, amen."

"Amen," Maggie repeated.

About that time, the face of Chief John Wilkins appeared at the window of the door. Seeing them there, he went right in. "Joe...Maggie," he said with a solemn look. "Any further word?"

"Nothing," Maggie answered.

"What have you found out, Chief?" Joe Lindsey anxiously inquired.

"Well, after I talked to Maggie, the first place we went to was Shooter Dobbins' trailer-house. The place was deserted, but his van was parked out front. We did a comparison of the fresh tire tracks we found at the site where they found Billy with the tires on Shooter's van, and it was a definite match—no question about it. So it's just about a hundred-percent certain he was at that exact spot when all this happened today."

"I knew it," Maggie said. "I just *knew* he was involved."

"We also found fresh blood in the van, and we think it might be Jenny's. There were two suitcases packed with women's clothing inside the van."

"That's what she had with her this morning—two small suitcases. Oh, God—I hope he hasn't killed her," Maggie said with a groan.

"It wasn't a lot of blood—more like a nose-bleed than a fatal wound—but, based on past history, I suspect he probably assaulted her, at the very least. We've sent a blood sample to the State crime lab for analysis."

"Oh, that poor, poor girl!" Maggie exclaimed.

Lindsey put his arms around her. "C'mon, Maggie—we've gotta be strong...for Billy."

"I'm trying, Joe," she said. "I'm doing my best."

"So what's next?" Joe asked the police chief as he held Maggie close to him in a comforting gesture.

"We've posted an all-points bulletin for all police agencies in this area to be on the lookout. You know...out here in this part of the world, it's pretty hard not to be noticed on these wide-open desert roads—especially a slimy-lookin' character like Shooter Dobbins, ridin' double with a beautiful redhead on a chopped-down Harley-Davidson."

"I can't believe somebody hasn't already spotted 'em," Lindsey said.

Wilkins nodded in agreement. "We found some tracks in front of Dobbins' house that looked like another vehicle draggin' a trailer had been there very recently—probably today—but we can't tell just from lookin' at the tracks what kind of vehicle it was, or what kind of trailer it was. But since Shooter's bike is gone and his van is still there, and nobody's spotted him on the highway, we think he mighta loaded his bike onto the trailer or put it in the back of the vehicle."

"Which would definitely complicate matters," Joe Lindsey offered.

"Oh, yeah," Chief Wilkins said with a nod. "We don't know what kind of vehicle it is, or what kind of trailer it is, or who's drivin' it, or which direction it might be goin'. If the motorcycle's inside the trailer, and Shooter and Jenny are ridin' inside a closed vehicle, nobody's even gonna see 'em. So that's a problem. And the other thing is...dependin' on how fast they're goin', they're puttin' sixty or seventy miles between us and them every hour. They're prob'ly at least two or three hundred miles away by now—but *which* way?"

"So it's just a matter of wait-and-see?"

"Not entirely. I've got my entire force canvassin' Shooter's known hangouts and associates to see if we can dredge up any information that way. There's bound to be somebody around town who knows somethin'. We just gotta find that somebody. But what I want you to know is...we're doin' all we can. Billy Braddock means a lot to all of us, and we *will* get to the bottom of this."

"We appreciate all you're doin', John."

"It's more than my duty. It's personal," Wilkins said with a stern look. "Billy Braddock's a friend of mine. I'll keep you posted, if there's any further developments on our end—and I hope you'll keep me posted as soon as you get any further word on Billy's condition."

"We certainly will," Lindsey assured him.

At that moment, Dr. Mendelson entered the room. "Good afternoon." He nodded to John Wilkins. "Chief."

"Doctor, this is Joe Lindsey, our assistant pastor," Maggie said.

"Nice to meet you, Pastor Lindsey." The doctor consulted some notes he had on a clipboard in his hand. "I know Reverend Braddock has no next of kin, so I assume you all are the closest thing to family he has?"

"Yes," Maggie said. "How is he?"

"Well, first of all, he did regain consciousness a few minutes ago."

"Oh, thank God!" Maggie exclaimed.

"Praise the Lord!" Lindsey fervently declared in a hoarse whisper, turning his eyes toward heaven as he did so. "Thank you, Dear Father!"

The doctor paused a moment, then continued, "He confirmed that he was assaulted." He looked through his notes. "I think he said it was Scooter"—

"Shooter—Shooter Dobbins," Chief Wilkins said.

"He was speaking in a whisper, so I couldn't understand him too well, but Dobbins was definitely the last name. He also said there was a girl"—

"Jenny," Maggie said.

"Yes...Jenny. He indicated that she had also been assaulted and taken away against her will."

"Kidnapping and aggravated assault," Chief Wilkins said, with a determined nod of the head. "That punk's gonna do hard time for this."

"Is Billy gonna be all right?" Maggie anxiously inquired.

"As far as the beating he sustained, the injuries are bad, but not fatal. As of now, we don't see evidence of broken ribs or any internal bleeding—but, at his age, this kind of injury has unknowable consequences. He told me his assailant kicked him several times." Maggie emitted a doleful moan, and the doctor paused a moment to allow her to regain her composure. "This is the part that gives me the greatest concern. It appears that the stress and the trauma caused him to have a heart attack."

"Oh, God!" Maggie cried, in a nearly hysterical tone. "That's horrible!"

"Now, don't panic," Dr. Mendelson said, as he made a reassuring gesture. "We don't yet know the extent of the damage to his heart, but it's for sure there is *some* damage. His pulse is weak and his heartbeat is somewhat erratic. We're gonna monitor him closely and let him rest tonight, and tomorrow we'll try to determine the exact state of his condition. The main thing right now is that he's alive and conscious. We've given him a mild sedative because he seemed to be in a state of extreme agitation over what happened to him and the girl, and we were afraid the stress might trigger another attack."

"When can we see 'im?" Maggie asked.

"Possibly sometime tomorrow. For now, I suggest you go on home and get some rest yourselves. There's absolutely no point in you folks staying here at the hospital tonight. I've called in extra help to keep watch on him, and I'm in touch with several of the best heart specialists in the country for ongoing consultations. Dr. Morton Abrams, who's probably the best heart doctor in the country, will be flying in here tomorrow from Houston. Just rest assured we're doing everything we can to ensure a good outcome."

"Oh, Billy...my poor, sweet Billy," Maggie moaned.

"We appreciate all you're doing," Joe Lindsey said, as he cradled Maggie in a reassuring hug.

Chief Wilkins extended his hand. "Thanks so much, Doc." He looked at Joe. "I need to get back to the station so I can update the alert on Shooter

Dobbins. Can you see to it that Maggie gets home safely?"

"She's gonna stay at my house tonight. You go ahead."

The doctor nodded to the two men. "That's all for now. See to it that the hospital has all the pertinent phone numbers, in case we have any reason to call you tonight."

"I'll do that," Joe assured him.

"Then I'll bid you good day. I have other patients waiting." He started to leave, then stopped abruptly. Taking out a prescription pad, he scribbled a brief notation and handed the slip to Pastor Lindsey. "You might want to have this filled on your way home. If Maggie continues in this emotional state, it'll help her relax."

"Thank you, doctor."

The doctor turned and left the room. Chief Wilkins paused a moment as he opened the door and gave a look back. "Take good care of her, Joe. I'll see you tomorrow."

The pastor nodded. "Until then." Putting his arm around Maggie's shoulders, he gently nudged her toward the door. "C'mon, Maggie. You're gonna stay at my place tonight. Mary and I will take good care of you. Billy's gonna be all right. He's gettin' the best of care. Come along now."

Lindsey guided Maggie down the hallway, patiently encouraging her as she shuffled toward the door. It occurred to him that she had never appeared so old and frail as she did now. He had never thought of her as anything more than Braddock's housekeeper, but her emotional response to the preacher's misfortune told him that her feelings ran much deeper than he had suspected.

"Have you known Billy long, Maggie?" he asked as they went down the hall.

She nodded. "Since first grade. We went all through school together until he went away to college, and then I didn't see much of him for a long time. But when he came back to town and decided to start the church, he found out that my husband had died, and he asked me if I'd like to come run his household for 'im. I've been with 'im ever since."

"I had no idea."

"Oh, yeah—Billy and I go back a long way."

When they came to the glass doors that led out of the hospital, they could see that a fairly large crowd was waiting outside. "Brace yourself, Maggie—it looks like word has already spread. I see a lot of faces from our church, God bless 'em." They went through the doors, and shouts from the crowd began immediately, people wanting to know Braddock's condition, and how he had been injured. Lindsey raised his hands for quiet and addressed the crowd from the top of the steps:

"Folks, Maggie and I wanta thank you so much for this show of concern. Here's what we know at this time: Reverend Braddock is conscious and resting quietly at this hour. As a precaution, he's being carefully monitored in the intensive care unit here at the hospital. Dr. Mendelson told us he has some injuries, but there's no sign of internal bleeding. So that's good news. And there's a specialist coming in from Houston tomorrow to help with Reverend Braddock's treatment. That's really all we know at this time."

"Joe! How did he sustain his injuries?"

Lindsey turned to look at the questioner, a man in a short-sleeved shirt and tie, wearing a straw fedora. "I know you," he said, trying to put a name with the face.

"Fred Whitcomb. I'm the managing editor of the Braddock *Bugle*."

"Oh, yes, Fred. Are you covering the story yourself?"

Whitcomb shrugged. "Hey, it's Billy Braddock."

"I understand," Lindsey responded. He then went on, saying, "I spoke with Chief Wilkins a few moments ago. There's an ongoing investigation into the cause of Reverend Braddock's injuries, so all such questions as that need to be addressed to the police department."

"He didn't give you any clues, any theories as to what happened...nothing?"

"That's a police matter you should discuss with the police, Fred. That's all I can say about it."

"Is there anything we can do to help, Joe?" a female voice called from the crowd.

The pastor recognized Rosie Dawson from the congregation. "Thank you for asking, Rosie. Actually, all I can ask any of you to do right now is to go back home and say prayers for Billy. That's what Maggie and I are gonna do, and that's what I advise all of you to do, too." There was another flurry of shouted questions, but Lindsey again raised his hands for silence. "Really, folks, I've told you all I know for now. If I hear anything further, I'll let you know. But we need to go for now. All you folks from the congregation know our dear Maggie, who's known Billy longer than any of us, and she's takin' this pretty hard. I need to get her home to rest. There's nothing any of us can do for now but—as I've already suggested—go home and pray. So...thank you for coming. We truly do appreciate your concern for Reverend Braddock."

The crowd parted to allow Lindsey and Maggie to pass. Many of the women in the crowd followed along, offering words of comfort to Braddock's frail little housekeeper. As they moved toward Lindsey's car, the pastor noticed two strangers in the crowd, one of them holding a large professional-looking camera on his shoulder, intently following the proceedings. In all the confusion, he took only passing note of their presence, but the fact that they were strangers in town left a distinct impression in his mind. He even had a split-second to wonder why they would be concerned with events surrounding a local preacher in a small town that was little more than a tiny oasis in the middle of the Texas desert. But the thought lasted only a moment. He reminded himself that the object of all this commotion was, after all, one of the richest men in the world. Lindsey helped Maggie into the car, then started slowly driving away, waving to the crowd and muttering words of reassurance as he passed by. The last thing he noticed in the rearview mirror was the image of the large man with the video camera standing in the road, filming their departure.

Dr. Mendelson arrived at the hospital at five a.m. and went directly to the intensive care unit. Upon his arrival, he stopped at the nurses' station. A burly black nurse in starched white uniform greeted him with a look of relief. "Dr. Mendelson! You don't know how *glad* I am to see you this mornin'."

"I understand our star patient's been bein' difficult."

"Oh, Lord—he's been threatenin' lawsuits, and swearin' he's gonna get us all fired and all sorts of stuff, if we don't let him out of the hospital immediately. We convinced him we couldn't do it without your approval, but he's in a really bad mood. He's been wide awake since three o'clock this mornin', and gettin' madder by the minute. I'm sorry

I had to call you so early, but considerin' who it is, I didn't know what else to do."

"You did the right thing. Let me see his chart." Mendelson took the clipboard from the nurse and studied it carefully for a moment. Handing the chart back to the nurse, he asked, "Is anyone with him now?"

"We've had a nurse stationed by his bedside all night, poor thing. She's been takin' the brunt of the assault. He's in a private room, ICU-101."

"Thank you."

It was only a few steps down the hall to the room where Billy Braddock was being monitored. Mendelson came through the door, and immediately the old man tried to raise himself out of bed. The nurse standing beside him grabbed his shoulder and said, "Just lie down and relax, Reverend Braddock. The doctor's here now."

Braddock pulled down the oxygen mask. "It's about time!" he shouted in a voice that had regained its strength since he had last spoken to the doctor. "Is this a jail, or a hospital? Get these tubes outta me!"

"Relax, Billy. We're just trying to keep you alive. We don't wanna lose you."

"David, I'm not a vindictive man, but if you don't take these tubes out of me right now and give me my teeth back, I swear I'll have my attorneys file a lawsuit that'll cost you and this hospital a fortune!"

"Where are his teeth, nurse?"

"They're right here," she said, retrieving a small container from the lower shelf of a portable table.

"Give 'em back to 'im."

The nurse washed off Braddock's false teeth and carefully replaced them in his mouth. "There you are, Reverend Braddock," she said, patting him gently on the shoulder. "Now you can talk better."

Dr. Mendelson looked at the nurse and gestured toward the door. "Take a short break. I wanta talk to Reverend Braddock alone."

"Thank you, doctor," the nurse said as she exited the room.

As soon as they were alone, Braddock said, "I know what you're gonna say, and I don't wanna hear it."

"What am I gonna say, Billy?"

"You're gonna tell me how all these wires and tubes and needles are all for my own good, and how you're gonna save my life, whether I like it or not."

"Are you saying you *wanna* die?"

"No, I'm not sayin' that. I'm sayin' I want outta this hospital."

"Look, Billy," the doctor began in a tone of gentle remonstration, "you are a very sick man."

"You think I don't know that?"

"No, actually, I think you *do* know that. In fact, I suspect you've known for a very long time that your health wasn't what it ought to be. We were afraid we were going to lose you yesterday, so we didn't try to run any meaningful tests to determine the full extent of the damage to your heart. But I suspect that things have been going on for awhile now—things that you knew about, but didn't mention to anybody. Your EKG doesn't look good, Billy. We have a specialist coming in from Houston to do some evaluations later today. Once we know the exact state of your physical health, we'll be able to determine the best course of action to keep you alive as long as possible."

"Well, you can call that specialist and tell 'im to stay in Houston, 'cause I plan to be out of this hospital within the hour!"

"Billy"—

"David, I'm telling you as seriously as I know how to say something seriously—I have a vicious wolf-pack of Harvard-educated corporate attorneys I can unleash with a single phone call. If I get them started on your case, you'll go to your grave wishing you *had* let me die. Don't do that to me, or to yourself. I have no desire to do you any harm. I just wanta go home. So get these tubes out of me and let me go."

The doctor had a look of regret on his face. "I wish you'd reconsider."

"Your concern is well noted, and I appreciate it. But you owe it to me as a human being to respect my wishes."

Pondering his options and realizing the risks involved if he didn't comply with Braddock's wishes, Mendelson gave a huge sigh. "All right, Billy. For legal reasons, I'll have to get you to sign a form that says you refuse treatment, and then I'll order your release. But I truly believe my release order will be your death warrant."

"We're all born with a death warrant, David," Braddock replied. "And, besides, I'm an old man. No matter what happens, I don't have much longer to live. I wanta die in my own bed. That's not too much to ask."

The doctor smiled, but the smile couldn't conceal the look of chagrin on his face. "All right, Billy. I'll have a nurse come back here and get you ready to be released while I'm getting the forms." He extended his hand. "I've enjoyed knowing you during the time I've lived here in Braddock. I only hope that the God you worship has the power to defy the wisdom of medical convention."

"Don't be so upset, David. I ain't dead yet. And just rest assured that, no matter what happens, I don't hold you in any way responsible." David Mendelson left the room without another word. It was a few minutes before the nurse returned. As soon as she stepped through the door, Braddock asked, "What time is it?"

She glanced at her watch. "It's getting on toward five-thirty."

"Is there a phone in this room?"

"They're not allowed in ICU."

"Well, before you start unhooking me, go call me a taxi right now. And hurry."

The nurse immediately went back through the door. She was gone for what seemed an interminable time to Braddock, and then she returned. "The taxi is on its way."

"Thank you," Braddock said.

Working quickly, the nurse removed the catheter, the intravenous tubes and the electrodes from Braddock's body, after which she retrieved his clothes from the small closet in the corner of the room. As he got dressed, Braddock was aware of the pain in his ribs and kidneys from the kicks the big biker had inflicted upon him. Feeling the pain actually brought the memory of the event back to life in vivid detail. As he laboriously struggled to dress himself with the help of the nurse, the old man felt a cold anger growing inside him, a feeling he hadn't known since his days as an athlete. He had the odd thought that it was that forgotten rage—that calculating killer instinct, coupled with his natural physical ability—that had made him so much better than so many others of similar abilities that he had faced on the athletic field. By the time he was fully dressed, the kindly look that people usually saw on his face was gone. The changes were subtle, indefinable...and yet they were discernible, like the subtle ferocity in the eyes of a tiger.

The nurse recognized it immediately. "Are you all right, Reverend Braddock?"

"I'm fine. Just a little sore."

"Are you sure? You look kinda funny."

"I'm fine. Go call Mendelson and tell him to get back here with that form—pronto. I have to be somewhere."

Before the nurse could open the door, Dr. Mendelson returned carrying a clipboard, accompanied by another nurse and a woman in business attire. "Billy, this is Madeline Smith. She works in administration, and she's a notary public. She's going to notarize the signatures of yourself and these two nurses, who will act as witnesses to this act of folly you're about to commit."

"Just gimme the paper."

Braddock signed the document with a flourish, and then the two nurses affixed their signatures, after which the administrator applied the notary seal. "All right, Billy. You're free to go. Hospital protocol requires that we take you to the front door in a wheelchair, and then you'll be a free man again."

"Thank you, doctor," Braddock said.

One of the nurses opened the door, and an orderly came into the room pushing a wheelchair. The orderly took solicitous care assisting the old man into the chair, and wheeled him out of the room, as the assembled group of hospital staff stepped out into the hall to watch the departure.

David Mendelson shook his head in disgust. "If any of you know him well enough to attend his funeral, you'd better go ahead and pick out your dress clothes now. It won't be long."

The taxi was waiting in the patient pickup area when the orderly wheeled Billy Braddock out of the hospital. With the young man's assistance, the preacher laboriously rose from the chair and then slowly managed his way into the taxi.

"Thank you for your assistance," Braddock said.

"You're more than welcome," the orderly replied. "It's always a pleasure to help a good man like you, Reverend Braddock."

"I'm not all that good, believe me," the preacher responded. "But I appreciate the thought."

Once Braddock was in the vehicle, the taxi driver, a black man in his twenties, looked at the old man in the rearview mirror. "Where to, boss?'

"Glory Road—as quickly as possible. The faster you get there, the better your tip's gonna be."

"Fasten your seat belt," the driver said. He drove away from the hospital as quickly as possible and maintained a fairly high rate of speed until he reached the highway. At that point, he stepped on the accelerator and went roaring toward Glory Road at eighty miles an hour. Looking at the old man in the rearview mirror, the driver asked, "Say, ain't you that preacher-guy who's the football player on the billboard outside o' town?"

"I am."

"I heard you was dead."

"Not quite yet."

"Are we goin' to th' church?"

"We're goin' to the estate behind the church."

"That big ol' mansion? Is that yo' house?"

"It is."

"Man, thass one fine place. I drove a State Senator over there from the airport one time."

"I'm glad you approve. But let's cut the chit-chat and get on with the drivin'."

Within minutes, the taxi was sitting beside the bungalow that served as Billy Braddock's private office. Braddock struggled his way out of the taxi, then told the driver, "Wait here. I'll be right back."

Taking his keys out of his pocket, Braddock unlocked the door and went inside. Once he was in the office, he went to what appeared to be a blank wall and pushed a button disguised as a knothole in the wood. The panel slid back, revealing a large safe hidden behind the wood facade. Braddock worked the combination and opened the vault. Inside the safe were dozens of bundles of crisp one-hundred-dollar bills wrapped in ten-thousand-dollar increments. He retrieved a large suitcase from the closet and emptied the contents of the safe, putting a couple of bundles in his coat pocket before throwing the rest in the suitcase. Then, leaving the suitcase open, he went to the desk and opened the bottom drawer, where he retrieved a large-caliber pistol that nestled in a shoulder holster. He checked the pistol to be sure it was loaded, then took off his jacket and strapped the holster to his body. There was a full box of ammunition in the drawer, and the old man threw that inside the suitcase with the money. After carefully closing the safe, he looked around the room for any telltale traces of human activity that might have occurred since the last time anyone knew he was in the office. Satisfied that he had restored the room to its original condition, he went to the main house. Taking the elevator to the second floor, he went to his bedroom and retrieved a cowboy shirt, a hat, blue-jeans and a pair of cowboy boots. He put the clothes in a small tote-bag and returned downstairs. Returning to the office, he locked the door from the inside, then went to the back door that led to the garage. Opening the automatic door, he stepped onto the driveway and motioned the driver forward. The driver pulled up in front of the garage and rolled down the window on the passenger side.

"You need any help, boss?"

Braddock walked around the car to the driver's side. "How does that meter work? Are you tracked by miles, or minutes, or both?"

"Why you askin'?"

"If you shut off the meter, and stop the car, and the car doesn't go anywhere for awhile—can they tell there's a discrepancy between where you were, and where you *said* you were, at any given point in time?"

"Now, say that again?" the driver said, scrunching his face into a questioning look.

The preacher pulled out a ten-thousand-dollar bundle of money. "Look—I don't have time to explain. Money talks, right? Does this say anything to you?"

"Yeah. It says ten thousand dollars."

"Okay. Park your taxi in the garage, stop the meter, turn off the ignition, take these keys, get in that Mercedes and drive me where I wanna go as fast as possible, and this money is yours. Get me *back* from where we're going"—Braddock pulled another ten-thousand dollars from his coat pocket— "and I got another one just like it to give you. Agreed?"

"Is this some kinda criminal shit?"

"No, it's not. It's a matter of life and death—my life—and there's no time to waste."

"Gimme the money first."

Braddock pulled several hundred-dollar bills out of the bundle and handed it to the driver. "This is good faith money. You'll get the rest when we're finished."

"Ma-an, somethin' 'bout this ain't right," the driver said, thumbing through the hundred-dollar bills. "All this money for a taxi ride?" He gave the old man a crafty look. "You got all this money on you—s'pose I was just to go ahead and rob yo' ass and kill you?"

Braddock pulled back the lapel of his jacket, revealing the weapon in the shoulder holster. "This is a .44-magnum, the most powerful handgun in the world" ...

The taxi driver's eyes widened perceptibly. "Yeah, I saw that in the movies," he said with a nervous laugh. "Dirty Harry, right?"

"This is real life," Braddock said with a serious look. "I have a proficiency with this weapon that Dirty Harry never dreamed of. The thing is—I have no intention of using it, except as a defensive weapon...like if some stupid-assed taxi driver tried to rob me."

"Aw, man, I was just kiddin' you."

"Well, I'm *not* kiddin' *you.* So let's get on with it."

The taxi driver was still hesitant. "So why are you doin' all this? It's gotta be somethin' criminal."

"Do you know how rich I am?"

"I got a pretty good idea," the driver said.

"So why would a man as rich as I am be doin' somethin' criminal?"

"Rich men is the biggest crooks in the world. Ever'body knows that."

The preacher made a gesture of frustration. "Look—this is pointless. I'm runnin' outta time." Braddock extended the keys. "Either you get in that Mercedes and drive me where I need to go, or you don't. I can do it myself, if I have to. But either way, time's runnin' out. I've only got a few minutes to get where I need to be."

"Twenty thousand dollars." The driver gave a shrug. "What the hell? I'll do it. If you *are* doin' somethin' criminal, you can hire us both a good lawyer." The driver pulled into the garage and got out of the taxi. Looking at the hat and bags the old man had set beside the car, the driver asked, "You want me to put this in the car?"

"Put it in the trunk."

The young man complied with the order, and then he got into the Mercedes and backed out of the driveway. Getting out of the vehicle, he helped the old man into the passenger side, and asked, "So where are we goin'?"

"You know the Camelot subdivision, just down the highway?"

"Sure do," the driver replied.

"We're goin' there. I believe the street is Lancelot Court."

"You're the boss, boss." The driver waited for Braddock to get into the car and then sped away from the house. "Now, this is my kind o' car, here."

"What's your name?" Braddock asked.

"Kareem. Kareem Lumumba."

"You seem familiar to me. Do you know the Johnsons...Willie and Evelyn?"

"They're my parents. They kept their slave names, but I was ashamed to be callin' myself Rufus Johnson. Now I'm Kareem Lumumba."

"Well, it's nice to meet you Kareem. You have some great parents. And now that we've been formally introduced—you can call me Billy."

"Okay...Billy."

"Now, look, Kareem—I'm gonna go see a man who's a big man in town—one of the world's top scientists. He's the only one who can help me. I wanna warn you in advance that I may have to pull a gun on 'im, but don't let that scare you"—

"You're gonna do what? *Pull a gun on 'im*? Are you fuckin' *crazy*?"

"Kareem, just shut your mouth and listen, or I'll throw down on *you*. It's not as bad as it sounds."

"Oh, no, *hell*, no. All you're gonna do is pull a gun on 'im." Seeing the scowl on Braddock's face, the driver raised his hands. "Okay—you da boss."

"Just don't get panicky. This pistol may not even come into play, but if I have to show it to 'im to let 'im know I mean business, I'll do that. I'm hopin' it won't come down to that."

"You gonna kill 'im?"

"No, nothin' like that. All I'm tryin' t' do is get him to give me some medicine that might save my life. I'm a very sick man. That's what this is all about."

"Well, if you're a sick man, why don't he just give you the medicine?"

"Because it's experimental and not approved for use on human beings. But that medicine's the only chance I've got. Anyway, I'm gonna get in his car and we're gonna go to the Braddock Institute. I want you to follow us into the employees' garage at the back of the building. Park the car and wait for me to return. This man has a private elevator that goes straight to his office, and I'm gonna go up there with 'im, where he's gonna give me the medicine I need to help me stay alive. Either that, or I'll be dead before the day is over." He paused. "Are you with me on this so far?"

"Yeah. After you kidnap 'im at gunpoint, I'm s'posed to follow you into the garage and wait for you to die. Couldn't be any plainer 'n that."

"Yeah, more or less. But if I'm not back in an hour, you can go with my blessing—I'll prob'ly be dead. If you *do* have to leave without me, go back to my house, park the car back in the garage, make sure the garage door is closed just like it was before, retrieve your taxi, and go on with your life. Forget this even happened." Braddock extended a bundle of money. "This is the rest of the money from the batch I took those bills out of. You're now ten-thousand dollars richer than you were when you woke up this morning. Just do what I ask, and if I make it back, you'll be twenty-thousand dollars richer." He held up a cautionary finger. "But if the medicine doesn't kill me, and I come back to the garage in an hour and find you gone, I'm gonna report this as a robbery. The serial numbers are consecutive and easy to trace. So you better hold up your end of the bargain."

"You know...this is some scary shit. I hope you're not gettin' my scrawny black ass in a sling."

"Trust me."

"Yeah, trust a rich white man—right. That's me all over."

Arriving at the subdivision, Braddock directed his driver to the house where Charles Keeler lived. The preacher instructed Kareem to stop in the driveway. Looking at his watch, Braddock said, "Six-thirty. I hope we haven't missed 'im. He always goes to work early." The old man pondered his options. "I tell you what—go ahead and park the car on the street. Leave the engine runnin'. I'm gonna find out for sure if he's still there."

Braddock struggled out of the car, grunting and groaning from the acute pain he felt from his injuries. He managed to stand erect and made his way to the front door, as Kareem backed the Mercedes out of the driveway and parked alongside the curb. Ringing the doorbell, the old man impatiently waited for someone to answer. A few moments passed, and Charles Keeler opened the door.

"Billy!" he exclaimed. "I thought you were in the hospital."

"They released me this morning. We need t' talk."

"Well, I was just about to go to work, Billy. I like to start an hour or so before the rest of the staff arrives and the place gets busy."

"No problem. I'll ride down there with you."

"Well...sure. But...what's goin' on?"

"I'll tell you on the way over there."

With an expression of uncertainty, Keeler said, "Well...okay." He stepped away from the door and gestured toward the back of the house. "It's this way to the car, through the utility room."

Braddock turned toward the street and motioned to Kareem. The driver rolled down the window. "Stay right behind us," the old man instructed. "We're goin' over to the research center."

The two men went to the rear of the house and out to the garage. They got into Keeler's car and backed out of the driveway. Kareem waited for them to pass and followed closely behind. As they drove away, Charles Keeler gave Braddock a questioning glance. "So...what's been going on, Billy? There's been all sorts of rumors flying around town."

"Well, Charles, what's goin' on is...one of our local thugs beat me up pretty bad yesterday."

"No! I heard you were hit by a car."

"I feel like I was hit by a car, but that's not what happened. He knocked me down and stomped on me."

"That's terrible!"

"Yeah, it is. But that's not the worst of it. It caused me to have a real bad heart attack. Dave Mendelson—you know him?"

"Yeah—over at the hospital? I know Dave."

"He's tellin' me I don't have much time to live—hours, maybe. So...I've got a number of things I need to do, and one of 'em is to leave some final instructions as to how I want the Institute run when I'm gone. I wanta be sure you're well-funded into the foreseeable future, and to make sure that certain kinds of research that I believe in are carried out in accordance to my wishes."

"Well...sure. But isn't this a little unusual? I mean, you came to discuss this at six-thirty in the morning?"

"I don't have much time left, Charles. And this is important."

Braddock extemporized the rest of the way to the research center, filling the time with conversation, being very careful not to arouse Keeler's suspicions that there was more in the offing than arranging plans for the future of the Braddock Institute. They drove into the employees' garage with Kareem in close pursuit. Inside the garage, Braddock and Keeler got out of the car, and then Braddock walked over to the Mercedes and instructed Kareem to park in one of the available spaces. He reiterated his previous instructions: "If I'm not back in an hour, go back and get your taxi, leave the keys in the car, make sure the garage door is closed and go on with your life like nothing ever happened. Buy your mother somethin' nice with some of that money I gave you. She's a real nice lady." With that, he followed Keeler to the elevator and the two men ascended to Keeler's private office.

As soon as they arrived upstairs, Braddock said, "I wanna go to the lab first. There's a few questions I need to ask you."

Keeler gave him a dubious look. "Well, sure, Billy—but there's nothing there that we can't discuss just as well right here."

"No. I wanna go to the lab."

By now, Keeler had his suspicions as to what the old man had in mind, but he held his tongue and led the way down the hall to the animal research laboratory. Once they arrived, Keeler leaned against one of the countertops and said, "I'm assuming we're going to renew the conversation we started yesterday, is that right?"

"Almost. Actually, we're gonna conclude the conversation we started yesterday. You're gonna shoot me up with that serum."

Emphatically shaking his head, Keeler said, "No. No, sir, I will not do that."

"Then I'll do it myself. Gimme the keys to that icebox."

"I can't do that, Billy. I don't have the keys. The security guards keep 'em down at the front desk. I have to call down and have one of the guards bring 'em up here."

"I think you're kiddin' me, Charles." Braddock reached under his coat and pulled out the pistol.

"Now, wait...there's no need for that."

Brandishing the pistol, the old man said, "Either you take out your keys and open that damn icebox, or I'm gonna shoot the lock off. And if I can't get to that serum before security gets up here, I'm gonna shoot you. And then me and the security guards are gonna fight it out to the death."

"Billy...you don't mean that. This is not like you."

"This is more like me than you would ever suspect," Braddock said. "What's it gonna be, Charles? I got nothin' to lose. But you—you got everything to lose. So...what's it gonna be?"

Keeler took the keys out of his pocket and offered them to Braddock. "It's this one. Go ahead."

"No, you go ahead. I'll just keep an eye on you."

His hands trembling almost uncontrollably, Keeler fumbled with the keys and opened the door of the refrigerator. He retrieved one of the vials marked *FYX-14* and handed it to Braddock. "Billy," he began in a pleading tone, "you have no idea what you're doing."

"You're right. And neither do you. But I like the odds—whatever they are. A million to one is better than the odds I'm facin' now."

"This is crazy, Billy."

"Look at it this way: I may be about to win you your next Nobel Prize and make you the second-greatest man who ever lived, just after Jesus Christ—or I'm about to be a desperate lunatic, lyin' dead in your laboratory, after forcin' you at gunpoint to make you give me the serum. No matter what happens, you can't be held responsible. So stop arguin' and gimme a needle."

Keeler went to one of the cabinets and retrieved a large syringe. "You don't even know what dose to give."

"Do you?"

"No. There's no way *to* know. That's what I'm trying to tell you. We just don't know enough about this drug to use it on a human being."

The old man took off his coat and unbuttoned his sleeve. Using the pistol to motion the scientist nearer, Braddock extended his arm and said, "In that case, just go ahead and fill 'er up."

"Billy, this is totally—totally—insane."

"Do it, Charles," Braddock ordered. "Either you shoot me, or I'm gonna shoot you. It's a simple proposition. Just think of it as the OK Corral, and play like you're Doc Holliday and I'm Ike Clanton. Fire away."

"You know, Billy"—

"Do it. Just shut up and do it," Braddock impatiently ordered.

Dr. Keeler uncapped the vial and loaded the syringe. He swabbed Braddock's arm with alcohol and inserted the needle, slowly forcing the contents into the old man's bloodstream. "If you start feeling sick or anything, tell me, Billy. I'll stop the injection before we do any more damage than I'm sure we're already doing."

Braddock smiled. "No. It feels good. It's like some kinda drug rush. It feels good. *Really* good."

Keeler emptied the contents of the syringe in to Braddock's arm and removed the needle. He put a cotton ball on the injection site and taped it down, then backed away to watch the results. The old man broke into a torrential sweat, and then he started to tremble violently. When Braddock's eyes momentarily rolled back in his head, the scientist started moving as unobtrusively as possible toward the telephone that was hanging on the wall.

Sweat pouring down his face, Braddock refocused his eyes and said, "Don't you even think about it, Charles. Sit down in the floor against that wall!" The doctor complied without a word. *"Oh, God, it burns!"* the old man exclaimed, as he convulsed in agony. Keeler tried again to move toward the phone. Braddock commanded, "Sit down, Charles! I don't wanna have to warn you again!"

Realizing that there was nothing he could do to stop the events unfolding before his eyes, the scientist in Keeler had to know what reactions were occurring in his subject. "What are you feeling, Billy?"

"Fire. It's like the Fires of Hell," he said with a tortured moan. "Oooh! It hurts so bad."

"Let me call 911. Maybe we can still get you some help."

"No. This is it, live or die."

For the next few minutes, Keeler watched helplessly as the preacher convulsed into a copious sweat that was accompanied by a grotesque howling noise that seemed to emanate from the innemost depths of his primordial soul. This horrific display went on for several minutes, his body trembling, shaking and quivering to various degrees of spasmodic violence until, suddenly, it was over. Breathing heavily, and looking drained from his reaction to the drug, Braddock returned the pistol to the holster and wiped the sweat away from his eyes.

"Are you all right?" Keeler asked with a solicitous expression.

"I...I feel woozy. Just let me get my senses. I feel like I did that time in the ring when I walked into a right hand and almost got knocked out cold." He shook his head to clear the cobwebs. "How long was I out of it?"

"I don't know. Maybe ten minutes."

"Well, guess what? I ain't dead yet."

"The day is young."

"I appreciate your help, Charles."

"I didn't help, Billy."

"Yeah, that's right. You didn't. But I appreciate it, anyway. At least I know that if I die now, I gave myself every chance to avoid the certain consequences I'm facin'.'"

"You need to go to the hospital, Billy."

"No. I don't feel much worse than I did when I got here. I'm gonna go now. I need you to accompany me back to the parkin' lot, and we'll call that good. When I get back to the office, I'll issue that memo about how I want increased funding for the Institute after I die. I'm gonna have you guys go full speed ahead on that stem-cell research you been wantin' t' do. There's a few other things, too, but it's all for the good. Let's go." The two men left the laboratory and returned to Keeler's office, where they descended the elevator to the parking garage. Braddock extended his hand. "Are you gonna call the cops on me, Charles?"

The doctor accepted Braddock's hand. "I ought to, but I won't. If I were in your situation, I couldn't swear I wouldn't have done the same thing. At best, I don't think it's gonna do any good. And at worst, you've probably just killed yourself. But like you said—your prognosis is bad, anyway. There's no point in getting the police involved. You've done a lot of good for a lot of people in your lifetime."

"Thanks," the old man said with a grateful look.

"I want you to do me one favor, Billy"—

"Sure, anything."

"I want you to let me know what side-effects you might experience from the drug, good or bad. Since you've made yourself a guinea-pig, I'd like to have the data for future reference."

"I'll do that."

"Good luck, Billy."

"Same to you, Charles."

Getting back into the car, the old man gave the doctor a brief salute as the vehicle drove away. As they neared the highway, Kareem asked, "Where to now?"

"Back to the house. I'm done here."

"Did you throw down on that guy?"

"Yeah, but he knows I didn't mean it."

"Man, you don't know how scared I was, waitin' in that garage. I was expectin' the cops to show up any time."

"I'm sorry for puttin' you through that, but I had to do it."

"Did he give you the medicine?"

"Yeah."

"You look pretty bad, man. Yo' face is red as fire."

"I feel pretty bad."

When they arrived at the house, Kareem parked the Mercedes back in the garage, and both men got out of the car. Braddock handed the second bundle of money to the taxi driver.

Grinning from ear to ear, Kareem said, "It's been a pleasure doin' business with you. If you ever need another ride, you be sure and call me."

"Lemme just put a bug in your ear before you go," the old man said with a serious look. "It might be in your best interest not to discuss anything about what happened this morning with anybody. I can't guarantee the cops won't get involved in this matter before it's all said and done, and the less anybody knows that you know *anything*, the better it'll be for you."

"I *knew* this was some kinda bullshit!" the driver exclaimed.

"All you did was pick me up at the hospital and bring me home. That's all you did and all you know. You got that?"

"Sho' 'nuff, boss."

The taxi moved slowly down the driveway as Braddock watched it go. He stood there for a few moments, a thoughtful look on his face, then turned and went back to the office. Sitting down at the desk, he took out a legal pad and wrote a brief message:

> *Dear Maggie,*
> *Just a quick note to let you know that I'm all right. I'll be gone for a few days, and I don't want you to worry. I'm taking a little sabbatical. Tell Joe to lead the congregation in my absence, and I'll return as soon as possible. Be assured of my love and concern for you—*
> *Always,*
> *Billy*

Leaving the note on the desk, Braddock got up and started walking toward the door. He paused on the threshold and gave a lingering look around the room, as if he were seeing it for the last time. Then, with an unmistakable look of sadness in his eyes, he turned away and closed the door behind him.

Maggie and Joe arrived at the hospital shortly after eight a.m. and proceeded directly to the intensive care unit. Going to the nurses' station, they asked to see Billy Braddock. The nurse looked surprised. "Hasn't he called you?"

"No," Lindsey said, "we haven't heard anything."

"The doctor released him early this morning."

"He did?" Joe asked with an astonished look. "Where's the doctor?"

"I think he's seeing patients right now."

"Will you please try to page him?"

"I'll call his secretary."

While the nurse was on the telephone, Lindsey took out his cell phone and called Braddock's house. The phone rang several times and then the answering machine came on. Lindsey hung up, a look of concern on his face. "There's no answer at the house. Let me try the office at the church." The church secretary answered the phone. "Annie? This is Joe. I'm fine. Listen, Annie—is Reverend Braddock around there anywhere? Have you seen 'im at all today? Well, if he shows up, will you please have 'im call me on my cell phone? Thanks, Annie." He exchanged worried glances with Maggie. "I don't understand it."

"I hope he's not lyin' there, too sick to answer the phone."

"Dr. Mendelson said for you to come to his office," the nurse interrupted. "It's near the reception desk in the main lobby."

"I know where it is," Lindsey said.

Going back to the lobby, they proceeded directly to the chief resident's office. The secretary immediately informed the doctor they had arrived and escorted them inside. Mendelson stood up to greet them when they came through the door. "Good mornin', folks," he said. "Come on in and make yourselves comfortable."

Once they were seated, Joe got right to the point. "They told us you released Billy early this morning."

"It wasn't anything I wanted to do," the doctor assured them. "Billy was furious that we wouldn't let him go home, and he was threatening to bring Braddock Oil Company's legal staff down on our heads. I know what kind of high-powered attorneys work for the company, so it wasn't a threat to be taken lightly. He signed a form, saying he refused treatment and releasing the hospital and medical staff from any further liability. I'm not a lawyer, but I felt I didn't have any legal justification to keep him here. He left me no choice." The doctor showed them the form Braddock had signed, and passed it to Joe and Maggie for their inspection. "I told him it was a suicidal decision, but he didn't care. We had no choice but to respect his wishes. I just assumed he went back home from here. It never occurred to me you'd be back up here today trying to find him."

"How'd he get home—in an ambulance?"

"I think he took a taxi."

"Doesn't that violate hospital protocol?"

The doctor shrugged. "What could we do? It *was* Billy Braddock, after all. And he *did* sign a waiver. There wasn't much else we *could* do."

"Well, see, Doctor...we don't know if he went home, or not," Joe said. "Maggie stayed at our house last night, and we came straight here from my house this morning."

The doctor gave a shrug. "Maybe he's there now."

"He's not answerin' the phone, if he is," Maggie said. "I'm so worried."

Mendelson gave them a sympathetic look. "I just want you to know...he was in very bad shape when he left here this morning. I don't mean to upset you, but you might as well be prepared for the worst to happen at any moment. He may already be dead." Maggie let out a plaintive moan, and he hastily added, "I'm not saying he *is* dead, Maggie—I'm just saying that you should start preparing yourselves now, because he won't last much longer if he won't let us help him."

About that time, there was a light knock on the door, and the secretary came in. "Doctor, Chief Wilkins is here."

"Send 'im in."

Wilkins came through the door. Skipping the formal greetings, he said, "I guess we all found out the same thing, huh?"

"Mornin', John," the doctor nodded. "I was just explaining to Joe and Maggie that we had to release Billy because he refused treatment."

"Why would he do that?" Wilkins said, with a perplexed expression.

"That's a question you'll have to ask Billy," the doctor answered.

"He's not answerin' the phone at home, John," Maggie said.

"Well, maybe we oughta go out and check on 'im."

Dr. Mendelson looked at the police chief. "Is that what you came to see me about, John? Billy's condition?"

"Yeah. Since I didn't get to talk to 'im yesterday, I just wanted to see if he could give us any more information about what happened. I been thinkin' Jenny mighta told him somethin' that would give us a clue where to look for Shooter Dobbins."

"When you see him, I hope you'll talk some sense into him and get him back up here to this hospital," Mendelson advised. "He desperately needs medical attention."

Maggie said, "I've known him for just about all his life, and I can tell you that Billy can be pretty stubborn when he gets somethin' in his head."

"I got a little dose of that this morning," the doctor said with an ironic smile. "Just do your best."

Opening the door, the police chief said, "Let's go see about 'im."

The three visitors thanked the doctor for his time and left the hospital. Chief Wilkins followed Joe Lindsey out to the Braddock estate. Inside the house, Maggie went upstairs with the police chief while Joe Lindsey checked the rooms downstairs. They conducted a thorough search of the house and eventually regathered in the living room downstairs. "Did you check the basement, Joe?" Maggie asked.

"Yeah. It looks like a big saloon down there—jukebox, pool tables, bandstand, dance floor...incredible. It looks like the old Copacabana Club in New York City. It's fantastic."

Maggie nodded. "That was Billy's playhouse, back in his younger days. His daddy's the one who actually built it. Wild Bill used to entertain his oil-business buddies down there. Back in the Thirties, when Prohibition was the law, people used to say that there was Prohibition everywhere in the country...except down in Wild Bill Braddock's basement. Billy told me some of the parties his Daddy threw down there woulda made the ancient Romans look like a bunch of choir boys by comparison. But Billy hasn't been down there in years."

"I didn't search thoroughly, but it was pitch-black before I turned the lights on, and there were no signs of life. I don't think we'll find 'im there," Joe said.

"Let's go check his office." Maggie led the way through the house to the bungalow out back. As soon as they entered the room, Maggie saw the note lying on top of the desk. Reading it, she showed it to the two men. "He's gone somewhere. He's takin' a...what was that word?"

"Sabbatical," Joe said. "It's like a vacation."

"As sick as he is, he's takin' a vacation? That can't be right," Maggie declared.

Wilkins rubbed his chin thoughtfully. "Hmm—I dunno...maybe he thinks he's gonna die, and he doesn't want anybody to be there with 'im when he does. Some people are like that."

"I wonder which car he took," Joe said.

"Well, let's find out," Maggie replied. The housekeeper led the way to the small two-car garage beside the bungalow, but the Mercedes was still there. She led them to the other side of the house, where a large garage held six other vehicles, all of them still parked in place. "If he's not still here on the grounds, he either called somebody or took a taxi. I doubt very seriously he walked."

"But why wouldn't he call one of us?" Lindsey asked. "We're closer to him than anybody in the world."

"I dunno," answered the police chief. "I'm gonna radio the department and have some of my boys come out here and conduct a thorough search of the premises. If we don't find 'im, I'll start an investigation."

"Billy...you crazy, stubborn" ... Maggie didn't complete the thought.

"How 'bout the hired help?" Wilkins asked. "You think any of them mighta seen 'im?"

"Except for a few permanent employees, we don't keep a regular staff. The people who work around the property are mostly poor folks who go to Billy's church," Maggie said. "They come in and work as needed. I doubt that any of the regular groundskeepers were here real early. There might be a few people workin' somewhere on the property by now."

"Well, let me get started with a search of the grounds, and then we'll figure out what to do next," Wilkins said. "If you can think of anybody else Billy mighta called other than yourselves, you might check with 'em." He paused. "But I'd like to caution you not to give people the idea Billy's disappeared. You know how gossip spreads in this town." The two listeners nodded their understanding, and Wilkins explained, "I don't wanna get a lot of reporters out here, buggin' the crap outta me while I'm tryin' to conduct an investigation."

"And I know how Billy is"—Maggie added— "he hates a lotta publicity. I can't even imagine how mad he'd get if his name was splashed all over the news around the country. I know he'd really get upset about that."

Nodding, Wilkins said, "Well, keep that in mind as you go about your business."

"We'll do that," Joe Lindsey assured him.

With that, the police chief left the office. Maggie looked as if she wanted to start crying again. "I don't know what I'll do without 'im. Takin' care of Billy has been my whole life, ever since my husband died. I just feel lost."

Putting his arm around her shoulder, Joe said, "I'm sure Chief Wilkins will find 'im. For now, we just have to carry on. I'm sure that's what Billy wants us to do."

Maggie directed a dark look toward the window. "I just have this feelin' I'll never see 'im again. Never again" ...

"Now don't be feelin' like that," Lindsey said in a voice of reassurance. "I'm sure Billy's just takin' a few days to commune with God, and he'll back before you know it." He gently nudged her toward the door. "Come on—let's go back to the house and get back to our normal routine. It's what Billy would want."

At the Tomahawk Motel, a long-haired man in casual dress attire was standing on the sidewalk, his luggage beside him, banging loudly on the door of one of the rooms. "Steve? Bobby? C'mon—open up! I know you're in there."

There were sounds of activity inside the room, and then a voice said, "Artie—is that you?"

"Yeah, it's me. Open up."

The door opened slightly, and a sleepy-eyed Steve Jackson peered out through the crack. "Artie? What the hell are you doin' here?"

"Open the door, will you?"

Jackson pulled the chain off the door and allowed Artie to enter the room. Setting his suitcases inside the door, the first thing Artie saw was a woman, naked to the waist, sitting upright in the bed where she had obviously been sleeping with Steve. In the other bed, two bodies were stirring to life under the covers, and Bobby rolled over to see who it was. "Holy crap! Artie? What're you doin' here?"

"I'll step outside while the ladies get dressed," Artie said.

In a few moments, the door opened again and two young women came out onto the walkway, closely followed by a shirtless Steve Jackson. "We had a great time," one of the women said, giving Jackson a lingering hug.

"Me, too, Sherry," Steve replied.

"Me, too, Alice!" Bobby shouted from inside the room as he struggled into his trousers.

"Me, too, Bobby" Alice shouted back, punctuating her comment with a little giggle. "Let's do it again soon."

"Are you guys gonna come over to the Country Club later on?" Sherry asked, directing her question toward Jackson.

"Yeah, if we don't get too busy. This is Artie. He's our boss from Houston."

"Hi, Artie," the girls said in chorus. Sherry smiled and gave him an enticing look. "You come with 'em, Artie. I got a girlfriend who'd just love t' meet you."

"I just might do that," Artie said with an insincere grin. The girls waved goodbye and went to their car, giving Steve a parting wave before they drove away. Artie came into the room and closed the door behind him. He gave his two subordinates a mildly disapproving look. "Is this what I'm payin' you guys for—to drink and fuck all night and lay in bed till ten a.m.?"

"It's not as bad as it looks," Jackson protested. "We've got an excuse."

"What excuse—a hard dick?"

"No, that came up after business hours," Bobby said, with a grin.

"Yeah, well...I don't have time for excuses right now. Get on your feet. It's time to get started."

Hastily buttoning his shirt, Steve, said, "So, really...what *are* you doin' here—just checkin' up on us?"

"That wasn't my original intention, although it appears to have been a good idea. When you called me and told me Braddock had been hit by a car, I decided I'd better come see about the situation myself, so I chartered a flight outta Houston. I told you we've been uncovering a lot of stuff from various film archives, things I doubt even the major networks have yet. But if this guy dies" ...he paused a moment, trying to think of an appropriate analogy... "Well, we're gonna be like a midget-league football team playin' against the Dallas Cowboys—billion-dollar corporations are gonna be rushin' to capitalize on the story of this guy's life. We'll be lucky to get any airtime at all, anywhere. So, to speed up the process, I put extra research staff to work yesterday to get more information about Braddock's business empire. We already know he's into everything from oil, to banking, to real estate, to defense contracting, and more. From what we do know, he's kinda like the Howard Hughes nobody ever heard about."

"Me and Bobby had a feelin' about that, too. But...you know, he doesn't seem like that kinda guy when you meet 'im. In a way, he's kinda—you know...likable. I never heard of anybody sayin' that about Howard Hughes."

"And you said he was gonna consider lettin' you interview him, right?"

"Yeah. He told us to call his secretary Saturday."

"Man, an exclusive interview with the man himself woulda raised the value of our stock unbelievably. Damn the luck!" Artie exclaimed. "Why'd a fuckin' car have to hit 'im *now*? Why not a month from now?"

"You're all heart," Steve chuckled.

Artie pondered a moment, then said, "I've been up for the past...I don't know...thirty hours or so, and I'm not thinkin' too clearly. I've gotta get a coupla hours' sleep pretty soon, but right now I want you to show me the lay of the land."

Bobby joined the conversation, saying, "We've shot a lot of exteriors around town, but Steve decided to hold off on tryin' to do any interviews until Braddock would tell us whether he was gonna help us out, or not."

"I didn't wanta spook 'im," Steve explained. "You know what happened to those guys from the BBC."

Artie took a moment to consider. "Yeah, I remember. That was prob'ly a good decision. No need to take a chance on pissin' 'im off until you could get an answer, one way or the other." He suddenly had a thought. "Have you got a video player in here, Bobby?"

"Yeah, it's right here," Pardo said.

"Crank it up," Artie ordered. "I wanna show you guys something." Immediately, Bobby Pardo retrieved the machine and set it up for his boss. Artie took a video disk from his briefcase. "Check this out." Once the disk was in the player, Artie took control and motioned them over to watch. "These are just some highlights I've assembled from the archives we've been collecting." Grainy black-and-white images of men in football uniforms appeared on the screen. "This is SMU against Texas...I can't remember what year. It was one of the biggest games of the year. See the big fullback, number forty-four? That's Braddock. Now, here we go—watch this." As the play unfolded, Artie did a running commentary. "Okay. The quarterback gets the ball and hands off to Braddock on a slant off tackle." He paused the video and rewound. "You see that? That big defensive tackle from Texas throws off his blocker and closes the hole." He paused again and backed up, then started the video again. "Now here comes number forty-four, and he's got no place to go. So he just lowers his helmet and goes head-to-head with the tackle, and knocks 'im on his ass—*boom!* See that?" Artie backed it up and played the collision again.

"Braddock knocked that sucker down like he was runnin' over a *cheerleader!*" Bobby Pardo said in a tone of approval.

"Now—check this out." On the screen, they could see that the big fullback ran past the tackle as he was falling to the ground and burst into the backfield, which was cluttered with defenders coming to the ball. With an incredible display of fakes, spin moves and sheer brute force, Braddock avoided tackles until he came to the last obstacle, a safety who had the angle on the runner and was closing quickly to make the tackle in the open field. Braddock made a move toward the safety as if to take him on the same way he had done the tackle at the line of scrimmage, and the safety slowed down a step, obviously thinking to brace himself for the collision. But there was no collision. Braddock put on a burst of speed that hardly seemed possible for a man of his size, and he blew past the defender, running untouched the rest of the way into the end zone. "Touchdown!" Artie exclaimed. "Ain't that somethin'?"

"Damn! That's fantastic!" Bobby exclaimed. "That's one of the greatest plays I ever saw! It's like Jim Brown and Walter Payton, all rolled into one."

"I don't know football as well as you do, Bobby," Artie said. "But I know a great play when I see one. And that right there was a great play." He smiled enthusiastically. "And we've found a whole treasure-trove of this stuff. I'm tellin' you, the guy was unbelievable." He again stopped the video and ran it fast forward. "Now, check this out—here he is in the Golden Gloves finals at Madison Square Garden." He stopped the action, then went fast forward where he wanted to start. "Wait a minute...okay, here we are—second round of a three-round fight, goin' for the national amateur heavyweight championship. Before I run this, I'll just tell you...the black guy moved and jabbed all the way through the first round, and then he cut Braddock's eye with what looks like an intentional head-butt near the end of the round. But here's the part I want you to see." He pointed to a spot on the screen. "You see that? Look at Braddock's face. You can tell this guy is severely...*pissed...off*...after the head-butt, and the black guy's actin' like he's got it won. So the black guy quits dancin' around and goes straight at Braddock, fightin' what normally woulda been Braddock's fight—I guess thinkin' to whip Braddock man-to-man, beat 'im at 'is own game, and humiliate 'im in the process. Whatever he was thinkin', he thought wrong. Now...watch"—The action went on a few seconds more, and then Artie exclaimed, "*Bam! The end!*" On the video, a crushing right hand from Braddock landed squarely on the opponent's chin and he dropped like a building imploding. The black fighter crumpled into a small pile in the middle of the ring, and Braddock raised his hands in victory. Artie stopped the video. "This is the kinda guy we're doin' a story on. Do you see why it's so important to me?"

92

"I sure as hell do," Bobby agreed. "Can you imagine Howard Hughes doin' somethin' like this? No fuckin' way!"

With an approving smile, Artie said, "I'll tell you—those interns we hired from Rice University are some hellacious researchers. They've found stuff in a coupla months it woulda taken me five years to locate. They really know their shit." Returning the disk to his briefcase, he said, "I don't suppose you've heard any further word on Braddock's condition."

"I'm sure he's still in the hospital," Steve said. "That assistant pastor said there was a specialist comin' in from Houston today."

"Well, why don't you call the hospital and see what they tell you?" Artie suggested.

Steve went to the phone and made the call. After a brief conversation, he hung up and directed a puzzled look toward his two companions. "He's been released from the hospital. That's kinda weird."

"Well, then, let's go over to the church and see what we can find out," Artie said.

"Yeah. That's a good idea," Steve agreed.

With Bobby Pardo behind the wheel, the three men got in the van and went straight to the Church of the Living God. As they drew closer to the church, they could see signs of unusual activity on the Braddock estate. Steve instructed Bobby to bypass the church and take the road leading to Braddock's property. Going through the main gate, they drove toward the house, where they saw John Wilkins standing beside his police car, talking to someone on the police radio. When Wilkins saw them, he cut his conversation short, dropped the radio in the car seat, and turned to greet them.

"Howdy, boys," he said, walking over to the driver's side of the van. "For a coupla whoremongin' drunks, you're out kinda early, ain't you?"

"You know about last night?"

"I know everything that goes on in this town. I hear tell Sherry and Alice have two o' the best pussies in the county—but then, they get a lotta practice. So who's your friend in the pony-tail?"

"Oh—this is Artie Davis, our boss."

"Artie," he said with a nod. "John Wilkins, police chief." He paused briefly, then asked, "So what brings you out this way today?"

"We heard they let Billy Braddock outta th' hospital. We just came by to see how he's doin'."

"They sent 'im to a specialist...Mayo Clinic, or somewhere like that."

"How bad is he?" Artie asked.

"Hey—I'm just a cop. You'll have to talk to 'is doctor about 'is condition."

"Who's 'is doctor?" Artie persisted.

Wilkins shrugged. "You have to ask somebody else that question. I got no idea."

"What's with all the police cars?" Steve inquired.

"There was a break-in last night. Nobody was here, and the housekeeper was too upset about what happened to Billy to remember to turn on the alarm. It's nothin' serious."

"Well, that's a lot of police cars, for nothin' serious."

"This is Glory Road. Folks around here don't take too kindly to criminal activity in this neighborhood. I think you can look at all the mansions around here and see where I'm comin' from." The men in the van nodded their understanding, and Wilkins continued, "Anyway, I gotta get back to work, and you'll have to get back to doin' whatever it is people like you do. We're treatin' the entire property as a crime scene at this point, so I'm gonna have to ask you to leave."

Understanding that the conversation was over, they left without any further questions. Back on the highway, they drove back toward the Tomahawk Motel and pondered the meaning of what they had just seen. Looking toward the back of the van, Steve said, "You're the boss, Artie—whadda ya think about half the police force bein' out there on a burglary investigation?"

Taking time to formulate an answer, Artie replied, "I'm not sure. It's prob'ly just what he said it was. I'd say over ninety-nine percent of the money in this whole town is concentrated right there in that neighborhood. I'd guess that cop's just keepin' 'is ass covered. You know the police motto: 'To protect and serve the rich.' He's just doin' 'is job."

"Well, where do we go from here?" Bobby asked.

"I dunno. It's obvious that the interview with Braddock is on hold indefinitely. I think we'll finish out the week, try to see if we can get a few interviews that might provide some insights into the man, and then we'll head back to Houston. Maybe after I get a few hours' sleep, I'll have some other ideas. For now, I just wanna go back to the motel and get some sleep."

"I just got a feelin' this whole thing is down the shitter," Steve glumly observed. "It'll prob'ly be a whole different kinda film than I was hopin' we could make."

"If we can't get Braddock involved, then we're gonna make the best film we can make without 'im. If he's fixin' t' die, we've still gotta get on with it, regardless. We've already spent a pretty good chunk of money—just on research—so we need t' come up with some kind of a product so we can recoup our investment. The good thing is—if we have to go to Plan B, I've got a connection who guarantees we can turn a profit by sellin' it in syndication. It's just that I had grander designs when we started all this." Artie paused, then added, "And—from what I've seen—once we get all this stuff put together, we may still have somethin' worthy of a theatrical release."

"I hope you're right, Artie," Steve replied. "I've just got a bad feelin' we've seen the last of Bronco Billy Braddock."

"I think you're wrong, Steve," Artie disagreed. "If I've really got what I think I'm gonna have when we finish gettin' all this stuff together, Bronco Billy—dead or alive—*will* ride again."

Several nights later, in a cheap motel on the outskirts of Houston, Billy Braddock woke up suddenly in the dead of night. He lay there motionless in the semi-darkness for what seemed like a very long time, aware of nothing but the relentless aching that seemed to permeate every muscle in his body. In all his years of playing violent sports, he had never experienced anything near this level of excruciating pain in so many places at once. The air-conditioner was going full blast and the room was very cold, but he was sweating profusely as he lay naked on top of the covers. Even his gums were aching, and the inside of his mouth felt hot. He forced himself out of bed and went to the bathroom to get a drink. Turning on the light, he removed his upper denture and rubbed a sore place at the center of the gum. He peered closely into the mirror to see what was causing him such extraordinary discomfort. Carefully studying the area where he could feel the rough spot that was hurting so badly, Braddock suddenly realized what he was seeing:

"Teeth," he said aloud. "*I'm cuttin' teeth!*"

END PART ONE

PART TWO

On a beautiful morning in early May, John Wilkins arrived at the Braddock estate and parked his vehicle in front of the house. As he started up the walk, the front door opened, and Maggie came outside to meet him. Giving him a warm hug as he stepped onto the porch, she said, "Thank you for coming, John. Joe just got here. Come on in. I've got the coffee ready and some nice hot cinnamon rolls fresh out of the oven."

"Thank you, Maggie. It's nice to see you again."

Leading the way, Maggie brought the police chief to the homey kitchen at the rear of the house, where Joe Lindsey was seated at the kitchen table, sipping a cup of coffee. He stood up when Wilkins entered the room and extended a friendly handshake. They exchanged brief greetings as Maggie brought coffee and a roll to the table. Pulling up a chair, Wlkins sampled the pastry and smiled in approval. "You make the best cinnamon rolls in Texas, Maggie."

Maggie smiled. "They came out of a can, but I appreciate the compliment, anyway. Since Billy's been gone, I don't get a lot of compliments on my cookin'."

Wasting no time, Wilkins got down to business. "Well, I know you folks have been wantin' to know what we've found out, and I'll just tell you straight out—it's not much. But here's what I do have: We know for a fact that Billy showed up for the meeting of Braddock Oil Company's Board of Directors a week after he disappeared. I've interviewed every one of 'em, and they all swear that the man who came to the meeting was the real Billy Braddock. They said he looked kinda sick, but he was in full control of his mental faculties and didn't look or act much different than he did the last time they saw him."

"Did he say anything to them about his immediate plans for the future?" Joe Lindsey asked.

"No. He didn't say much at all that day, other than to take care of business. That was the one thing that was unusual about his behavior—he didn't go out to dinner with them after the meeting, and he didn't stay any longer than he absolutely had to, before he left the meeting. Normally, he woulda spent some time...you know...socializin' with everybody. But not this time. They all told me they really didn't think too much of it at the time—they just figured he had pressing business elsewhere."

He paused to take a sip of coffee, and Maggie used that moment to ask, "Is that the last time anyone saw 'im?"

"Well, no...a coupla days later, he met with his personal attorney and made some changes in his will. And then a few days after that, he met with one of his financial advisors and did some kinda restructuring involvin' the funding of the research institute here in town. And I found out that while he was there, he borrowed one of the secretaries to dictate a letter to Dr. Keeler, who runs the institute, tellin' him about some pet research projects he wants 'em to put on the front burner. And, as far as I know, that's the last time anyone actually saw 'im."

"That's not too reassuring," Maggie said, with a worried look. "He's been gone quite awhile now."

Chief Wilkins held up an index finger. "There's one more thing—about six weeks after he disappeared, he called Dr. Keeler from a pay phone at the Hyatt Regency in Dallas. I've confirmed that from the phone records. And I've also talked to Keeler, and he says he's positive it was Billy because they talked about some stuff that only the two of 'em could possibly know about. So he was definitely still alive around the first of the year."

"I just don't understand it," Joe Lindsey said. "I mean—how could he manage to disappear so *completely?*"

"Well, that's partly because I'm respectin' what we all think would be Billy's wishes—he wouldn't take too kindly to us turnin' this into a full-blown missing-persons investigation and gettin' the press and the FBI and everybody else involved. Somethin' tells me that if he's still out there, alive and well, and we call that kind of attention to the case, he'll go ballistic. I got a family to provide for, and I'm not gonna jeopardize their well-being by gettin' Billy all upset with me."

"No," Maggie said, shaking her head, "that wouldn't be the thing to do at all."

"Here's somethin' else, just so you'll know: I have a friend who works for the FBI in El Paso. With permission from his supervisor, he's been conductin' his own private investigation, usin' resources we don't have at our disposal in our little local police department. I'm not totally sure what all we been doin' is completely legal—let's just say we're operatin' in a gray area for the greater good—but we've been monitoring for any sort of activity involving his cell phone, bank accounts and credit cards...and there's nothing. I have a feelin' he tore up his cell phone and threw it away so he couldn't be traced that way. And as for money...he's bound to be operatin' on a cash basis, unless he's got a credit card in some other name. Or maybe there's a third party involved, funneling cash to him as he needs it. I don't know. But if he's still alive, he's gotta be payin' 'is way somehow."

Maggie bowed her head in frustration. "This is just so...strange. Why wouldn't he take the time to call us and let us know he's all right? He's bound to know I'm worried about 'im."

Wilkins shrugged. "I don't know."

"What about that taxi driver?" Joe asked. "Did you get any more information out of him?"

"Rufus Johnson. He swears up and down all he did was pick Billy up at the hospital and bring him back here, but I think he knows more than he's tellin'. Like I told you awhile back...he's never explained the discrepancy between the time he picked Billy up and the time he checked back with the taxi company. He says he was out in the country, takin' a nap, but I don't believe it. I know he's been flashin' a lot of cash around town lately, and there's no way that taxi job pays him enough to be doin' that. We're keepin' an eye on 'im, but since Billy was alive several weeks after he left the hospital, I haven't got any reason to arrest the taxi driver."

Interrupting, Maggie said, "Oh—I been meanin' t' tell you—I may know how Billy left here, if no one came and picked 'im up."

"How's that?"

"You know that little building at the very back of the property?"

"Yeah...the little workshop building?"

"Yes. One of the boys who works on the property asked me yesterday what happened to that old pickup truck that Billy had stored back there. I think it was a Ford they made back in the Fifties. A long time back, Billy bought it from a junkyard or someplace like that, had 'em bring it to the shop, and he tinkered with it off and on for years till he got to feelin' so bad he didn't wanna mess with it any more. I know he had it runnin' at one time, but it didn't have any plates, or a title, or anything, as far as I know. But it's gone, and I know I didn't call anyone to haul it off. Then again, Billy mighta done that himself, and I didn't know anything about it. I just thought that might explain how he left here without a trace."

The police chief was thoughtful. "Hmm...you know...that could be it. Maybe he just got lucky and avoided gettin' a ticket until he made it to El Paso, or somewhere, and then abandoned the vehicle. If it was an old junker, somebody woulda just towed it off and never thought anything about it."

"Chief, have you been gettin' calls from some reporters in Houston?" asked Joe Lindsey. "They work for DocuTex?"

"Yeah, those jerks. Have they been callin' you, too?" Lindsey nodded, and Wilkins said, "They're not exactly reporters...they're some kinda filmmakers. I hope you haven't told 'em anything."

"Well...I did," the pastor admitted with some reluctance. "I hope I haven't talked outta school, but their questions were makin' me nervous. They were talkin' about Billy bein' hit by a car, and I told 'em he simply had a heart attack. But then they were sayin' somebody at the hospital told 'em he had other injuries, and I said that was because he fell out of the van. I mean"—he clasped his hands and turned his eyes toward heaven— "Lord forgive me for lyin', but I was afraid they might get somethin' stirred up."

"No, that's a good cover story," Wilkins said with a grin. "If you ever decide t' give up preachin', you oughta go into politics."

"I'm not sure if that's a compliment, or not," Lindsey replied, returning the smile.

The police chief glanced at his watch. "But, really, folks—that's all I've got, as far as Billy's concerned. We're still tryin' t' locate Shooter Dobbins and his wife, too, but no luck on that so far, either. I have a feelin' he's crossed the border into Mexico. But we're gonna keep lookin'. He'll turn up somewhere, sooner or later."

Maggie gave him an understanding look. "I know you have a tough job, John, but we appreciate all you're doin'."

"Some days are better than others," Wilkins agreed. "But your kindness is well taken. Anyway, I need to be gettin' to the office, so with your permission" ...

"Thanks for comin' by, John," the pastor said.

"I'll walk you to the door," offered Maggie.

"I know the way. You folks finish your coffee and we'll see each other soon. If anything new comes up, I'll let you know."

In Houston, at the offices of DocuTex Productions, a large old house in the Montrose district, Artie Davis was sitting at his desk when Steve Jackson and Bobby Pardo returned from assignment. Looking up from his work, Artie gave them an unenthusiastic glance. "Okay, guys—what? More of the same?"

Steve repressed a look of celebration. "No, not entirely."

Davis leaned back in his chair. "Okay...so partial me."

Steve motioned to the cameraman. "Get that interview cued up, Bobby." While Pardo was getting the video ready, Steve Jackson explained: "Before we show you this, I wanna ask you: Did you ever hear of a football coach named Tom Langston? He coached with several pro teams back in the day."

Artie shook his head. "I don't know that much about football."

"Well, back in the Fifties, he was with the Baltimore Colts. It was his first job in the pros. He remembered Billy Braddock really well, and wasn't a bit shy about talkin' about 'im. We didn't even try to do any editing yet. This is the raw interview, but I think you're really gonna like this."

"Okay, Steve—it's ready."

Jackson nodded. "Roll it, Bobby."

Onscreen, a leather-faced old man wearing a baseball cap and a good-natured grin appeared. He was sitting in a lawn chair in what looked to be his back yard, holding a can of beer in his hand. In the background, Steve Jackson's voice could be heard asking the questions:

"So, Coach Langston...do you remember Billy Braddock?"

"Oh, Billy?" The old coach chuckled aloud. *"Yeah, hell, yeah—who could forget a crazy guy like that? Bronco Billy, they called 'im. Great football player."*

"So what's the story on him and the Baltimore Colts? Why didn't that deal work out?"

The coach gave a disdainful wave of his hand. *"Oh, hell...that was a total cluster-fuck from the beginning."*

"Tell me what you recall about it."

"Well, I was a young coach then, kind of an assistant to the assistant's assistant, you know what I mean? I was a gopher, is what I was," he said with a laugh. *"Nobody listened to me at all. But I remember Billy joined the Colts the same year Johnny Unitas came to the team—same year I came to the team, too. He had just graduated from college, made All-America*

103

the year before, and I know he thought he was gonna set the world on fire. He was a big, cocky, kinda arrogant kid—real friendly, but...I don't know—kinda cocky in a way that pissed some people off. Now me— I liked 'im, us both bein' from Texas and all, 'cause I understood where he was comin' from...it's a Texas thing, you know? But the big coaches...I dunno...they didn't get it. Wasn't none o' them from Texas, as far as I ever knew."

"You mean all that Texas braggin' and blowin' pissed 'em off?" Jackson asked.

"I think everything about Billy Braddock pissed 'em off. But that wouldn't-a made any difference in what happened...you know...even if Billy's personality didn't rub some people the wrong way, because the powers-that-be had already made decisions about Billy's future with the team that pretty much guaranteed it was never gonna work."

"How so?"

"Well, see...the Colts already had a startin' fullback—Alan Ameche? Alan the Horse, they called 'im. You remember him?"

"My cameraman knows who he is. What about Ameche?"

"Well, all the coaches liked Alan and his blue-collar work-ethic and no-frills style of running—he was just a straight-ahead fullback—good blocker, hard runner—and Weeb"—

"Did you say dweeb—good blocker, hard runner...and dweeb?"

"No, Weeb—Weeb Ewbank. He was the head coach."

"Oh, I gotcha," Jackson said. "So go ahead."

The coach continued, "Anyway, Weeb was completely sold on Alan. So right from the git-go, there was no way Billy Braddock was gonna get Ameche's job—I don't care how good he was—unless Ameche got hurt. That was pretty much the only way. And, *really...personally—I thought Billy had a lot more to bring to the field than Al did—Billy had power, plus moves, plus speed, plus size, plus good hands for pass catchin'...and he was also a helluva blocker. For my money, he was what you'd call the complete package. I tried to state my opinion about it...but nobody was gonna listen to a little piss-ant like me, so it didn't do any good."*

"Why wouldn't they listen to you, if what you were saying was right?"

Tom Langston chuckled. *"I hate to admit it, but it's just possible I wasn't necessarily right. Ameche was an All-Pro player himself. Plus, he had a professional discipline that Braddock didn't have. So the way it worked out was...you had Alan the Horse Ameche, and Bronco Billy Braddock, and both of 'em wantin' t' be the startin' fullback—and I guess that was just one too many horses in that particular corral."*

"Sounds kinda like a wild-horse versus work-horse situation," Steve Jackson suggested.

"I couldn't-a said it better myself," Langston agreed. *"And what the Colts needed at that time was a good, reliable work-horse at that position. And Ameche was perfect for the part."* The coach stopped and took a sip of beer. *"But if you wanta know my opinion—and I've always believed this—I think Braddock's career was doomed from the first day they signed 'im with the club, because the coaches never intended to let him play what he thought was his natural position."*

"Why weren't they gonna give 'im a chance? Wouldn't they want the best man available at every position?"

"I know it sounds crazy, but...not necessarily." He made an equivocating gesture. *"It all depends on how you define the term* best man. *Like I say—for what the Colts wanted, Ameche was the best man.*

And since he did make the All-Pro team several years in a row, it's hard to argue that he really wasn't the best man for the position."

"*So that was that,*" Jackson suggested.

"*Pretty much,*" Langston agreed. "*But Billy had played both sides of the ball in college, and he was just about as good on defense as he was on offense—he was a great all-around player, no kiddin'. He'd-a made a great defensive back. But he didn't join the Colts to play defense. Billy was kind of a glory hog—offense was* what *he wanted, and* all *he wanted, and he was never gonna get a chance to do that on his terms. He had it in 'is head he wasn't gonna play any offensive position but fullback—period. I'm sure he coulda started at a number of other positions, but he just wasn't interested in playin' anything but fullback.*"

"*That sounds kinda self-defeating to me,*" Jackson observed.

Langston nodded. "*Self defeating? Try plumb stupid. That's what it was—plumb stupid.*"

"*Why do you think Braddock was so hard-headed about it?*"

The coach shrugged. "*Who knows? Maybe growin' up rich and talented and good-lookin' and always gettin' everything he wanted, when he wanted it...maybe all that turned 'im into a spoiled brat. I dunno. But in a way, that's kinda what he was—a spoiled brat.*"

"*So what happened?*"

"*What happened? They gave 'im a token tryout at fullback, and no matter what he did, they found fault with it. And I'm tellin' you—I was watchin' the same thing the other coaches were watchin', and I was seein' flashes of somethin' that looked like a true potential for greatness. Seriously. Billy was a raw rookie, and he was doin' some incredible things out there on that field—a rookie! But it didn't make any difference. It just wasn't gonna happen. So, one day they called 'im in and told 'im he just wasn't cuttin' it at fullback, and they didn't think he'd ever be able to, and they were gonna start trainin' 'im to play defense, and that's when things went all to hell."*

"How did things go to hell?"

Tom Langston shrugged. *"Billy just quit givin' a shit...started breakin' all the rules...doin' whatever he damn well pleased, when he pleased."*

"Can you give me a for instance?"

"For instance, like—you name it. Everything. If there was a rule about somethin', he found a way to break it." The coach paused to think a moment, and then grinned as he recalled something: *"One of the things he started doin' that I thought was funny was when the senior coaches would come over and try to explain how they wanted 'im to do somethin', and Billy'd play dumb so they'd get up closer to show 'im what they were talkin' about, and then he'd hawk up a big ol' slimy oyster and spit on their shoes and act like it was an accident...stuff like that—crazy shit."*

"Anything else like that you recall?" Jackson asked.

"Anything else" ...Langston muttered, as he thoughtfully rubbed his chin. His expression brightened as he suddenly recalled another example. *"Oh, yeah—this was funny as hell: If he'd see one of the coaches sittin' down, lookin' at 'is clipboard, Billy'd kinda ease over and get 'is ass close to the coach's head and fart like a motherfucker, and then he'd put on like it just slipped out."* The coach laughed out loud, recalling the memory. *"By the time he left the Colts, he had the whole coachin' staff on edge— me included—wonderin' when that crazy bastard was gonna sneak up and fart in your ear."* The coach laughed again. *"Anything to piss 'em off—that was Billy Braddock"*

"Any other prime examples you can think of?"

107

"Oh, I don't know...he'd come to practice hung over, and only half try. A few times, I think he showed up for practice about two sheets in the wind. I mean, the guy just got to where he didn't give a damn. I think he suspected that he'd got himself in a rigged game, but he couldn't prove it, and he couldn't do anything about it. I'm sure that's what made 'im mad—he thought it was politics that was keepin' 'im from realizin' his dream."

"Do you think that was the case—office politics?"

Langston shrugged. "Maybe some. Seems like there's politics in everything—even football." He paused for a thought. "But, really—I ain't gonna lie about it—Braddock's hard-headed attitude created some of the politics that aggravated the situation."

"Can you think of any specific incidents that would kinda crystallize Braddock's time with the Colts?"

The old man threw his head back and gave a rich laugh. "Yeah, I can. One Saturday night before we were supposed to play the Rams, Billy disappeared. The senior coaches were all pissed off about it, and discussin' what to do about it, and I decided while they were busy plottin' their revenge, I'd go out for awhile and have a coupla drinks myself. It was somewhere around midnight, and I was takin' a taxi back to the hotel where we were stayin', when I see a coupla gorgeous women gettin' out of a taxi that was stopped in front of us, unloadin' passengers at this hotel. So these two women got out, and then Billy Braddock gets out with a big bottle o' whisky in each hand, and then two more women get out of the taxi— and all of 'em were in the back seat. It was like one of those things at the circus where twenty midgets get out of a car the size of a cracker box. I could tell right off the bat that Billy was drunker'n a skunk. But these four gals he had with him were all different colors—white, black, yellow and brown."

108

"*Were they hookers?*"

Laughing, the coach said, "*Well, lemme put it this way: If they* weren't *hookers, that guy was the greatest pickup artist of all time.*" He nodded his head. "*But, yeah, I'd guess they were on the high end of the hooker trade. All of 'em were* hot mamas, *I do mean to tell you. I stuck my head out the window and yelled at 'im, but I guess he didn't hear me because of the horns honkin' 'cause traffic was blocked. So, anyway, him and the girls started into the hotel and my taxi started movin', and just when my taxi got about even with 'em as they were goin' through the door, the last thing I heard was Billy singin' 'Jesus Loves the Little Children' at the top of his lungs.*" He laughed again. "*Can you believe that? 'Jesus Loves the Little Children'!*" Coach Langston started singing in a raspy voice, "*Red and yellow, black and white, they are precious in his sight*" ... This remembrance was followed by another hearty chuckle, then Langston paused and took a sip of beer. "*That's the last words I ever heard outta his mouth and the last time I ever laid eyes on 'im. But yeah—that Billy Braddock was a character, all right.*" Langston paused, nodding, then added, "*And you know—I heard he's turned preacher since then.*"

"*Yeah, he did,*" Jackson said. "*Even started his own church—big fancy church he built at his own expense out in West Texas.*"

"*No kiddin',*" the coach said, with a thoughtful expression. "*Who woulda guessed? Crazy bastard like that.*"

"*So, what finally happened with Billy and the Colts?*" Jackson asked.

"*What finally happened? Well...that next day, when we played the Rams...Billy didn't bother to show up for the game. As far as I know, he never came back again. It was kinda funny, though. Nobody on the coachin' staff ever discussed the matter in front of* me after that. It was like Billy Braddock never happened. But deep down, I know they knew they had lost a kid who probably woulda had a good career if they'd-a found some way to work with 'im. I used to wonder if they signed 'im just to keep some other team from gettin' 'im."

"Do you actually think that's a possibility?"

The coach pondered momentarily. "Oh...prob'ly not. I think it just wasn't in the cards—which is really kind of a shame. Billy told me hisself he'd always dreamed of playin' for the Colts, 'cause he was Bronco Billy, and he just knew it was a perfect match, just like when he was playin' for the Braddock Broncos in high-school, and the SMU Mustangs in college. You know—he had that horse-thing goin' on...Broncos, Mustangs, Colts... He thought it was Fate that the Colts drafted 'im. But when he got to the Colts, the Colts had their own ideas about Billy Braddock's fate." Then the coach hastily added, "Don't get me wrong, though—the problem wasn't all caused by the Colts. Billy coulda made the team easy...just not the way he wanted to. In a lot of ways, he kinda shot hisself in the foot, if you know what I mean. That kid was really bull-headed." Shaking his head, the old coach stared into the distance. "It's kinda sad, really, when you think what mighta been" ...

"What do you think might have been, Coach?" Jackson asked.

"Well, the game was on the verge of changing in really big ways about that time...a lotta spread formations, play action—more of a wide-open, speed-and-finesse type offense focused more on the passing game—and Billy woulda been perfect for that style of football. The future was coming, but there was no way to see that far ahead. If he'd-a just hung in there a little longer, he woulda found himself playin' a game that was tailor-made for his skill set." The coach gave a shrug. "But I don't know...I guess that's just the *way it goes sometimes—it's all there for the taking, and you just don't see what you have to do to take it all. That's what happened to Billy Braddock."* Coach Langston paused thoughtfully, drank the rest of the beer, then crushed the can and tossed it aside. Then he added, *"But, yeah, he really was a great football player"* ...

"Okay, Bobby—go ahead and stop it," Jackson said. There's not much else after that." He looked at Artie. "So, whaddaya think?"

Artie thought about it, then gave an approving nod. "Yeah, I think we've got some usable footage here. We've got the old-time insider story for the hardcore football fans, and the candid glimpse of the preacher as a young man to add shadings of character to the portrait of the man himself. I like it. You got anything else?"

"We talked to a few other people, too. It's on here. You can look at all the footage we've got and make your own decision, but I don't really think there's much we can use. A lotta people who prob'ly do know some stuff like the old coach told us won't give us the time of day. Others talk, but you can tell they're bein' careful not to say anything but what they think Braddock might wanta hear. I think some are afraid of repercussions. Others...I think they're honestly tryin' to protect his reputation out of loyalty to the man. But I know there's gotta be some more people out there like this Coach Langston. I just gotta find 'em."

"Any more word about Braddock's whereabouts, or his condition?"

Jackson shook his head. "Nothin'. The story I'm gettin' now is that all that happened to Braddock was he had a heart attack while he was drivin'. Those other injuries he sustained were supposedly caused when he fell out of the van. He's stayin' at an undisclosed location for rest, recuperation and further treatment. That's all I can get out of anybody."

"Well, keep digging. This thing is shaping up quite nicely, and I'd like to get some more interviews like this one you got from the coach. I'll hold off as long as I can before I start puttin' this in final form, just in case Braddock does show up and gives you an interview, but we *will* have to be wrappin' this up, one way or the other, within the next few months. The research staff is still lookin' for stuff, too, so there's time left before we have to go all the way to the mat with this thing."

"Did they get that list of Braddock's old teammates at SMU? The ones who are still alive?"

"I believe so, yeah," Artie nodded. "I think they've also got the name of a few rodeo guys who were on the circuit the year Braddock won the championship. I know they were workin' on it. You need to check with Doris on that."

"Well, we're gonna head on out. There's a guy who's on the Board of Directors at Braddock Oil I'm gonna try to talk to."

"Board of Directors? Good luck with that. You'd prob'ly have a better interview with the Sphinx."

"We know where he does lunch downtown. We're gonna do a little Mike Wallace-style ambush journalism. Maybe he'll be so flabbergasted, he'll talk outta school."

As they started out the door, Artie called after them, waving a paper in his hand. "Oh—you guys come in early tomorrow before you head out, okay? I wanna talk to you about some of the items you've listed on this expense account."

Steve and Bobby exchanged dubious glances. "Will do," said Jackson, and then hurriedly closed the door behind them.

As they headed toward the van, Bobby could be heard complaining under his breath, "I warned you about usin' that damn credit card at the topless club" ...

There was a bustle of activity at the Resistol Arena as cowboys were arriving to register for the Mesquite Rodeo. Through the milling crowd, a tall, muscular, fresh-faced cowboy wandered around the premises, gawking like a tourist, as he absorbed the sights and sounds of everything around him. The fact that he stood at least a head taller than just about everybody in the building would have made him stand out in any crowd, but the rippling muscles that were barely concealed under the tight-fitting cowboy shirt and blue jeans he wore made it practically impossible for anybody in his proximity not to take note of his imposing presence. His childlike interest in everything that was going on around him did absolutely nothing to diminish the aura of supreme confidence that seemed to radiate from every pore in his body. As he roamed about, a beautiful woman with platinum-blonde hair, dressed in western regalia that served to call attention to every feminine curve of her voluptuous figure, watched him from a distance with an expression of keen interest. After a few moments, she started walking directly over to talk to him. As the big cowboy turned to go to the other side of the building, she stepped in front of him.

"Hello, long, tall and handsome," she said in a sexy voice. "I'm Mary Lynn Bradley. I work with the rodeo."

The cowboy shook the tiny hand the woman offered. "Mary Lynn? I'm Buck Rodgers."

She smiled skeptically. "Buck Rogers? Like the outer space guy?"

"Well, yeah, you *could* say that about me. I *am* kinda out there. But I spell *Rodgers* with a *d*, if that helps any."

"Oh, I didn't mean it like that," she said.

"I'm just kiddin'," he said with a grin. "Actually, my *real* name is Royen Dale Rodgers—and *that's* all kiddin' aside."

"Roy 'n Dale Rodgers?" she repeated with a skeptical chuckle.

"Yep—that's me. It's actually spelled *R-o-y-e-n*. But, yeah, that's me—Royen Dale Rodgers. My ol' man met the King of the Cowboys at a shoppin' mall in Dallas when he was a kid, and he was a lifelong fan after that. So when I was born, the fool actually had the gall to name me Royen Dale. Can you believe that?"

The woman laughed and said, "Well, it's possible, I guess."

Enjoying the story he was telling, the big cowboy continued, "My mama told me he was gonna throw Trigger and Bullet in there with Roy and Dale, but she talked 'im outta *that*, thank God. As crazy as I am, I can't imagine how crazy I'd be if I'd-a spent my childhood bein' called Royen Dale Trigger Bullet Rodgers."

By now, the beautiful blonde was laughing at everything the handsome young cowboy said. "So, how'd you become Buck?"

"Well, my ol' man insisted on callin' me Royen Dale against my will until I got big enough to buck 'im. At the time, I was a big Buck Owens fan, and I got to thinkin' that Buck was a good name for me, too. So I told ever'body to start callin' me Buck from now on. And ever'body did, except my old man—to him I was still Royen Dale. Then one Saturday night, when I was about fifteen years old, I was alone at the house gettin' drunk on some home-brew I'd cooked up out in the toolshed, and here came my ol' man home from the beer joint. He was drunk, too, so I figured now was the perfect time to get this matter straightened out, once and for all. So I just flat-out told 'im I wanted 'im t' start callin' me Buck—or else—and *he* told *me* to go buck myself. Well, that made me mad, and the fight was on."

"Really? You mean, like...a real fight?" she asked with a mild expression of shock.

He gave a casual shrug. "Well...it really wasn't much of a fight—more like a drunken rasslin' match. But after I pinned 'im down, the old man knew I could kick 'is ass if I wanted to, so he quit buckin' on callin' me Buck. And I been Buck ever since then...buckin' the rules, buckin' the system, buckin' in the rodeo, buckin' for a buck...you name it. Buck—that's me. And that's the entire buckin' truth, I swear. So help me Buck."

Getting fully into the spirit of the conversation, she laughingly inquired, "Are you sure you're not just buckin' with me?"

"No, I swear," he said with an obviously feigned expression of sincerity. "I'm so honest, a lotta people call me Buck *Truth* Rodgers."

"Buck Truth? Well, doesn't that bother you? That sounds a lot like Buck *Tooth*," she said with a teasing smile.

"No, not really," he said. "Actually, it kinda makes me feel good, like Abraham Lincoln. You know—real honest, and all that."

She laughed and said, "I don't know if you're actin' like a Texan, or if you're just havin' fun with me, but that's one crazy story, Buck."

The big cowboy gave her a friendly smile. "Hey, I'm a crazy guy."

"But don't you have to put up with a lotta kiddin', bein' Buck Rodgers?"

"Not so's you'd think," the cowboy said with a confident smile. "There's not too many guys a whole lot stupid enough to even *think* about raggin' me. But if somebody gets too insistent and tries to get smart about it, I got a real convincin' way of wipin' that smile off their face." As he said this, the big cowboy patted a large fist into the palm of his other hand as if to say: *Bad things might happen.* "You wouldn't believe how many people have accidentally run into my fist...in broad daylight."

Her eyes flickered with glittery interest, the hint of danger in what the cowboy implied appealing to the adventuress in her. "I bet you *do* have a way of convincin' the doubters. I sure am glad *I* believe you."

"Oh, hey—you can call me Gene Autry, if you feel like it. A pretty thing like you—I don't care what you call me—as long as you call me when you're lonely on a Saturday night."

Mary Lynn tried to conceal how much the flattery pleased her. She gave him a look of mock-disapproval. "And on top of everything else, you're a flirt."

"I ain't flirtin'—I'm serious. You're incredibly beautiful."

"You are too kind," she said, making an effort to change the direction of the conversation. She adopted a slightly more formal attitude. "So—are you new here? I mean...I've never seen you around before."

"I just joined the PRCA, if that's what you mean. And I'm kinda new to the Dallas area, too. But this ain't my first rodeo."

"Well, listen...I serve as an advisor to the people who run the rodeo, and if you need any help or advice, you call me." She took a business card out of her back pocket. "Put this in your wallet," she said, with a smoldering look in her eyes.

The cowboy took the card and did as she said. "I sure do appreciate your interest, ma'am."

"Well, listen—I gotta go mingle, but I'll keep an eye out for you. What all events are you gonna be in?"

"Uh...I signed up for everything, includin' bareback, saddle-bronc and bullridin'. I ain't expectin' to do a whole lotta damage my first time around. I hear the competition's pretty tough at this level."

"I'm sure you'll do just fine," she assured him as she backed away. "Good luck. I'll be watchin' for you."

The cowboy said goodbye, and then stood admiring the graceful movements of Mary Lynn Bradley's extraordinary body as she moved through the crowd to attend to her official responsibilities as an ambassador for the sport. Under his breath, Rodgers muttered, "Whoo-ee!"

From behind him, a voice said, "Looks like you just made a real good friend, amigo."

Buck Rodgers turned to look at the speaker. It was another cowboy, obviously one of the contestants, who greeted him with a friendly smile on his rodeo-battered face. "Who am I talkin' to?" Rodgers asked.

The cowboy extended his hand. "Clete Justus. I'm a regular on the circuit."

"Yeah, I heard o' you," Rodgers said, shaking the proffered hand. Then, by way of introduction, he said, "Buck Rodgers."

Justus laughed. "Well, that's a good name for the rodeo, whether you stay on the ride or get launched into orbit. Either way—competin' with me is scientifically impossible. But it's nice t' meet you, anyway, Buck."

"It's nice t' meet you, too, Clete. I heard a lot about you. So how do you figure I made a real good friend just now?"

"You don't know who that gal is?" Clete asked with an incredulous look.

"Nah, who is it?"

"That's Mary Lynn Bradley. Her husband's a big oilman here in Dallas."

Rodgers had a look of consternation. "Don't *tell* me her husband is Carter Bradley."

"That's him—Mr. Tex-Mex Oilco, his goddamn self."

"I know Carter Bradley. He always struck me as a combination of a snob and a fuckin' prick." Rodgers shook his head thoughtfully and looked in the direction of the beautiful woman who had just introduced herself. "And she's his wife?'"

"Sure is," Clete said.

Rodgers shook his head in disbelief. "That old sonofagun. Got himself a trophy wife. I'll be damned."

"Hey, Carter's a good guy," Clete said. "You don't know him like I do."

"You know Carter Bradley?" Buck asked.

"Oh, hell, yeah. He's a great guy. All those stories they tell about him? A total pack of lies. He's just a regular guy, like you and me—except a whole lot richer."

"Is that right?" Rodgers asked, trying to conceal his disbelief. "I never woulda guessed."

"You just gotta get to know 'im. Then you'll see what I'm talkin' about."

Buck nodded. "Yeah, you're prob'ly right."

"So you got all your registration done?" Clete asked.

"Yeah, I'm good to go. Lookin' forward to it."

"Well, I wanna warn you—the competition's pretty rough, and I'm one o' the roughest. I placed third overall last year, and I'm lookin' to do better this year. But I'm always glad to welcome the new guys, and I wanta be the first to wish you all the best. I just don't want you t' beat me." He gave Rodgers a good-humored smile.

Buck returned the smile. "Well, Clete, I appreciate the thought. And...just so you'll know—I'm gonna do my dead-level best to beat the hell out of you."

"I expect no less." Justus gave a small salute, touching the brim of his hat. "So I guess I'll be seein' you this evenin'."

"Oh, yeah—you're gonna see me. You're gonna see me *real good.*"

"Until then, podnuh," Clete said.

"Till then," Rodgers said with a friendly wave goodbye.

Once Justus was gone, Buck roamed around the building for awhile longer, and then he started toward the door. Near the front exit, Mary Lynn Bradley watched Rodgers move through the crowd, as she spoke to a group of rodeo fans. When the big cowboy neared the doors, she yelled at him and gave him a vigorous wave of the hand that caused her shapely breasts to jiggle conspicuously. "Buck! Hey, Buck! Good luck tonight!" He nodded briefly, gave her a friendly smile, and touched the brim of his hat as he walked out the door.

Outside a ramshackle house in a remote area of the New Mexico desert, Shooter Dobbins was finishing a joint with Bubba, one his biker friends. Shooter took a big puff and passed the joint. "Go ahead—finish it," he said. He held his breath a few seconds, and exhaled the residue of smoke. Leaning back in the chair, he smiled with satisfaction. "That's what I like about pot—it pumps up the high, and smooths out the drunk, all in one fell swoop. That's some good shit, Bubba."

"Yeah, it is. I'm s'posed to get a pound of it next week," Bubba said, putting out the joint and dropping it in the ashtray. "If I wasn't so low on cash, I'd get five pounds o' this stuff."

"Yeah—money. That's gettin' t' be a problem." Bubba offered no response, so Shooter continued, "I wanta tell you, bro'—I really appreciate you lettin' me lay low here these past few months. I'll make it up to you, I swear."

"Hey, man—you'd-a done the same for me."

"Yeah, but still...it really means somethin' to me. I mighta been in jail by now, if it wasn't for you." When Bubba offered no reply, Shooter continued, "Did I tell you I talked to Chopper—that friend o' mine in Braddock?"

"I don't think so."

"He said there ain't been nothin'—not nary a word about that phony preacher bein' dead, or nothin'. Chopper said he was in the hospital overnight, and that's all that's been said about it since that whole thing happened."

"Is he back preachin'?"

"Naw. He's been outta town, or somethin'. The assistant preacher's been runnin' the church. I'm thinkin' maybe I ran that old sonofabitch outta town. Or maybe he's waitin' till I get arrested to show back up, I don't know. I'd like to think I threw a scare into that old bastard. Maybe he'll keep 'is nose outta other people's business next time."

"I dunno, man. If he's as rich as you say he is, he's got the local cops in 'is back pocket—right up next to 'is billfold."

"Yeah, but...if he ain't dead, what's the worst they can get me for—misdemeanor assault? Hell, I can do that standin' on my head."

"Didn't you say that whole deal happened 'cause your ol' lady was givin' you shit about goin' with you that day? S'pose they was to say it was kidnappin'?"

"They could say it, but she'd never testify to somethin' like that. She wouldn't fuckin' *dare*."

Bubba gave an emphatic shake of his head. "I dunno, man—she ain't been actin' right, ever since you guys came up here."

"Man...I would chop that dirty bitch into little pieces and feed 'er to the dogs, if she did some shit like that," Shooter replied, with a look of repressed rage.

"Yeah, you'd do that—once you got outta the penitentiary, after servin' twenty years. I'll be honest, Shooter—I've told you before—I don't trust the bitch."

"Oh—and you think I do? *Not even*." They passed a few moments in silence, then Shooter continued, "I gotta get some money, man. I'm down to it. I'm takin' the bitch and headin' out for Houston in the mornin'."

"Whadda ya gonna do in Houston?"

"I got a coupla old friends who run with the Bandidos. I'm gonna see if they can't turn me on to some action...you know—runnin' dope, or somethin'. There's gotta be some way I can get some money fast—short of goin' on a robbery spree."

Bubba suggested, "You can always put the old lady out on the street sellin' pussy. I can't tell you how many times Kitty's hot little ass has bailed me out of a jam."

"Yeah, but your old lady...you know...she kinda digs it—or at least she ain't got no hang-ups about it. But my old lady...I dunno...I dunno why I ever got involved with that bitch. She's worthless."

"Well...she's goddamn good-lookin', for one thing. The way she looks, she could cause the Pope t' do somethin' crazy."

Shooter pondered the remark. "I used to think that. But now when I look at 'er...all I see's a fuckin' ugly bitch. I fuckin' hate 'er. I'll prob'ly wind up killin' 'er, one o' these days."

"Well, you better start gettin' 'er trained now, before you head out for Houston."

"What're you talkin' about? Gettin' 'er trained for what?"

"I'm talkin' about...s'pose that deal don't work out with your Bandido buddies? I mean—you know 'em and all that—but you ain't one of 'em. As far as they're concerned, you're just another asshole ridin' a chopper—you're like a groupie to them. There's thousands o' guys like you out there, goin' through all the right motions, actin' like they're one of the Bandidos...except for one thing—they ain't no Bandido. They walk the walk, they talk the talk—but if you ain't won your colors—you ain't no Bandido. Those guys got their own thing goin' on. You might get along great and all that, but that don't mean they're gonna cut you in on their business. That's *their* thing—and you ain't one of 'em. That's like goin' to the Mafia and tellin' 'em you want a piece of the action 'cause you eat a lotta pizza. Just think of the Bandidos like the Mafia, 'cause it's really the same thing: If it was the Mafia, you know for sure they'd laugh at you—and then they'd prob'ly kill you for bein' too stupid to live. Same deal with the Bandidos. I mean...I think you're countin' on too much with these guys."

"So...what're you sayin', exactly? I ain't gettin' this," Shooter said.

Bubba gave Shooter an assertive look. "I'm sayin' you better get your old lady used to the idea o' takin' a strange dick on command, 'cause that may be where you get the money you need to get goin' again—unless you wanna pull some armed robberies, and *really* get some heat on yo' ass. You wait till you're desperate for money, and you *have* to put 'er on the street—with no preparation at all...and I guarantee you—a bitch like that—she'll rat you out to the first guy she sees, and she'll get you arrested, and the next thing you know—you'll be doin' some big time in the penitentiary for panderin'. And I heard the penalties are pretty stiff for that in Texas."

"Yeah, I heard that, too," Shooter agreed.

Bubba continued with his thought. "But it's like a horse—you break it to the saddle, and you don't have any more problem with the buckin'. Same thing with women. That's how I got Kitty saddle-broke—I made 'er let some of my friends fuck 'er till she stopped complainin' about it and started doin' it whenever I told 'er to, with whoever I told 'er to. Now she's got no problem with it. Actually, I think she spends all her time, hopin' I'll go broke so she can go back to trickin'. You're right—she likes it, no doubt about it. But she didn't at first. First—I had to get 'er broke to the saddle. Now, she's my own personal ATM machine—just slide it through the slot, and out comes the money."

Shooter laughed, and then suddenly gave his friend an accusing look. "Oh—I get where you're comin' from—you wanna be the one to help me saddle-break my bitch, right?"

Bubba shrugged. "Hey—I'm just tryin' to help. Somebody's gotta do it. And it ain't like you ain't gettin' nothin' in the bargain—you can have Kitty. She'll do anything you can think of—and then some stuff you'd *never* think of. It never ceases to amaze me, all the different forms of perversion she can come up with. We can make a regular orgy out of it. So what's the beef? You said you hate the bitch, anyway."

A silence passed while Shooter considered the possibilities. "You know...you're right. It's because of *that* goddamn bitch I been hidin' out here in the sticks all this time—not to mention the time I spent in jail when she ran off to that preacher's shelter, and he ratted me out to the cops." Taking a long sip of beer, Shooter sat up straight in his chair. "You know what? I always thought your old lady was kinda hot—but I want you to know—I never hit on 'er, outta respect for you. But if you're willin' t' let me fuck your old lady, as hot as she is—I say, let's swap out. Everything you been sayin' is right. That bitch needs t' learn who's the boss, once and for all."

"Damn right," Bubba agreed.

"And she *does* need t' be saddle-broke before we get to Houston, 'cause she *is* gonna start sellin' that pussy, regardless o' what happens with the Bandidos. I done made up my mind. And I ain't doin' no more jail-time because o' her, neither. I tell you what: Let's have a couple more beers, and then we'll throw them bitches a surprise party."

Bubba raised his beer can in a toast and grinned through his grizzled beard. Rubbing his crotch, he said, "Yeah, baby—*surpri-ise!*"

Inside the house, the two women could hear raucous laughter coming from the front porch through the open door. Sitting at the kitchen table, Jenny watched with idle interest as Kitty rolled a joint. Finishing her work, Kitty inspected the result.

"Damn! Another camel! I never can get that hump outta the middle. Bubba's joints always look like ready-rolls. I don't know why I can never get mine to look like that." There was another loud burst of laughter from the front porch, and Kitty observed, "Sounds like they're startin' t' feel no pain." She offered the joint to Jenny. "You sure you don't wanna try this with me? It's really good."

"No, thanks," Jenny said. "I don't really like that stuff."

From the front porch, Bubba yelled through the door. "Hey, Kitty—bring us a coupla beers out here!"

"Oh, shit," Kitty said with a look of disgust, as she dropped the joint in the ashtray. "I'll be right back." Kitty got up from the table, retrieved two beers from the refrigerator, and left the room. In a few seconds, she was back. "You sure you don't want a beer? Maybe some wine?" she asked.

"No. I don't want anything."

Lighting the joint, Kitty took a long drag and held her breath a few moments. When she exhaled, she asked, "What's with you, Jenny? You haven't partied with us since you've been here. You just sit in the corner, and mope around, and stare off into space...you got some kinda hang-up about booze and pot?"

"Not really. I used to party like that, but"—

"But what?" Kitty asked.

"Oh...these last few years, Shooter's got so bad about wantin' t' beat me all the time, I just feel like I have t' know what's goin' on at all times, 'cause I never know when he's gonna go off on me. And even if I do stay sober and watch out, I never know what's gonna set 'im off."

"They're all like that," Kitty asserted. "A buncha bastards, all of 'em." She took another hit, and added with a cynical smile, "If Bubba didn't beat me at least once every five or six months, I'd start thinkin' he didn't care about me anymore."

"How do you *stand* that?" Jenny asked, with a look of consternation.

"It's part o' the life. That's what you sign up for when you get involved with guys like Bubba and Shooter. Didn't you know that when you married him?"

Jenny shook her head. "No. He wasn't like that when we first met. He was really nice. He brought me flowers and candy...you know, he just really treated me good."

"How old were you when you married 'im?"

"Sixteen."

Kitty gave her a knowing nod. "Young and dumb. He saw you comin', girl."

"I guess he did. But now...now I only stay with 'im 'cause I'm scared he's gonna kill me. He's really, really mean. You just can't imagine. I'm sorry to say this, but I just hate 'im."

"Listen, honey—I've had my rounds with Bubba, too. I got a pretty good idea how it is with you and Shooter."

"I just can't figure out how to get away from 'im. I had a chance, and I didn't take it."

"That preacher?"

Jenny nodded. "Yeah. He was so kind and good. I just hate myself for not lettin' 'im help me. And I hate myself even more for gettin' 'im hurt. I just feel awful. Sometimes I wish Shooter *would* just go ahead and kill me, so I wouldn't have to live with my conscience. Reverend Braddock was such a nice man."

"Well, honey...we all make our mistakes. You prob'ly can't tell it, but I have my regrets about gettin' involved with Bubba. Did I ever tell you my daddy was a Pentecostal preacher?"

"No!" Jenny exclaimed in surprise.

Kitty nodded. "He was. I was brought up real strict. And in our church, the women couldn't use makeup and had to dress in these old ugly-ass clothes that made you look like a bag-lady...and I

126

was just a young girl and—you know, girls wanna be pretty—but that was against the church. I hated it. I felt like a freak when I was at school. And one day I was walkin' down the street to go to the store, and Bubba pulled up on 'is motorcycle. Back then he was really handsome...you'd never know the guy I met that day was that fat slob sittin' out on the front porch right now."

Jenny laughed. "No, I can't believe Bubba was ever handsome."

"Well, maybe not handsome—call it semi-good-lookin'. Or maybe not even that. At least he was kinda slim and had hair on his head," she said with a giggle. "Anyway, he talked me into lettin' 'im give me a ride on the back of 'is bike—and within an hour of the time he picked me up, I was lettin' *him* take a ride on the front of my pussy. It was my first time, and I loved it. We fucked that whole day, and I made a point to do everything my daddy hated—fuck, suck, up the ass—everything. Bubba had the time of his life. I never went back home after that. I called my daddy a few days after I left and told 'im what I'd done, and he condemned me to the flames of Hell, and I've never been back to see my family or been inside a church since then. And, for better or worse, I've been with Bubba ever since. Mostly worse, but...that's the choice I made."

"I just don't know how you handle it so well."

"It's all a matter of lettin' go, honey. Accept your fate. That's what I did. You can do it, too. Just go with the flow."

"I just can't do that, Kitty. There's just somethin' in me that wants somethin' better."

"Well, good luck with that, sweetie. I hope it works out for you."

About that time, the men came into the house. As they entered the kitchen, Bubba said, "Girls, me and Shooter have talked it over, and we got a surprise for you."

"A surprise?" Kitty asked, her eyebrows skeptically raised.

"Yeah, a surprise," Bubba said. "C'mon—let's all go to the bedroom. That's where we got it hid." The women hesitated, and Bubba repeated, *"C'mon, damn it!* You're gonna get a kick outta this."

Reluctantly, sensing that the behavior of the men was not quite normal, the two women rose from the kitchen table and went into the bedroom with Bubba and Shooter following right behind. Once they were together in the room, Bubba said, "Shooter, why don't you tell 'em what we got for 'em?"

Shooter started rubbing his crotch. "Well, what we got for you girls is a coupla good, stiff dicks." He paused a moment, then added, "Of course, you already knew that. But here's the surprise: To make it interesting, we're gonna do a little switch-and-swap-thing tonight. For starters, I'm gonna fuck you, Kitty—and Bubba's gonna fuck Jenny. And then we'll trade off, dependin' on how the fuckin's goin' at any given moment in time."

"No!" Jenny immediately protested. "You won't treat me like this, Shooter!"

"Get naked, Kitty," Bubba ordered.

Kitty immediately started taking off her clothes, but Jenny backed up against the wall, cowering in the face of the onslaught that she knew was coming. Shooter's face was a picture of rage. "Bitch, get your clothes off! You see Kitty over there? You see how she does what she's told? She's doin' it—why the hell can't you do it? You're disrespectin' me in front o' my friend. I'm tired o' this shit. You get naked—now!"

"No! No, I won't! I don't care if you kill me—I won't!"

Shooter grabbed her by the hair and aimed a fist at her face. Bubba grabbed his arm. "Hey, man—

128

don't hit 'er in the face. You don't wanna bust up somethin' that beautiful—that's your money, man. Besides, I don't want 'er bleedin' all over me while I'm fuckin' 'er. Shit like that might make my dick go limber. Just give 'er a good body shot. That'll get 'er mind right."

Shooter thought about it for a second. "Yeah. Yeah, you're right." He directed a brutal blow to Jenny's midsection, and she fell to the floor, completely immobilized, and curled up in a fetal position.

"Don't hurt 'er, like that, Shooter!" Kitty protested. "She's just a tiny thing!"

"You stay out of it!" Bubba ordered, pointing a warning finger in Kitty's direction. "This is between him and her."

Shooter pulled Jenny to her feet by the hair and leaned her up against the wall. She was crying, and coughing, and gasping for air. He drew back his fist again. "Start takin' those clothes off," he said in a pitiless voice. "Either that, or I'm fixin' t' beat your ass to death, bitch."

"Don't do this to me, Shooter," she pleaded.

"Get 'em off!"

Afraid of the brutality that he might inflict upon her next, Jenny reluctantly started removing her clothes, crying and pleading all the time for Shooter to change his mind. When at last she was completely undressed, Bubba said, "Now, that's a money-makin' machine right there, Shooter. That's one fantastic bitch."

"Well, you have at 'er, buddy. Don't leave any opening in her body untouched. You talkin' 'bout saddle-breakin'? Well, saddle up and ride her ass bloody." He looked over at Kitty, who was standing naked by the bed. "I ain't got no more time for this shit. Looks to me like I got somethin' pretty good to work on over here, too. You have a good time, bro.' I know I'm goin' to."

Bubba stripped himself naked, his hairy, blubbery body quivering in the light shining into the room through the open bedroom door. "Well, it's a dirty job, but somebody's gotta do it." He grabbed Jenny by the arm and violently threw her on the bed. "C'mere, bitch—it's *party time!*"

Outside the rodeo arena, Buck Rodgers stood beside his pickup, studying the check he had just picked up for his winnings. Grinning with satisfaction, he stared at the check for a full minute before unlocking the pickup and placing it in the passenger seat, being very careful to keep it in pristine condition. From behind him a voice said, "Typical rookie mistake."

Turning around to see who was speaking, Rodgers found himself face-to-face with Clete Justus. "Clete! What're you doin', sneakin' up like that?"

Justus shrugged. "I gotta lotta Indian in me," he said with a grin. "Can't help myself."

"I'm startin' t' think that," Rodgers agreed. He extended a handshake. "Congratulations on winnin' first place."

"Thanks," Clete replied. "Lord knows I needed the money."

"What're you sayin' about a rookie mistake?"

"Oh, yeah. You leave your check lyin' in the seat like that, and it's liable t' blow out the window. Put it in your billfold, where you know it'll be safe. That's how the pros do it. Layin' it in the seat like that's as rookie as it gets."

"I ain't *that* big a rookie. I was gonna put it in the glove compartment when I got in the truck. I'm thinkin' about takin' it somewhere and havin' it framed."

"That's gonna be an expensive picture, cowboy."

"Yeah, but...you just don't know what it means to me," Rodgers replied.

"Hey...I was a rookie once, so I kinda got an idea," Justus said, then added, "'Course, I *never was* a rookie like you're a rookie. That ridin' you did in this rodeo? That was top-notch. You know that first bull you drew—Widowmaker? That's one o' the meanest bulls in the world. I drew him three times last year, and that sucker threw me every time. But you rode 'im like you was takin' a Cadillac down the freeway—easy as pie. All the way through the rodeo—top notch...as good as it gets—until that last ride. And then you fell off a kiddies' bridle horse, goin' at a full walk. What was that? It almost looked like you took a dive. I don't get it."

"Uh...I don't know...he zigged when I thought he was gonna zag. Caught me by surprise," Rodgers answered with a deceitful glimmer in his eyes.

"Hell, he wasn't even buckin', podnuh," Justus argued. "When you drew that horse for your last ride, I done kissed that first-place money goodbye. You had it all sewed up. And then you just fell off that damn nag who was takin' you for a walk in the park. It don't make no sense t' me."

"I don't know...typical rookie mistake, like you said."

Clete Justus had a thoughtful look in his eyes. "Yeah, like I said." Justus looked as if he had more to say on the subject, but he decided not to discuss it further. "Well, listen...uh...the reason I made a point to catch you before you left is because Mary Lynn Bradley is havin' a little get-together for some o' the rodeo crowd, and she specifically requested that I invite you along."

"Oh, no, Clete, I gotta be gettin' on."

"You headin' out for another rodeo?"

"Not immediately. I just got things I gotta do tomorrow."

Justus made an emphatic gesture that commanded full attention. "Now, listen, Buck...you need to do this. It don't sound like much, but it is. This ain't gonna be just a buncha crazy cowboys. There's gonna be some people there who got money—*big* money. You need to get to know these people, 'cause they can really help you somewhere down the line. As young as you are, I know you can't see it right now, but these rodeo days ain't gonna last forever. You need to take your chances when they come."

"I don't know"—

"Aw, come on! An hour or two ain't gonna hurt you. Besides, I wanna get to know you a little better. It ain't every day a first-class rider like you shows up outta nowhere. I wanna find out a little more about you. If I can figure out your weaknesses, it might help me get an edge somewhere down the line." As Buck thought it over, Justus tugged gently on a muscular arm. "C'mon, podnuh—my pickup's right over here. I promise to have you back here in an hour, so your mama won't be mad at you for comin' home late."

"Well...I guess, for an hour" ...

"Now you're talkin'!" Clete said, slapping him on the back. "Let's go."

"Just lemme put my check in a safe place and I'll be right with you."

Buck Rodgers carefully placed his precious check in the glove compartment and locked the vehicle. Getting into Clete's pickup, they drove to the estate of Carter Bradley, the wealthy oil baron. As they were arriving on the property, Clete offered some helpful advice:

"Now, look, Buck—don't let this fancy house and all these rich people throw you off your game. Once you get past the money part, it all boils down to this: They're just people like us. They eat, drink, shit, piss and fart like everybody else. So act natural, be yourself, and you'll do just fine."

"I'll do my best, Clete," Buck assured him, his eyes sparkling with silent laughter.

The cowboy raised a cautionary finger. "One thing, though: If one of 'em tears off a fart anywhere near you, move away as fast as you can. Those caviar farts are absolutely *rancid!*"

"I'll keep both feet on the floor, just in case," Buck said with a laugh. "Just kinda stay close by till I get my sea-legs under me, okay?"

Justus gave him a reassuring glance. "Hey, no sweat. I got your back."

As they followed the drive completely past Carter Bradley's large mansion, Buck said, "Hey, Clete—I think you just went by the house."

"We're goin' to a little house out back. Carter built it for Mary Lynn's little playhouse. It's sort of a miniature ranch-house. That's where she entertains the rodeo crowd. She's big on this rodeo stuff."

There were already several vehicles parked along the drive that led to the house. Clete stopped his vehicle a distance away, and the two men walked side-by-side up the driveway. The small house at the back of the property was a picturesque little structure that looked as if it had been built by Hollywood craftsmen for a scene from an old Western movie. As they approached the front porch, Clete looked at Buck with a questioning glance. "Pretty cool place, isn't it?"

"I like this better'n I do the big house," Rodgers agreed.

"Well, stand tall and get ready. It's time to meet and greet some of the big-time financial players of the Dallas social set."

When the two cowboys entered the house, all eyes turned toward them. Mary Lynn saw them as soon as they came through the door and rushed over to greet them. "There you are! I was afraid you weren't gonna make it." She turned to the assembled crowd. "Hey, everybody—say hello to our two star attractions. I think you all know Clete Justus, who won the big prize tonight." There were shouted greetings mixed with mild applause, which Clete acknowledged with a tip of his hat. Mary Lynn continued, "And this is our second-place winner in his first PRCA competition, and one of the future stars of the national rodeo circuit—Buck Rodgers!" The applause the handsome young cowboy received from the assemblage was even louder than it had been for Clete Justus. Buck touched the brim of his hat and nodded shyly to the crowd. Mary Lynn said, "Clete—grab yourself a drink. There's everything in the world over there at the bar." She turned to Buck. "And you—I want you to come over and meet my husband Carter." She pulled him by the arm across the room toward a distinguished-looking man of advanced years, who was chatting with a group of expensively dressed men and women near the far wall. She touched the old man on the arm and said, "Carter, I want you to meet Buck Rodgers."

The oilman turned to look. "Buck? Carter Bradley." The two men exchanged handshakes. "It's a sincere pleasure. Mary Lynn's done nothing but talk about you for two days. I hear you're one helluva bronc rider."

"Well...I try. I'll get better when I get in a little more practice."

"So where do you hail from?" the old man asked.

134

"All over, really. Here and there. I lived in San Antonio for awhile, so I guess you could say I'm from San Antone."

"Beautiful town. Beautiful town." The old man looked more closely at the young cowboy. "You know...you look so familiar to me. Have we ever met before?"

Rodgers seemed somehow uncomfortable with the question. "Not that I could say. I've seen your picture in the paper before."

"Who hasn't?" the old man said with a laugh. He patted the cowboy on the back and added, "Well, you just make yourself t' home here, Buck. Drinks are on the house, and enjoy your visit. It's always good to meet young people with talent and promise. You're the future of America."

"Well, thank you, sir. You're very nice to say that."

Mary Lynn touched her husband on the arm again. "I'm just gonna show Buck where the bar is. I'll be right back." Linking her arm in his, she led him across the room toward the bar. "You did just fine talkin' to Carter. I think you made a real good impression, even if you did seem a little nervous. But you'll get over that, once you get to know him." When they reached the bar, she said, "Just fix anything you like. It's serve yourself around here. If beer's your poison, it's in the cooler behind the bar."

Buck nodded. "Well, thank you so much."

She lowered her voice to a confidential tone. "I gotta get back over to Carter. He doesn't like it when I stay away too long. You just help yourself."

Leaning up against the bar, Clete was sipping on a large glass of whisky on the rocks. "Damn, cowboy—I think you done made a big hit with Mary Lynn." When Rodgers offered no reply, he asked, "Ain't you drinkin'?"

Rodgers shook his head. "I haven't drunk a drop in a long time."

"Well, hell, I haven't either," Clete said in a tone of mild complaint. "Damn near three days, as a matter o' fact. How long's it been for you?"

"Uh...a *long* time," came the vague reply.

"Well, that's *too* long." Clete Justus went behind the bar and popped open a large can of beer. He set it on the bar and came back around. Picking up his whisky glass, he raised a toast. "Here's to victory."

Not wishing to seem rude, Rodgers reluctantly picked up the open can and raised it in the air. "To victory."

They drank the toast and Justus leaned back against the bar. "Look, Buck—you been real mysterious about your plans for the future. Have you mapped out your career strategy?"

"Whadda ya mean?"

"I mean...yeah, you picked up a little cash this weekend, but that won't last too long. Then what?"

"I dunno...I guess then I'll pick up a little more cash somewhere else."

Justus gave a disapproving shake of the head. "No, son—that's not how you do it. If you're gonna make any real money doin' this, you need to figure out where you're goin' from one event to another, week after week, for the whole season. You ain't gonna get nowhere, ridin' every now and then, when you need the money."

"Well, I really haven't thought much about it," Rodgers said.

"Look, podnuh—I don't know why, but I kinda like you. You remind me of myself when I was your age—not sure what to do, and no one to tell 'im what to do...but that's where you could be different from me."

"How's that?"

"If you'll let me, I'll help you work up a game plan. With your talent, I'd bet money you'll be in the top ten in no time—prob'ly not this year—but next year, for sure. Two years, tops, if you do it right."

Rodgers gave Justus a curious look. "Hey, Clete, you may not realize it, but I'm the *competition*. Why would you wanna do that?"

"'Cause I love this sport. It's my life. And I love guys who can promote the sport for the future. As big and good-lookin' as you are, with the way you ride, you could become the face of professional rodeo." He looked across the room toward Mary Lynn Bradley, who had positioned herself to have a clear view of the bar as she conversed with her husband and his friends. "I been seein' how Mary Lynn's been lookin' at you. Man, her panties are drippin' wet right now, I guarantee you."

"You're crazy, Clete."

"Yeah, I'm crazy—crazy like a pussy-hound. Man, you could bring the women to the rodeo in droves. And where the women go, the guys follow. With my brains and your looks, we could kick this sport up a notch or two."

Rodgers again addressed a quizzical look toward his companion. "You know, Clete—I don't think I'm understandin' where you're comin' from."

Clete lowered his voice and said in a confidential tone, "Listen—just between me and you—Carter Bradley told me he'll stake me so I can get into rodeo promotion when my ridin' days are over. Hell, I'll be thirty-one my next birthday. Rodeo's a young man's sport. Every year, those horns and hooves and two-story falls hurt a little worse than they did the year before. Every year, it takes me a little longer to heal up from the injuries. I got two, three more years, and then I'm gonna be goin' downhill at a full gallop. But I do have a backup plan—I'm gonna get into the business side of the rodeo. So I'm thinkin' of my future, as well as yours. Why don't you let me help you, amigo? In the long run, it'll be good for both of us."

Rodgers took a long draught of beer, draining the can at a gulp. He gave a vigorous shake of the head. "Whoa! It's been a long time since I did that!" Going to the back of the bar and grabbing another beer, Buck opened the can and continued the discussion. "I'm gonna tell you the truth, Clete: I just joined the rodeo to find out if I could do it. It never once crossed my mind to try to make a career out of it. I don't know where my next rodeo's gonna be. The only plans I have for the future are to wake up tomorrow. That's it. And there ain't no guarantee of that."

"See? Just like me, when I was your age."

"Well...not exactly," Rodgers said with a shrug.

Clete gave him an apologetic look. "Look, man— I'm sorry. I'm talkin' shop, and this is s'posed t' be a party. Just tell me you'll at least consider it."

Rodgers nodded. "I will, Clete. I'll consider it."

Justus slapped him on the back. "Good deal!"

"You know," Buck suddenly interjected, shaking his head side to side, "I'm feelin' kinda woozy. I shouldn't-a killed that beer like that."

"Yeah, that first drink does that to me sometimes, too."

"I think I'll step outside and get some fresh air," Rodgers said.

"Take your beer with you. No need to waste it. Check out the back yard, man. It's nice out there," Justus said, pointing toward the door.

Taking the direction Clete Justus indicated, Rodgers found the door and stepped out onto a spacious patio. He sat down on a large outdoor couch, alone with his thoughts, and sipped on his beer. A few minutes passed, and Mary Lynn Bradley came outside. "There you are," she said with a smile. "Clete said you weren't feelin' too good."

"It's this beer," he explained, holding up the can. "I haven't done any drinkin' in a long time. That first beer made me feel like I was kicked in the head by a mule."

She sat down beside him. "Are you gonna be all right?"

"Oh, yeah. I just gotta get it back together. I'm gonna be gettin' outta here pretty quick."

"Oh, no!" she exclaimed in disappointment. "Carter just went to the big house. He's gone to bed for the night, and the party's just warmin' up. The evening's still young—and so are we, Buck."

"It's been a long day," Rodgers said. "I need to get back to my place. I got a lotta stuff to do tomorrow."

"Where are you stayin'?"

"Aw...it's a cheap motel on the outskirts of town. One of those weekly rental joints—Deluxe Motel, I think they call it."

"I know that place. It used to be the busiest hot-sheet motel in Dallas, from what I hear tell."

"Yeah...well, it's just a dump now."

"You can stay here tonight, if you want to. It's just a tiny little house, but there's a bedroom that almost never gets put to use, unless one of my guests gets too drunk to drive."

"No. No, thanks. It's nice of you to offer, but I need to get on with it."

Without any warning, she leaned over and kissed him on the lips, a lingering, yearning kiss, full of unbridled passion...a kiss that betrayed boundless depths of unfulfilled longing and desire. As she clung to him in that unguarded moment, Rodgers could feel the hunger roiling inside her, a kind of animal lust that would not be denied. His first impulse was to turn her loose immediately, but the temptation was too great. He put a powerful arm around her and pulled her body to him. As the moment became moments, it was Mary Lynn who finally pushed herself away.

"Oh! I'm sorry," she breathlessly exclaimed. "That's not like me. I just"—

"No, don't explain," he said, with a look of sincere understanding. "Me, too" ...

She stood up, her face flushed. "So you and Clete are gonna be leavin'?"

"Yeah, I think that's all for the best. I'm a little drunk, and you are...much...*much*...too beautiful."

Regathering her composure, she said, "Well, thank you for coming, Buck." She paused uncertainly, then said, "If you wouldn't mind...just finish your beer, and I'll go back to my guests."

"I understand completely," he said with a wave of his hand.

"I'll see you again soon," she said, with a smoky glimmer in her eyes.

"Soon," he smiled back.

Buck Rodgers finished his beer and went back inside. He told Clete he was ready to go, and Clete took him back to his truck. Returning to the arena, they exchanged their goodbyes, promised to keep in touch, and Rodgers went back to the motel where he was staying. Unaccustomed to the alcohol he had consumed, he felt very tired, and still a little dizzy. Rodgers stripped naked, throwing his clothes in the floor, and fell heavily into the creaky motel bed. As he drifted into unconsciousness, visions of the beautiful face of Mary Lynn Bradley and memories of the softness of her lips and the sweetness of her perfume filled his mind...

It seemed he had only been asleep a few moments when he was awakened by a loud knocking on the door. Retrieving his pistol from a tote-bag under the nightstand, he went to the door. "Who is it?"

"It's me—Mary Lynn."

Opening the door, he said, "Mary Lynn? What are you doin' here?"

"I need to talk to you."

"Hold on a second. I gotta put somethin' on."

"No, *now!* It's scary out here."

"I wanna warn you—I'm buck-naked."

"I won't look," she assured him as she pushed the door open. She stepped into the room and closed the door behind her. Buck sat down on the bed, fumbling for his pants in the semi-darkness. "Has somethin' happened?"

She hesitated a moment by the door, then said, "Yes, it did." There was an expectant pause, and then she added, "You happened." Walking over to the bed, she dropped the long overcoat she was wearing onto the floor right where she stood. In the twilight glow of the motel room, he could see that she was completely naked. Even after having seen her in the form-fitting attire she normally wore, he saw that her body, revealed in all its glory, was even more beautiful than he ever could have imagined. She leaned over and kissed him, and repeated, "You happened. And now I need you to fix me."

He wanted to protest, but the words would not come. As if they had a mind of their own, his hands reached greedily toward her warmly inviting flesh. Cupping her pendulous breasts in his hands, he kissed her lips, and then he put his arms around her and pulled her down onto the bed beside him. He embraced her with an uncontrollable ferocity, his fingers touching, feeling, exploring the hidden wonders of her magnificent body. In the raging moment of unbridled passion, as their yearning bodies intertwined, Mary Lynn heard him whisper, "Oh, God! It's been so long" ...

Charles Keeler strode into the laboratory at the Braddock Institute, where Dr. Chris McKenzie and a lab assistant were completing their examination of Kimba. The chimpanzee reached out toward Keeler as he approached the table, and Keeler gave the animal an affectionate pat on the head. "Hey, fella," Keeler said. "Have these mean old people been putting you through hell this week?" He looked toward his colleague. "Chris," he said with a nod. "Have you completed the tests?"

"All done. Do you want to examine Kimba yourself?"

"Let me just take a quick listen." Keeler put on his stethoscope and listened to the chimpanzee's heartbeat. He asked the assistant to lay Kimba on his back so that he could monitor the flow of blood through the aorta. As he listened, his face took on an expression of deep concern. "Bruits? It can't be. Surely not."

"I'm afraid so," the other doctor replied.

The two men exchanged ominous glances. "Well, I guess we'd better discuss it now," Keeler said.

"Let's go to my office."

The two men went to Chris McKenzie's office, and McKenzie handed Dr. Keeler a large file folder. "This is the full report in detail. You can read it at your leisure."

"I'll do that. I have a meeting scheduled, but I'd like to have a quick summary of the facts."

Dr. McKenzie sighed. "Well, you heard the bruits in the aorta. The arteriogram showed that plaque is building up throughout his vascular system at a fairly rapid pace. And that's troubling, because we've had him on the best diet and exercise program we could devise ever since his veins cleared up." McKenzie picked up two X-ray films and put them on display. "Here's Kimba's dental X-ray as of this week. You know how he had that hyper-spurt of bone regeneration after we gave him the serum, before he started growing new teeth?"

"Yes," Keeler said with a look of concern.

"Well, the bone is degenerating. See the bone loss...here...here...especially around these back teeth?"

"Yes. Could it be a staph infection?"

"No. We ran tests to be absolutely certain. We've had him on a rigorous program of dental maintenance. This is not my area of expertise, but the bone cells are just...dying—that's all I know to tell you. We can't attribute the bone loss to any of the usual suspects. It's a complete mystery. Dr. Brooks and his team are delving into the questions of causes and possible cures."

"So he's going to lose his teeth?"

"Well, we're in uncharted waters here, but I would say...yes, definitely. I can't say how long, but—let me show you a comparison." He put another X-ray of Kimba's teeth on the screen. "This was taken six weeks ago. You see the difference? In the earlier picture, you have to look close to see the irregularities in the jawbone around the teeth. But in this X-ray, which we took yesterday, you can practically see the bone-loss from across the room."

Keeler shook his head in dismay. "I assume there's more?"

"Yes, I'm sorry to say. You'll find the specific numbers in the paperwork, but his testosterone levels are down, his muscle tone is degenerating, his metabolism is slowing down, he's putting on weight, his hair is beginning to turn gray...and there's other stuff, too. And we've had him on the healthiest regimen of diet and activity that our experts can devise. And yet...he's still falling apart. I hate to state the obvious, but the effects of the serum are wearing off."

Keeler swallowed hard, as if he were choking back some strong emotion. "Damn! Damn!" he muttered.

"Are you okay, Doctor?" McKenzie asked with a look of concern.

"Yes, of course," Keeler said, gaining control of himself. "I guess I liked that little monkey better than I thought I did. I was hoping for better results."

"He's done better than any of our test subjects so far. You've gotta look at it this way—whatever happens next, he *did* get to be young again, at least for a little while. How many of us are ever gonna get to do *that*?"

"There must be a way to prevent this," Keeler said. "But—what?"

"Well, we could try to give him another dose of the serum" ...

"No," Keeler disagreed with a shake of his head. "I'm certain a second dose would kill him, like it's done every other subject we've tried to do that on. It's true that he's done better than any other of our other experiments, but he's still following the same pattern—regeneration, restoration, degeneration. The only difference is that in Kimba's case, we've had better initial results, and the reversal of those results has taken longer to occur." Charles Keeler stared thoughtfully down at the floor, then said, "Let's just observe the process, give him the best of care to keep him alive as long as we can, and learn what we can from the experiment."

"I'm sorry you're taking this so hard, Dr. Keeler," McKenzie consolingly stated.

Keeler sighed. "I suppose I was just hoping against hope that this experiment would achieve the impossible."

"It's come as close as we would have ever dared to dream, not so long ago," McKenzie asserted.

Charles Keeler nodded his agreement. "You're right—it has. I just can't help wishing that" ... Keeler didn't finish the thought. Picking up the file folder, he said, "I'll read this later on today. Come by my office in the morning, and we'll compare notes, okay?"

"I'll do that."

Taking his leave, Charles Keeler went directly to his office. He looked up the number to the Church of the Living God and called Joe Lindsey. "Pastor Lindsey? This is Dr. Charles Keeler, over at the Braddock Institute."

"Dr. Keeler! How may I help you?"

"Pastor Lindsey, have you heard anything from Billy Braddock?"

"Not a word, Doctor. Chief Wilkins told me you were the last person to talk to him—I mean...the last person we know of."

"Do you know anybody whom he might have called, or someone he might be likely to call?"

"The two most likely people in the world are me and Maggie, who's been his housekeeper for the last twenty years. She's also probably his oldest friend in the world who's still alive. As far as I know, she and I would be the most likely parties he would call. Why? Is something wrong?"

"It's a private matter between me and him, involving the Institute. I really need to talk to him."

"Well, if I hear from 'im, I'll have 'im call you."

"Would you mention this to Maggie, too?" Keeler requested. "It's imperative that I speak with him. Tell her it's an urgent matter of the highest priority."

"I certainly will, Dr. Keeler."

"Thank you, Pastor Lindsey. If he calls, just be sure Billy understands that it's very important."

"I will. I promise you I will. And I'll see to it that Maggie understands the importance as well."

Keeler ended the conversation and turned his chair toward the window that looked out on the scenic grounds around the Braddock Institute. He stared thoughtfully at the world outside. "Billy," he muttered, "if you're still alive out there somewhere, I hope you're living your life to the fullest" ...

Steve Jackson and Bobby Pardo strode onto the porch of the small frame house in an old working-class section of Waco. They were greeted at the door by a portly woman wearing an apron, her hair tied back in a bun, who appeared to be in her mid-sixties. She peered at them through very thick glasses that gave her an owlish appearance. "Can I help you?"

Steve Jackson smiled at her. "Are you Miz Smith? Betty Jean Smith?"

"Yes. Are you the fellas from Houston?"

"We are." Jackson made the introductions, and the woman invited them inside. "Is your dad feeling well enough to talk to us?"

"Oh, sure. He's been kinda cranky today, but I'm sure he'll be glad to have some company for awhile. Come on back."

She led them to a bedroom at the back of the house, where an old man sat in a lounge chair with a breathing apparatus hooked to an oxygen bottle, the end of which was lodged in his nostrils. Betty Jean led them over to meet him. "Daddy, this is Steve and Bobby. They're reporters. You remember I told you about them?"

"Yeah. Sure as hell do," the old man said.

"Well, they're gonna take a few pictures and ask you some questions about your days in the rodeo, okay?"

"Okay."

The woman brought two chairs into the room while Steve and Bobby set up their equipment; and then, once they were comfortably situated, Steve began the interview. "So you're Hank Wooley, the famous rodeo cowboy?"

"Sure as hell am."

"Well, Hank, we're wantin' to ask you about a guy you knew back in your rodeo days—a guy by the name of Billy Braddock. You remember him?"

The old man riveted his pale blue eyes on Steve Jackson. "Yeah, I remember that sorry sonofabitch."

"I take it you weren't too fond of 'im."

"Hell, no! I'd like to put a bullet in 'is goddamn ass."

"What did he do to make you so mad?"

"He fucked my first wife, is what he did. The sorry sack o' shit! He ruined my life."

"You mean...him sleeping with your wife ruined your life?" Jackson asked.

The old man gave a vigorous shake of his head. "No, that's just what started it. That—and everything that happened *after* that—is what ruined my life."

"And what was that?" Jackson asked.

"Well, when I found out about what him and my wife had done, I went kinda crazy. I wanted revenge in the worst way. And that's pretty much what I got— revenge in the worst way."

"How so?"

"Well, see...my wife had this homely sister who'd been wantin' me to put it to 'er for awhile, but I wouldn't do it 'cause I was scared my wife would find out. Plus, like I say, she was ugly as hell, so it really wasn't worth the risk. But when I found out my wife had been screwin' Billy Braddock, that caused me to get drunk and go screw her sister, just to get revenge. But then, later on, when my wife found out I fucked 'er sister, that caused her to run off with the kid and divorce me."

"So that's how Braddock ruined your life?"

"Yeah, pretty much. He set the wheels in motion, and it was all downhill after that. And the reason I still think about that bastard right down to this very day is because I still don't know if Betty Jean's *my* daughter, or if she's *Billy Braddock's* daughter, 'cause me and him both were puttin' it to my old lady about the time she came up pregnant with Betty Jean. For all I know, *I'm* the chump who helped raise *his* kid all these years. And *that* makes me so mad every time I think about it, I feel like goin' back and fuckin' my ex-wife's sister all over again. And if you knew what a goat-smellin' skank *she* was, you'd realize just how mad I get."

Jackson suppressed a giggle. "Well, did you ever confront Braddock about what he'd done?"

"Well, yeah...eventually. I had to figure out what to do first. I wanted to kick 'is ass—but as big as he was, that woulda been a all-day job. Plus, ever'body said he was some kinda ex-boxer, and there wasn't nobody who knew 'im who wanted to take 'im on in a fistfight. And I ain't gonna lie about it—I prob'ly woulda got my ass kicked if I'd-a tried to jump on 'im. He was a lot bigger'n me. So that's why I did the next best thing."

"What was that?"

"Instead o' physically jumpin' on 'im, I tried t' shoot the bastard."

"You tried to shoot him? With a gun?"

"Well, hell, yes! Whadda ya think I'm gonna shoot 'im with—my dick?"

Steve laughed. "No, I guess not. So what happened?"

"I *missed*—that's what happened. Like I say, I got all whiskied up when I found about him and Betty Jean's mother, and I stayed shit-faced for days—or maybe it was *weeks*—after that. But eventually I loaded up my pistol and went lookin' for 'im, and one night I finally found 'im in a beer joint in Fort Worth. He's lucky I was drunk and he saw me first, or I'd-a got 'im. But I got off a coupla shots before some guys jumped on me and got the gun away from me. And while I was rasslin' with them for the gun, Braddock went hoofin' it out the back door on a dead run and got away clean."

"And then what happened?"

"Well, what happened after that is...I got five years' probation with a stipulation that I couldn't enter any rodeo that he was in. And I couldn't come around 'im, or anything else, or I'd have to go to the penitentiary. So, because of all that shit, I never did get a clear shot at 'im after that. And after my wife left me and took the kid—Betty Jean wasn't even a year old when that happened—I took t' drinkin' real heavy. And, you know—whisky for breakfast and wild bulls for lunch don't go together too good...so I ended up gettin' hurt real bad up in Tucson. After that...I don't know...I just kinda drifted away from the rodeo and into the bottle. Ended up workin' on the oil rigs out in the Gulf of Mexico. But if you ask me, it all goes back to that sonofabitch Billy Braddock. If he'd-a kept his dick outta my wife, me and her mighta stayed married. Plus...I'd-a prob'ly had a better career than I did, 'cause I wouldn't-a took to the whisky the way I did, and ended up gettin' myself hurt. So if you're wantin' the true story on

Braddock...well, here's your story: That worthless pile o' crap was the sorriest bastard on the rodeo circuit...not to mention, the *nastiest.*"

"He was a pretty big womanizer, was he?" Steve asked, suppressing his laughter.

"You just can't imagine. But I know 'im for exactly what he was. I mean, I will admit—he was a tall, good-lookin' sonofagun. And everywhere he went, he had these good-lookin' gals throwin' their pussies at 'im, right and left—and he didn't turn nothin' down. But I guarantee you—if there hadn't been any good lookin' gals after 'im, he'd-a fucked the ugly gals. And if there wasn't no ugly gals around, he'd-a fucked the livestock. And if there wasn't no livestock, he'd-a found a knothole in a fence somewhere, and fucked the knothole."

Steve and Bobby both burst into laughter at the old man's description of Billy Braddock. "So...so Billy was a pretty raunchy guy, huh?"

"I'll put it this way...if you ever run into 'im, don't turn your back on 'im, unless you're wearin' iron underwear. You never know what a nasty bastard like that might do next."

Bobby and Steve were convulsing with laughter for a few moments, but when Steve finally regained control, he asked, "So...do you have any rodeo stories involving you and Billy Braddock that you'd like to tell?"

"*Hell, no!* Just talkin' about that sonofabitch is gettin' me as pissed off as I was all them years ago. Only thing I can't figure out is how I'm sittin' here, barely able to walk to the bathroom, and he's still ridin' in the rodeo."

"Billy's not in the rodeo any more, Hank," Steve Jackson said.

"The *hell* he ain't! I just saw 'is picture in the paper a few days ago."

"That couldn't have been a recent picture, Hank. Billy's about the same age you are."

"I don't give a shit how old he is. I saw 'im in the paper." The old man looked around the room. "Gimme that stack o' papers, right over there," he instructed, pointing to some newspapers that were lying on top of a small table. Steve Jackson retrieved the papers and handed them over. Hank Wooley thumbed through the pile. "Now, where did I see that? Yeah, here it is." He handed them a section of the sports page from a recent edition of the Dallas *Times-Herald*. "If that ain't Billy Braddock, I'll kiss your ass."

He showed them a picture of Clete Justus and Buck Rodgers, accepting their winnings from the Mesquite Rodeo. Steve held up the picture for the camera to see. "You know, Hank—I do see the resemblance, but this isn't Billy Braddock. This is someone who looks like him. This is a young guy named...Buck Rodgers, it says here."

"The hell you say! I'd know that bastard anywhere."

"It *does* look like him, I will admit," Jackson diplomatically offered. "But that's not Billy Braddock."

"It's *him*," Hank insisted. "Same shit-eatin' grin, same pussy-hound expression on 'is goddamn face...same everything. Hadn't changed a bit. That's him. That's Billy Braddock."

Since old Hank continued to get more and more agitated the more Jackson persisted in trying to draw Billy Braddock stories out of him, Steve wound up the interview and the two reporters returned to the van. Once they were inside the vehicle, they looked at each other and simultaneously burst out laughing. "Wasn't that the funniest shit you ever heard?" Steve asked.

"Yeah, Artie was talkin' about that interview with Coach Langston addin' shades of character to the portrait of the man. We oughta title this segment, 'Portrait of the Young Man as a Shady Character.' You think Artie'd go for it?"

"Aw, you know Artie. His sense of humor falls somewhere between a rattlesnake and a tarantula. He'll prob'ly scrap this whole interview."

"Yeah, you're prob'ly right. That's a shame, though. That's one of the best interviews about the real Billy Braddock that we've been able to get."

"What about that cowboy at the Mesquite Rodeo?" Steve asked. "Can you believe the resemblance?"

"That was weird," Bobby agreed. "But they say everybody's got a double out there somewhere."

"Well, I can see why old Hank thought he was lookin' at 'is old nemesis. The guy's a dead ringer for the young Billy Braddock."

"So where are we headin' now?" Bobby asked.

"Over to Nacogdoches. There's a guy livin' there who was on the same team with Braddock at SMU. We'll see what he has to say."

In a seedy section of Houston that was once informally known as "The Strip"—called that by the locals because of the heavy concentration of topless bars on both sides of the street—Shooter Dobbins peered through venetian blinds as he sized up the terrain. He nodded with satisfaction.

"Yeah, this is just perfect. This setup couldn't be more perfect if I'd-a called in an order and had 'em build it for me." Turning toward the bed where Jenny was warily watching him with both feet on the floor, he directed a hateful look toward her and motioned her toward the window. "Get over here. I want you to see this." She got up from the bed and cautiously approached him. He grabbed her by the arm and positioned her in front of the window. Pointing across the street, he said, "Okay—you see that place over there, with the garage doors open?" When she didn't immediately respond, he squeezed her arm and gave her a hard shake. "Damn it, bitch—do you see it?"

"Yes," she said in a dull, lifeless voice.

"You better get off this act, bitch," he said, waving a warning finger in her face. "You answer me when I speak to you." Turning back toward the window, he said, "That's what they call an icehouse around here. They licensed these places for the shift workers, so the graveyard guys at the oil refineries can have a drink and shoot some pool when they get off work. They start sellin' beer at seven a.m., and stay open till the regular bars close. That street out there has whores sellin' pussy day and night. So here's how this deal's gonna work: I'm gonna station myself at the bar in the icehouse, where I can see what's goin' on over here at the motel. And what you're gonna do is walk along the street over here in front of the motel, where I can keep an eye on you. Sooner or later, somebody's gonna pull up alongside the road, and you're gonna ask 'im if he's lookin' for a date. If he says he is, you ask enough questions to make sure he ain't a cop. If you're sure he ain't a cop, discuss the money up front. I think you could get fifty pretty easy. Not too many people are gonna pay more than fifty for a street-whore. If you can't get fifty, go for thirty-five. Don't sell it for less than thirty-five. If the price is right, you tell 'im to drive around the corner and meet you here in the room. You collect the money up front once the trick's in the room, and then you do whatever you agreed to. I'm gonna expect you to pull about twenty tricks a day until we get a good stash goin', and then I'll decide after that what I'm gonna do with you. But for now, you're gonna sell that pussy till you get me outta this jam you got me into."

She pulled away from the window and walked to the middle of the room. "I didn't get you into anything, Shooter. That was all you."

"Am I gonna have t' kick your ass again?" As he asked the question, he stood menacingly over her.

She seemed to wilt at the threat of further violence. "No, Shooter. I just can't take any more beatings."

"That's more like it," he said decisively. "A lot more like it. Now, get into them clothes I bought you, and put on some makeup. It's almost showtime."

"Shooter," she said in a tone of pleading, "why are you doin' this to me? Why?"

He glared angrily at her. "I ain't doin' *nothin'* t' you. You brought this all on yourself."

"You know, Shooter—I used to think you loved me. Even through all the times you beat me and all the times you cheated, I kept tellin' myself that, deep down inside, you really loved me. But when you beat me up and let that fat slob Bubba"—

"Now, don't start on that again. You loved it, and you know you did."

Her face turned red with anger. "*Loved it*? How can you even *say* that?"

"Hey, I heard all the moanin' and screamin' you was doin' all night long. You was moanin' so loud, I could barely concentrate on what I was doin' in the other room. Don't even *try* to tell me you didn't like it."

"He was hurtin' me!" she protested. "I felt like he was gonna kill me! Do you have any idea what all he did to me that night?"

"Bubba told me all about it the next day. And he said you loved every minute of it. He told me he felt like he was bein' attacked by a fuck-monkey."

"Oh, God! You make me sick!" She made a helpless gesture. "You don't care about me. Why don't you just go ahead and kill me, Shooter? I know you're gonna do it sooner or later, anyway."

"Yeah, you're prob'ly right about that," the big biker nodded in agreement. "With your attitude, you're prob'ly gonna force my hand eventually. But right now, you're the workin' part o' my business. I'm management, and you're labor. So get your ass in that shower and get cleaned up. It's time for you to start earnin' your keep."

Unable to think of any way out of her predicament, Jenny obeyed his orders. After taking a quick shower, she dressed herself in the tasteless miniskirt and tank-top outfit he had bought her, put on the high-heels and mesh stockings, and applied her makeup in gaudy fashion. When she was finished, she stood up from the dressing table. "Are you satisfied with the way I look?"

"Yeah, now that looks classy," he said in approval. "So I'm gonna go over to the icehouse, and you watch out the window. Once you see me go to the bar, you come on outta the room and start shakin' that ass out there on the street. The way you look, I give it no more'n ten minutes and you'll be pickin' up your first trick."

Shooter got on his bike and went across the street. Jenny watched as he sat down at the bar. "God...can't you help me—please, God?" she said aloud. But no answer came, nor did any ideas come immediately to mind. Reluctantly, she turned away from the window and walked out into the humid Texas twilight. She went to the street and started walking casually along the side of the road. Shooter was right: In less than five minutes, a car pulled up alongside the road. Inside the vehicle was a man in his late forties, dressed in business attire. He rolled down the passenger-side window. "Hi, honey! What's a pretty girl like you doin' out here tonight?"

"Can you give me a ride somewhere?" she asked. "I might do you a real special favor, if you'll help me."

"Why, sure, honey," the man said, reaching over to open the door. "Where would you like me to take you?"

Jenny jumped into the car. "Let's just get outta this part o' town, as fast as possible. Then we'll talk about what arrangements we're gonna make."

"You got it," the man said with a smile of anticipation. He put the car in gear and drove away from the motel.

Inside the icehouse, Shooter incredulously watched what was transpiring on the street. "What the fu"— He didn't finish the question. Shooter jumped off the stool and told the bartender, "Save my place. I'll be right back." Running outside, he got on his bike and started off in pursuit of the businessman's vehicle.

Jenny looked back toward the icehouse and saw Shooter mount his bike. "Could you hurry? Turn somewhere, or something...go faster—please!"

The man's face took on a look of concern. "What's goin' on?"

"I'm not a prostitute. My old man's tryin' to make me start bein' one. Please help me get away from him."

"Now, listen—I can't afford any trouble. People know me in this community."

"Please...please, just help me. I'll do anything you ask."

The man stopped the car at the curb. "No. Get out. I'd like to help you, but I can't afford any trouble like this. It would ruin me."

About that time, Shooter rode up on his bike. He pulled onto the sidewalk, got off the bike, and jerked open the passenger door. "Get outta there, bitch!" he said, pulling Jenny out of the car by her hair.

The businessman held up his hands in a placating gesture. "Hey—I don't want any trouble, buddy."

"I ain't your buddy, Fancy Pants. You just keep drivin'," Shooter said. The driver sped away without looking back. Shooter pulled Jenny between two buildings, away from prying eyes passing by on the street. "You just won't learn, will you, bitch?" he said, choking her. He pulled a small-caliber pistol out of his belt and put it up against her head. "You know, I oughta blow your brains out right here," he said through clenched teeth. "But that would be too easy. You're gonna learn to do what you're told before you die. I tell you what: I came here to do some business with the Bandidos. I know how to get you saddle-broke. I'll just let the Bandidos have a little fun with you. By the time they're through with you, you'll be *beggin'* me t' let you sell some pussy. And, besides, that'll prob'ly make it easier for me to make some kinda business arrangement with 'em." He held her there, pinned against the wall by her throat, until it looked as if she were about to pass out. He let her go, and she fell to her knees, gasping for breath. "Yeah, that's what I'll do. It's just a little change of plans, that's all. It'll still be the same result in the end." He dragged her to her feet. "Get on the bike. We're goin' back to the motel."

Inside the private office of Carter Bradley, a short, pudgy man in a gray fedora hat, multicolored plaid coat and green polyester pants was handing a manila envelope across the desk to the oilman. The envelope was clearly marked *Edgar Gross Detective Agency: Confidential File.* "Here's the photographs," the man said, as he passed the envelope. "Two weeks' worth." He took a stack of video disks out of his pocket. "And here's some live-action stuff, if you really wanna see a show."

Bradley opened the envelope and spread the pictures out on the desk. His face remained expressionless, but the stiff manner in which he was sitting in the chair betrayed the strong emotions that he was struggling to control. "Where were these taken?"

"You know Linda Tooman, don't you? Used to be a Dallas Cowboys Cheerleader the same time as Mary Lynn? Married that big insurance guy?"

"I know who she is," Bradley said.

"Well, she's lettin' Mary Lynn use her guest house for her little love-nest. It's almost perfect—you can park in the back, go in through the rear entrance, and nobody drivin' down the street would even suspect you were there."

The old man continued thumbing through the photographs. "And how did you get these pictures?"

"When I found out where they were meetin' up, I went in and planted some cameras in a few strategic places, and then I just zoomed in on the action as necessary from the comfort of my remote-TV van. These shots are professional quality. Ain't no lawyer in the world can argue that's anybody but her." As Bradley continued to thumb through the pictures, the fat man added, "Look at the size of that guy's pecker. The way I figure it...if the ratio of his pecker-length to his overall-body-height is considered to be normal, then I oughta be a midget." He laughed at his own joke. "I don't know how she takes that damn thing."

Carter Bradley directed a withering stare at the little man. "Edgar—will you please restrain yourself from indulging your crass sense of humor in my presence?"

Edgar gave him an apologetic look. "Uh...sorry, Mr. Bradley. I just thought it was kinda funny."

"What have you found out about this Buck Rodgers character?"

"Well...his full name is Royen Dale Rodgers, according to 'is drivers' license."

"You're kidding me."

"That's what it says on the license—Royen Dale Rodgers. I had a buddy o' mine down at the Police Department run a check on 'im, and he's clean as a whistle—almost too clean. It's like he suddenly dropped outta the sky. His driver's license is valid, even though it was issued less than six months ago. I mean, what is he—like, twenty-two years old—and he's just gettin' 'is drivers' license? That's kinda unusual, to say the least. Most kids get their license as soon as they're old enough to drive."

"That *is* unusual," Bradley agreed.

"That's pretty much all I could find out about 'im. He appears to be who he says he is, even though what little I could find out about 'im really doesn't seem to fit a normal pattern. His address is a weekly rental motel out on the edge of town, but he rarely shows up there. The manager said he's paid up for the next six months, but he's only seen him on the premises once or twice. He's not on any social websites, or anything like that, as far as I could find. You said he might be from San Antonio, but there's no record he ever attended school under that name in the San Antonio school district. I did find out he's got a horse stabled out at Tumbleweed Ranch, and most of his rodeo gear is rented from them. He doesn't even haul his own horse and equipment around—they do it for him."

"Isn't that unusual for a struggling rodeo cowboy?" Bradley asked.

"*Real* unusual," the detective replied. "But what about him ain't? Oh—and as far as I could find out, he's got no credit history of no kind, neither. I swear, this guy's like the mystery man who came from outer space. So, if there's somethin' more to find, I need somethin' more to go on."

"I see."

"And as far as the surveillance goes...is this enough evidence? Do you want me to get my equipment outta that guest house before somebody finds it?"

"Yes. As soon as possible. This appears to be more than enough to serve my purposes." The oilman dropped the pictures on top of the desk and directed a look that commanded attention from the pudgy detective. "I want to tell you a story, Edgar—and I warn you...this is not to leave my office."

"Oh, sure...I understand. I'm a professional, Mr. Bradley. Anything you tell me is strictly confidential."

Gathering his thoughts, the old man said, "When I was finishing my last year of college at SMU, there was a young man who was a grade behind me—a star football player named Billy Braddock. Like me, he was the son of a wealthy oilman. But that was where the resemblance ended. The Braddock family was new money, and they were the worst representation of all that *nouveau riche* implies to some people. The daddy was a gambler, a drunkard, a barroom brawler, a shameless blowhard, a degenerate sex-fiend—the walking definition of white trash with money. And the son...the son was just like him—big, loud, rowdy, uncouth...just a filthy gorilla unfit to be around decent society. That's all he was."

"I know the type," Edgar said in agreement. "All-around sorry sonofabitch."

Ignoring the comment, Carter Bradley rubbed his hands together and stared into the distance. "At that time, I was engaged to marry a girl named Anita Van Heusen, an heiress to the Van Heusen insurance fortune. Anita had class, taste, style—incredible beauty in the true classic sense of the word—everything you could ever ask for in a woman...or so it seemed. Our pending marriage promised to be a marriage made in heaven—Old Money marrying Old Money, and everybody living happily ever after in Champagne Paradise."

"Sounds good to me," Edgar said.

The oilman got up from his desk and walked across the room, where he unlocked a large file cabinet, continuing to speak as he did so. "During spring break that year, I had to accompany my father on a business trip to New York. Anita stayed in Dallas to spend the time with her friends." Retrieving a file he was searching for, he closed the cabinet and returned to the desk. He sat down and resumed: "When I returned from New York, I knew almost immediately that something had changed between Anita and myself. I couldn't say what it was...it was just one of those things you sense, deep down—something...some indefinable *something*...had changed."

"I know what you mean. I been there myself," Edgar said. "It's like...you can smell shit in the wind, but you can't tell where it's comin' from. Reminds me of my third wife—the dirty bitch!"

Bradley directed a distasteful glance at the little man, but said nothing. He then continued his narrative: "As I was saying...her behavior altered in subtle, but noticeable, ways. She would disappear at times without even telling me where she was going. Then, when she would finally show up, she would offer some lame explanation of her whereabouts that just didn't ring true. I won't bore you with the details, but I eventually became extremely suspicious of my lovely bride-to-be. When I finally told my father about the situation, he hired the best detective agency in Dallas to look into the matter for me. What they found out was that Anita had been seeing that barbaric slob she knew I detested more than anybody in the world—Billy Braddock, the filthy jock...the big man on campus. It broke my heart. I broke off the engagement, but I never got over what she did to me. I do not exaggerate when I tell you that the experience scarred me for life." He paused, then added, "I've never fully trusted a woman ever since." Opening the file, Bradley handed some pictures to the detective. "Tell me what you see here."

Edgar eagerly eyed the photographs. "Yeah, man—that Anita was one hot mama! Look at the ass on that bitch!"

"Edgar"—

"I mean it! If this is what millionaire pussy looks like, I'm gonna go out and rob a bank this afternoon! I gotta get in on this action!"

"Damn it, Edgar! I've asked you to restrain yourself from making such insensitive comments."

"I'm sorry, Mr. Bradley," Edgar said with a contrite expression. "I was just showin' my appreciation."

"Look at the man in the pictures."

The pudgy detective studied the pictures. "Holy shit!" Edgar exclaimed. "It looks like the same guy...right down to the dick and balls. Only thing different about 'im is the haircut. But it can't be the same guy, right?"

"I don't know. I don't know how it *could* be. But that Braddock family has been a thorn in my family's side ever since the roughneck father got lucky in the oilfield back in the late Twenties. We've been competing with them ever since. And I will tell you that very often, over the years, because of the total lack of scruple embodied and practiced by that family and their corrupt company, my family's interests have often suffered in the process."

"So...what? You think this guy here might be Braddock's son...grandson, maybe?"

"I don't know what to think. I can tell you this: I met this Buck Rodgers fellow at a party one night...and for a brief moment, I actually thought it was Billy Braddock standing there in front of me. But then I realized that couldn't be possible."

"Couldn't it just be a strong resemblance?"

"The resemblance was more than strong—it was uncanny. But, again—I don't know. However, I do know that Billy Braddock was a rodeo cowboy—a world champion, if I recall correctly. And this...this Buck Rodgers, as he calls himself...is also a rodeo cowboy. And he's a dead-ringer for Billy Braddock...right down to the oversized penis, as you so astutely observed."

"Yeah, but if he was in college the same time you were, it couldn't be the same guy. It doesn't make sense."

"No, it doesn't." Carter Bradley contemplated for a moment, then leaned forward on the desk. "I want you to get a line on Billy Braddock. Find out where he is, and what he's doing these days. Find out if he's got any wives, mistresses, children or grandchildren somewhere. There's a little town out in West Texas named after the family...Braddock, Texas. That's been his home base for years. That's probably where he is now. I want you to find out what you can about him, and then get back to me."

"Will do." Edgar hesitated, then added, "Uh...I don't mean to be crass, Mr. Bradley...but I *will* need some more money to keep goin' on this."

"Certainly." Bradley took a checkbook from the desk drawer and wrote out a check for ten-thousand dollars. "That should keep you going for awhile. Get back to me as soon as you know anything."

"I'm all over it," Edgar gratefully replied. "And thank you, Mr. Bradley. I'll leave no stone unturned."

When the detective was gone, Bradley picked up the pictures on the desk and started thumbing through them. Although his expression never changed, tears started, ever so slowly, to trickle out of his eyes and down his wrinkled cheeks onto the desktop...

Outside the Rock-N-C arena in Crosby, a tiny bedroom community near Houston, Buck Rodgers was accepting accolades from Clete Justus on taking first prize in the competition. "Well, Big Slim—you finally beat me. Congratulations."

"Aw, well, it was a small rodeo. Nobody's gonna notice. Besides, I didn't beat you, Clete. You were out o' the money early. I beat them other chumps."

"Yeah—and you did it in style. This is...what? Our fourth rodeo? And every time I've won first place, you came in second because of some stupid rookie mistake. But not this time. The one time I'm completely out o' the money, you ride like the wind. I tell you what—I've seen the best...at their best...and I never saw anybody better than you were these past two days."

"Aw, Clete"—Buck protested— "you exaggerate."

"I'll be damned!" Justus replied. "As soon as I was out o' the runnin', you went through that livestock like a hot knife through butter—no mistakes, not one...not even *close to one*—perfect. Every other time, when I *was* in the runnin', you'd do somethin' stupid and find a way to lose to me. Why is that, Buck?"

"I don't know. I guess you just make me so nervous when it's me and you, head-to-head, fightin' it out for top prize, I choke. Maybe I can't handle the pressure. Who knows?"

"I don't know, man. It's kinda strange. I almost think I don't believe you. If I didn't know better, I'd swear you were throwin' the competition. You been makin' side bets on me?"

"No, hell, no," Rodgers said with a laugh. "I'm just a stupid rookie."

Justus gave a thoughtful pause, then asked, "So...you sure you're not goin' over to Louisiana with me? It's gonna be a whole lotta fun."

Shaking his head, Buck said, "Naw...there's a guy comin' t' Houston I wanta try to talk to sometime in the next few days, and I'm gonna hang around for that."

"So where you headin' from here? I mean...you goin' t' Houston now?"

"Yeah. I'm gonna find a cheap motel to bunk down in till I see that guy I came to see," Rodgers said.

"Well, look—my sister lives in Pasadena. I'm gonna stay at her place tonight, before I head out in the mornin'. Why don't you follow me to Pasadena, and we'll have a coupla drinks at a bar I know there? The drinks are cheap and nobody bothers you. I know a few people there."

Rodgers thought about it. "Yeah, I can do that."

Clete gave an approving smile. "Follow me."

The two men got into their trucks and drove to Pasadena. Once there, Clete led the way to a dingy-looking bar in a seedy part of town. Clete pulled up in the parking lot, got out of his truck and waited for Buck near the dozens of motorcycles that were parked in front of the club.

Taking note of all the bikes out front, Buck lifted his eyebrows ironically as he approached the door. "Hey...looks like my kinda place."

"Oh, it ain't so bad, once you've had about forty-two beers," Clete said with a grin. "After forty-five beers, the women even start lookin' good to you."

"The anticipation's killin' me," Buck grinned. "I never drank forty-five beers and danced with a female wart-hog before."

Inside the bar, Buck noticed that most of the men in the place were wearing the colors of the Bandidos motorcycle club. Several of the bikers eyed them suspiciously as they entered the bar, but no one seemed to take particular exception to their presence. Sitting down at the bar, they ordered beer and resumed their conversation.

"So when you get done here in Houston, what 're you gonna do—go back to Dallas?" Justus asked.

"I haven't made up my mind," Buck answered.

"Well, I need t' tell you somethin', hoss—Mary Lynn Bradley actually called me at my house before we headed this way and asked me to keep an eye on you. I think she's worried you're fixin' t' fly the coop." When Rodgers offered no comment, Clete persisted: "You and her got somethin' goin' on, man? You can tell me."

"Nah. I ain't got nothin' goin' on nowhere."

Clete gave a skeptical shake of his head. "Well, I don't know...that's kinda funny. She's never done that before. Maybe she's wantin' t' *get* somethin' goin'."

About that time, a very large man with long hair and a full beard, wearing Bandido colors, and sporting skull-and-crossbones tattoos on both forearms, came up beside Justus and placed a big hand on his shoulder. "Clete? How ya been?"

Justus turned to look, and broke into a smile. "Hey, Crossbones...how you doin'?" The two men shook hands and exchanged a friendly hug.

Crossbones answered, "Aw, you know...just livin' the life."

"Well, I'm glad t' see the life ain't killed you yet."

"So far, so good," Crossbones said, knocking his big knuckles on the bar for good luck. "You still rodeoin'?"

"Yeah—gettin' a little older and a little tireder, but still at it."

"Who's your friend here?" Crossbones asked.

"This is Buck Rodgers. He's a rookie on the rodeo circuit...but he's gonna be big, man—really big. I'm predictin' world champion in the near future, if he'll just start listenin' to me." He turned to Rodgers. "Buck—meet Crossbones."

Crossbones reached around Clete and shook Buck's hand. "Buck? Any friend o' Clete's is a friend o' mine. Nice t' meet you."

"Same here," Rodgers said.

Crossbones slapped a meaty hand on the bar. "Well, if you guys have any trouble, or need anything of any kind, you just come see me, and I'll get you squared away—pussy, dope, whatever...if I ain't got it, I know where to get it."

"Thanks, Cross," Justus said, as the huge biker walked away from the bar.

"You know these guys?" Buck asked, directing a look of disbelief toward his companion.

"Well, most o' the older guys. I used to ride with the Bandidos."

"You're kiddin' me," Rodgers protested.

"No, it's true," Clete nodded. "Started right after I dropped out of high school. You never had a chance to know this about me, but I ride a motorcycle better'n I ride a horse. I met up with the Bandidos through some biker friends...I started hangin' out...and one thing led to another. It was actually Crossbones who took a likin' to me and ran interference for me as far as joinin' the club—and...after a few fights and some other shit I don't wanta talk about—they inducted me. It's a long story better left untold. But I ran with 'em for about...oh, maybe a little over two years."

"I never woulda guessed," Buck said in amazement. "How'd you get out?"

"I just wasn't wantin' to...you know...live that life. They were goin' a direction I didn't really wanna take. I always liked the rodeo. I wanted t' make somethin' outta myself. So one day I just talked it over with 'em, told 'em how it was...and we all parted friends. That's when I cleaned up my act and started rodeoin' full time. Did my first rodeo right here in Pasadena."

"Well, who woulda ever thought?" Buck said, leaning back on his stool. "Clete Justus—outlaw biker."

"I guess we all have our little secrets, don't we?"

"Yeah...I guess we do," Rodgers agreed.

About that time, a fat biker with a beautiful blue-eyed redhead in tow came into the bar. Looking into the mirror behind the bar, Buck's eyes flashed with a spark of recognition. He watched as the big biker walked over to a small round table situated near the pool table and directed the redhead to sit down. "You stay put and don't move, bitch," he said.

"Of all the gin joints in all the world," Rodgers muttered under his breath. He turned around on his barstool to be sure his eyes weren't deceiving him.

"What'd you say?" Clete asked.

"Uh...nothin'," Buck answered, turning back toward the bar, still watching in the mirror as the big biker started talking to Crossbones. He looked at his companion. "Hey, Clete—you packin' heat?"

"Heat? Why are you askin'?"

"Cause I'm fixin' t' start some shit with that fat sonofabitch talkin' to Crossbones."

"What for?"

"Are you packin' heat?" Rodgers repeated.

"Well...yeah. I got a derringer in my boot," Clete answered.

"Well, get it out where you know it's handy. If that fat motherfucker pulls a gun on me, put that derringer up against 'is head and disarm 'im. I'm about to show you somethin' you won't believe."

"What?"

"Well, you never had the chance to know this about me, but I actually fight better'n I ride horses. Get that pistol out of your boot."

"Are you drunk, man?"

"No, but I'm fixin' t' be drunk—on pure power." Buck Rodgers got up from the bar and walked over to the little redhead who had come in with the big biker. "Howdy, ma'am," he said. "Would you like to dance?"

"I don't dance," she timidly replied.

"Well, could I buy you a drink?"

"I don't drink. I don't do anything. You really should get away from me, if you know what's good for you."

"Well, I'd say *you're* good for me. But since you don't dance and you don't drink, maybe I oughta just pull up a chair and talk for awhile."

The big biker, engaged in conversation with Crossbones, suddenly noticed the tall cowboy talking to his woman. He held up his hand in the middle of the conversation and said, "'Scuse me, Crossbones." Then he yelled toward Rodgers. "Hey, you—Big Tex...get your ass away from her. She belongs to me."

Rodgers turned to look. "Well, I was only askin' the lady to dance."

"She don't dance. Now, take a hike."

The big cowboy squared his shoulders. "Who am I talkin' to?"

"My name's Shooter Dobbins. And if you don't get your ass away from that bitch, it's a name you're gonna remember till the day you die."

The pool game stopped, Crossbones backed away from Shooter, and the crowd in the immediate area who realized what was going on watched to see what would happen next. Rodgers said, "There ain't no way you're that good a dancer."

Shooter looked confused. "What the fuck you talkin' about?"

"Well, if I'm gonna remember you till the day I die, you must dance like Fred Astaire. That's what I'm talkin' about. I just wanna dance. But if you won't let me dance with this pretty little woman, maybe you'd like to dance with me yourself."

"Don't push it, cowboy," the little redhead warned him. "He'll hurt you."

"Don't you worry your pretty little self, ma'am," Buck reassured her. "I've danced with some of the best, and I've still got every one of my toes."

Shooter looked at Crossbones. "Who is this stupid motherfucker?"

"I don't know. He says he's a dancer."

"Well, let's see if he can dance around this!" Dobbins angrily exclaimed.

Grabbing a pool cue, Shooter ran at the cowboy and swung the stick, aiming directly at his head. Anticipating the motion, Rodgers stepped inside the swing and threw a devastating uppercut to Shooter's ribs. Shooter exhaled violently, dropping the cue stick, and stumbled against the pool table, gasping for breath. Immediately, as if he were working by some prearranged plan, Buck Rodgers grabbed Shooter Dobbins by his long pony-tail, put a leverage hold on his wrist that made resistance all-but-impossible, and pushed him outside the bar, all the way around to the back of the building. The bar emptied out immediately, as the whole crowd gathered under the security floodlights, anticipating some unscheduled entertainment. Once Buck had the big biker at the place where he wanted him, he gave a mighty shove that sent Dobbins flying to the ground. Shooter immediately picked himself up, his face a portrait of animal rage.

"Now here we are"—Buck said— "alone at last...with a hundred or so other people as witnesses. Kiss me, you fool."

The total fearlessness in this unexpected adversary prompted Shooter to reason. "What's this all about, man? I didn't cause you no trouble."

"The hell you didn't," the big cowboy disagreed. "I wanted to dance with the pretty lady, and you wouldn't let me. So now I only wanta dance with you."

Dobbins was trembling with rage. "Man—I will...totally...beat your fuckin' brains out if you don't quit with this shit. You have no idea who you're fuckin' with."

"Yeah, actually...I do. You're a bully, and a coward, and a woman-beater...and generally a worthless piece of shit. I just want all these other people to know it, too. If I'm lyin'...here's your chance to prove yourself. These rough guys would prob'ly get a kick out o' seein' me get my brains beat out by a bad motherfucker like you. Before we start, just tell me—would you like to waltz, or do you prefer boogie-woogie?"

Shooter started toward him. "Okay, that's it, motherfucker—you asked for it."

Buck gave him a taunting grin. "C'mon—beat my brains out. C'mon. C'mon, girl." Rodgers held up his hands in the posture of an old-time bare-knuckles fighter and started dancing around. "You can do it, bitch—beat my brains out."

Humiliated and enraged by the display the big cowboy was creating in front of people he was hoping to impress, Shooter charged blindly toward the taller man, swinging wildly as he ran. The cowboy laughed and stepped aside, throwing a left hook to Shooter's ribs as the biker stumbled forward and fell to the ground. Dobbins immediately felt a stabbing pain in his side from the bone-deep bruise his adversary had inflicted upon him. Not wanting the stranger to know how badly he had hurt him, Shooter quickly regained his feet.

"Why don't you stand and fight me like a man?" the biker said, hoping to antagonize Rodgers into a barroom brawl. "You scared?"

"Oh, hell, no," Buck said with a laugh. "But the *real* fightin's gonna come later, after I finish dancin' with your fat, no-good, sissy-boy, woman-beatin' ass. Now, if you're already through dancin' after only two steps of a whole full-length Texas two-step marathon, you can just go ahead and rip your britches down, and I'll cornhole you right here in front of all these people, and we'll call it love."

This kind of taunting in front of the Bandidos absolutely enraged Shooter Dobbins. "You sonofabitch! You're gonna die!"

Shooter charged again, but Rodgers easily handled the charge, making a point to inflict pain on his opponent again, as he did with every other attempt that followed. Laughing, the cowboy stuck out his chin and said, "C'mon—hit me right here. Right on the chin. You can do it." Shooter swung wildly, only to have a big fist slammed into his face. The blow opened a huge gash over Shooter's left eye. Laughing, the cowboy said, "Ooh, that looks bad. You gonna be okay?"

"I'll be okay when I kill you, motherfucker!" Shooter answered, as he wiped the blood out of his eye.

Shooter charged again, and the brutality continued, as Rodgers methodically chopped his helpless adversary down to size, one futile charge after another. When Dobbins would slow down, appearing to tire, Rodgers would sadistically taunt his adversary—daring him to come after him, making fun of him, teasing him, challenging his manhood, goading him to attack again...and, sooner or later, Dobbins would make another attempt. And with every futile effort Shooter made to do the big cowboy harm, Rodgers always laughed and turned the tables, inflicting pain as he pleased—depending on the whim of the moment—in greater or lesser measure. Eventually, Dobbins was spent, his body battered, his hands down at his sides, gasping for air, sweat pouring off his body, a beaten man. Buck Rodgers walked up to him and stood before him, triumphant—smiling at him with a sadistic, pitiless leer.

"Let's take a minute before we finish the dance," Rodgers said. "I want you to get your breath." He turned toward the crowd. "Somebody give this motherfucker a drink of water, or a beer, or somethin'. We can't have the grand finale until he gets 'is wind back."

Five people rushed over to hand Shooter a can of beer. He took one of them, drank it down, and then stood panting for awhile, staring silently, while the big cowboy waited patiently. "Why are you doin' this, man?"

Buck Rodgers shrugged. "Oh, I dunno—call it revenge. Or maybe I just fuckin' feel like it. You shoulda let me dance with the lady when I wanted to."

"Is that what this shit's all about—that fuckin' red-headed whore?" When the cowboy offered no reply, Shooter said, "Man, she's *shit*. You can have 'er."

173

"No, *you're* shit. I want you." Buck Rodgers paused a moment to allow the biker to reply, but no reply was forthcoming. "Okay—we've been kiddin' around long enough. You got your wind back?" Shooter stood up straight, as if to get ready for the next round. "You said you wanted me to fight you like a man. So get ready, fat boy. It's time for you to pay for your sins. Court's in session, *and here come da judge.*"

Remembering the words he had uttered to Billy Braddock just before he knocked the old man down, Shooter stopped in his tracks. "Do I know you?"

"You're about to."

Without another word, Rodgers moved toward Dobbins like a ferocious beast of prey in a frenzy of bloodlust. To the amazement of the crowd, who had watched in astounded silence as this incredible display of brutality had unfolded, Rodgers directed a flurry of punches at such speed and from so many directions that it was impossible to count the number. Unable to defend himself, and devastated by the fusillade, Dobbins tried to fall to the ground, but Rodgers stood him up with a punch that snapped his head back and sent teeth flying through the air. Shooter fell, choking on other teeth that he was swallowing, and Rodgers waited until the biker caught his breath before kicking him in the kidneys.

"Get up, bitch," he said.

"Hey, man—the fight's over," Dobbins breathed. "You win."

"Oh—no, no, no!" Rodgers exclaimed, standing over his devastated opponent. "The fight's not over till you scream like a bitch." When Dobbins did not respond, Rodgers said, "Either you scream like a bitch, or you get up and take your punishment."

When Shooter refused to stand up, Rodgers rolled him over on his back, sat down on his chest, and straddled him. He directed another punch to the biker's face. "Scream like a bitch, damn you!"

"Please, no!"

"Scream!" Another punch landed, and blood splattered in all directions.

"Aaarrrgh!" Dobbins let out a blood-curdling scream.

Rodgers hit him again. "Louder!"

"AAARRRGH!"

Again Rodgers slammed a fist into the bloody face. "Louder, damn you!" And, saying that, he sadistically directed two more brutal blows into the gory face of his hapless victim. "Louder!"

"AAARRRGH! EEEYAAAH—AAH—AAH!" The scream at last became a plaintive howl. "Please! Please don't hit me again! Ple-eease!"

By now, Shooter Dobbins was sobbing openly, tears running down his battered face for everybody to see. Rodgers stood up, towering over the prostrate form of his vanquished foe. "Okay, bitch. I've taken...lemme guess—three or four teeth? Five, maybe? I've taken what little dignity you might have ever had in front of all these people. What else can I take? You got any money?"

"No, please"—

"Roll over on your stomach, bitch. I wanna see how much money you got." The big man allowed Rodgers to turn his body over with a push of his boot. Buck took the biker's wallet out of his back pocket. Removing the cash, he counted the amount. "Two hundred and eighty-five—is that all you got? Big, bad bitch like you? That's all you got?" Dobbins lay sobbing in the dirt, begging Rodgers not to hit him again. Rodgers threw the billfold on the ground. "Pull your pants down and get your butt out here where I can see it. Me an' you gonna make love, fat boy."

"Oh, please, man...don't do that!"

"Get your pants down, or we're gonna start dancin' again."

Shooter Dobbins loosened his belt and exposed his buttocks to the assembled crowd. The bikers started laughing. "Fuckin' punk!" one of them said.

Buck Rodgers laughed and kicked Shooter's naked behind. "Aw, never mind. I just wanted to see if you were weak enough to do it." He looked at the crowd of bikers. "Any of you boys want any pussy? I got it all hot and juicy for you." The bikers laughed derisively, and Rodgers continued to torment his hapless victim. He grabbed Dobbins by his pony-tail and started pulling him to his feet. "C'mon, fatass—stand up." With Rodgers pulling his hair, the big biker struggled to his feet, his pants down around his ankles, begging for mercy. Rodgers grabbed the front of Shooter's shirt and stood nose-to-nose with his beaten adversary. "Okay—I took your dignity, I took your teeth, I took your money...I coulda took your butthole, but it's too damn nasty—and I need to tell you...I'd like to take your bike—but since I ain't got no place to keep it, I'm gonna destroy it before I go. The only reason I'm givin' you a break on your butthole is because you stink too bad for me to even consider fuckin' you. And, one final thing, just so you'll know...I'm takin' your woman."

"Take the bitch...*take* 'er," Dobbins said.

"Oh, yeah...I can't forget this"—Rodgers said, knowing that he was in total control— "I want you to strike a pose for me...you're gonna go to sleep now."

"Please...please don't hit me again."

"Hold your arms down at your sides, and stick your chin out." Starting to cry again, Dobbins hesitantly did as he was told, and when he was positioned to Buck's satisfaction, Rodgers said, "There you go. Now, say—*cheese*" ...

"Please" ...Shooter pleaded.

"No, not *please...cheese*. Say it, motherfucker—
cheese!"

Against his will, but too afraid of what even
worse might happen if he refused to obey, Shooter
stood, arms at his side, chin out, as Rodgers backed
a step away to get the proper leverage on the punch.
Once Rodgers determined he was at the ideal
distance, he said to Dobbins, "Okay—you ready?
Now, say what I told you to say."

"Cheese," Shooter obediently declaimed. With
that, Buck Rodgers threw a right hook that flew so
fast toward its target that it was hard for the
spectators to follow the trajectory. The punch
connected with a sickening thud, and Shooter
Dobbins fell to the ground like a boulder dropping
from the sky. Rodgers removed his hat and took a
bow. The crowd who had witnessed this brutal
exercise in unmitigated sadism roared their
approval.

"Man, you got class!"

"You da man, bro'!"

"Yeah, I like that! *Kick* that goddamn ass!"

Buck walked directly over to Jenny Dobbins and
took her by the hand. She came along without
question, and they went to Buck's pickup. Unlocking
the door, he retrieved a .44-magnum from under the
seat. He looked at Jenny. "Which one's Shooter's
bike?"

"That one, over there," she said, pointing.

"Hey, you're not gonna shoot the gas tank and
get a bunch o' cops and fire trucks out here, are
you?" Crossbones asked with an anxious expression.

"Nah," Rodgers assured him. "I'm just gonna
blow a little hole in the engine." Buck turned the bike
on its side and fired three shots into the engine.
"That oughta give 'im somethin' to remember me by."
He grabbed Jenny's hand. "Let's go."

Clete Justus shouted after him, "Hey, Buck! Where you goin'?"

"I'm ridin' out ahead o' the posse."

"Well, hey, man—see you in Dallas?"

"Maybe. So long, Clete."

Buck Rodgers drove his pickup out of the parking lot, leaving behind an excited crowd of people who were laughing and exchanging impressions of what they had just seen. Clete Justus watched the pickup fade into the distance and shook his head in amazement. He looked at Crossbones. "That's one wild cowboy there."

Crossbones nodded his agreement. "I've seen some ass-whoopin's in my time, but that was the cat-daddy of 'em all. If he hadn't left so soon, I was gonna ask 'im if he'd like t' join the Bandidos. We need more guys like that."

As Buck drove away from the biker bar, Jenny said, "I wanta thank you for what you did back there."

"Oh, you don't have to thank me," Buck said. "I enjoyed it. That punk's been long overdue for a good ass-whoopin'."

"Do you know Shooter?"

"I've run across 'im before. That's why I knew he deserved everything I did to him. I think at the very end, just before I brought the hammer down, he realized who I was."

"Have we met before?" she inquired.

"Why do you ask?" he replied.

"I don't know. Just something about you seems so familiar."

"If we'd-a met before, I'd sure remember you," he said. "You're just about the most beautiful woman I've ever seen."

There was a moment of silence, and then she asked him, "So what are you gonna do with me?"

"I thought we'd get a motel room...get a good night's sleep."

Unenthusiastically, Jenny said, "Oh, sure—I forgot. Time to collect your reward."

"Reward?"

"You know what I mean," she answered.

"What? You mean"— Rodgers left the question unasked, as he directed an incredulous glance her way. "Do you think that's what I did that for?"

Jenny looked confused. "Well...I don't know...I just assumed" ...

"Don't assume," Rodgers said. "I kicked that fool's ass just for the pleasure of doin' it." He drove a little further in silence, and then asked her, "Do you want a room of your own, or would you like to get a double, and have a bed of your own in the same room with me?"

She thought about it a moment. "Well, if you wouldn't mind, I'd like to stay in a room with you. I'd feel safer that way."

"Okay—we'll get a double."

Rodgers checked into the first motel he saw. Putting his pistol in a tote-bag he carried behind the seat of the pickup, the two of them went to the room together. Once they were situated inside, Buck sat down on the bed and started taking off his boots. Jenny began to disrobe in front of him.

"Wait—don't you want me to at least turn the lights out, before you do that?"

"I thought you'd wanta see what you're gettin'," she said.

Rodgers got up from the bed and gently led her to the other bed, where he sat her down. "Listen—I don't know what you're thinkin', but don't think that. I just put that life you've been livin' permanently to rest. There ain't gonna be no more Shooter Dobbins. This is a new beginning for you." He pulled out his wallet and took out ten one-hundred-dollar bills.

"Here—I'll just leave this on the nightstand. If you wake up in the middle of the night and wanta leave—take this money and go with my blessing. Nobody's keepin' you here, and nobody's gonna hurt you, and you don't need to feel like you have to go to bed with a total stranger just because he kicked the shit outta that animal who was makin' your life miserable. You're a free woman now. Make the most of it." Rodgers turned out the lights, then sat down on the bed and started removing his shirt. "Let's rest up...regroup and reconnoiter...and, if you're still here in the mornin', we'll decide where we go from here."

Jenny had a look of disbelief on her face. "Cowboy—you are one weird dude."

"Good night," Rodgers said, as he climbed under the covers. "I hope you'll still be here when I wake up."

"You know," she said, peering at him in the semi-darkness. "I believe I will be."

The next morning, having left Jenny still sleeping in the motel room, Buck Rodgers strode into the downtown Hyatt Regency and went through the lobby to the information desk that had been set up for the medical convention. "May I help you?" a well-dressed woman behind the desk inquired with a smile.

"Yes, ma'am. This is where they're havin' the big medical convention, right?"

"It is," the woman replied.

"Well, I'm tryin' to locate Dr. Charles Keeler. I saw in the paper he was goin' to be makin' some kind of speech here today."

The woman consulted her schedule. "Yes—he's going to address the Alzheimer's research group in about"—she glanced at her watch— "twenty minutes."

"Thanks," Rodgers said as he abruptly walked away. He walked through the hotel, looking for an employees' entrance, until he noticed a Hispanic-looking man dressed in a hotel uniform walking toward him. Rodgers approached him. "Hey, amigo—do you speak English?"

"Yeah. I grew up right here in Houston."

"Well, look here—I got a hundred bucks if you'll get me back where I can catch one of the doctors who's about to make a speech here today in front of the Alzheimer's group. I got another hundred for you if I actually get to talk to him."

The hotel employee didn't hesitate. "Follow me." The man led Rodgers down a back hallway to a door that opened on a large convention room. "You said Alzheimer's group, right?" Buck nodded agreement. "It's right here." He looked through the door. "I don't see anybody on the stage. If he doesn't come in through the front door, this is where he's gonna go in." The employee hesitated. "But...listen...I gotta get back to work. And if security comes back here and sees you, I don't wanna be here with you. I could lose my job." He held out his hand. "So...would you mind?"

Buck handed him the other hundred-dollar bill. "Ah, what the hell? Thanks, amigo. Appreciate the help."

At that moment, Charles Keeler came around the corner, looking at the notes he had prepared for his speech. Rodgers approached him with a big grin. "Excuse me, but aren't you the famous researcher, Dr. Keeler?"

"I don't know how famous I am, but I am Charles Keeler."

"Well, could you spare me a coupla minutes, Doc? I really need to talk to you."

Keeler glanced at his watch. "I don't mean to be rude, but I'm scheduled to make an address to a group of prestigious scientists in just a few moments. Maybe after the meeting."

"Thank you so much, Doctor," Rodgers said. "I knew you'd give me a moment of your time."

Buck grabbed the smaller man in a viselike hug and dragged him further down the hall, away from the door that led to the ballroom. Caught by surprise, Keeler barely had time to sputter out a feeble protest before he was whisked several feet down the hall by the powerful man who held him captive. Having gone what he considered a safe distance away, Rodgers turned the doctor loose. Keeler backed up against the wall, afraid of the crazy cowboy with the strange grin on his face.

"Please...don't hurt me. I'll give you my money."

"Charles? Don't you recognize me?" Paralyzed by fear, Keeler didn't answer. "It's me, Charles—Billy. Billy Braddock." The look in Keeler's eyes changed from fear, to confusion, to doubt, to tentative belief, to absolute certainty—all in barely more than a scintillating moment of epiphany. The wave of emotion that swept over him was so great that he almost collapsed in the hallway. The cowboy reached out to steady him, for fear that Keeler was about to faint. "Hey, c'mon, Charles—I didn't mean to give you a heart attack."

"Billy?" Keeler studied the face, unable to believe the words he was hearing. Then, recognizing what he was seeing, he exclaimed, "It's you! It's really you!"

"In the flesh," Braddock grinned.

Awestricken, Keeler breathed, "Oh, my God! My God! You look...wonderful!"

"Hey, I feel wonderful," Braddock said. "That serum really did the trick."

Keeler fumbled for words, realizing the magnitude of what he was seeing, and all that was yet to be done in the name of scientific advancement. His mind was racing a thousand miles a second, but all he could say was, "Billy...Billy...I'm absolutely speechless." He tried to gather his thoughts. "You have to come back with me to Braddock, Billy. There's so much we have to do...so much we have to learn. This is a true miracle of science. Nobody will believe it, if you don't come back with me." He shook his head. "I can't believe it myself, and yet...there you stand, in all your youthful glory, the Billy Braddock I never knew. It's more than I could ever dream."

"I just looked you up because you wanted me to tell you how it all came out. The last time we talked, I was growin' teeth, my hair was changin' colors, and the wrinkles were disappearin' one by one. So here's the rest of it"—he held out his arms to show his magnificent physique— "it's me. It's the old Billy Braddock, back from the dead."

"Oh, Billy...this...this" ... His eyes filled with tears.

"Hey—I didn't come up here to make you cry," Braddock said. "I thought you'd be happy."

"Billy, I am overcome with joy," Keeler said, wiping away the tears. "I'm happy for you, I'm happy for our Institute...I'm just thrilled to death." He stopped and directed a pointed look at Braddock. "But you need to come back to the research center with me, Billy."

"No—that's not gonna happen any time soon, Charles. I'm livin' my life all over again."

"You don't understand. You remember Kimba— our chimpanzee?"

"Yeah, I remember him. Cute little guy."

"Listen—he was doing so well, it looked like he was going to live another fifty years, and then some. And then suddenly, for reasons we can't explain or understand, he started deteriorating. Now he's going downhill fast. We've done everything we can, but we can't stop the process, or slow it, or fix it, or change it. His days are numbered. The serum will not last, Billy. It didn't last on him, and it won't last on you."

Braddock's look turned serious. "Well, I coulda done without that, Charles. Seems like every time I see you lately, you start tellin' me I'm gonna die." He paused a thoughtful moment. "Do you have any idea how much time I've got?"

"No. There's no way to know. The deterioration might start tomorrow, or it might start a year from now—two years, maybe. I don't know. But I'd say the inevitable onset of symptoms is more likely to occur in the near future than it is five years from now."

"Well, then...I guess I better live my life while I got it." Braddock gave the smaller man a hug. "I'll see you, Charles. Thanks for everything."

Keeler reached out and grabbed one of Braddock's powerful arms. "Come back to Braddock with me, Billy. Maybe we can do something."

Braddock's eyes were distant. "Goodbye, Charles. It was nice knowin' you."

Billy Braddock started walking away down the hall. Charles Keeler called after him, "Billy! Think of the contributions you could make to science! To the future of mankind" ...

As soon as he left the hallway, Billy Braddock once again became Buck Rodgers in his own mind—at least as far as self-willed cognitive dissonance and conscious denial of the facts would allow. He tried to tell himself there had never been such a person as Billy Braddock, that he was a new man of his own creation...that he was, and would be, Buck Rodgers from now on. He got into his truck and returned to the motel room in Pasadena, stopping by a liquor store along the way. When he got back to the room, he opened the door, and the first thing he saw was

Jenny, sitting on the bed in a sexy negligee. He could smell the fragrance of expensive perfume as soon as he closed the door. She smiled in a shyly enticing way that he found to be disarming in its simple charm.

Even though he was still upset by what Charles Keeler had told him, he forced the thoughts to the back of his mind and allowed himself to smile back at her. "I see you didn't leave."

"No," she said. "I made up my mind I don't wanta leave. I don't ever wanta leave. I wanta be with you."

Trying to appear casual about the fact that she was sitting there in a negligee that left nothing to the imagination, Rodgers said, "It appears like you been out shoppin' while I was gone. Did you...take a taxi?"

"Sure did."

He poured a stiff drink and sat down on the other bed. "So...you say you wanta stay?"

"I do," she said. "And I don't ever wanna go away. You're my hero, and I wanna be with you forever."

"Nothin' lasts forever, Jenny," he said, taking a large sip of whisky.

She got off the bed and came to the bed where he was sitting. She put her arms around his neck, her beautiful breasts almost touching his face. "Then let's make it last as long as we can."

She leaned over and kissed his lips, and he returned the kiss with a passion he had long denied in his own mind that he had ever felt for this beautiful creature of desire. But now—with her offering herself to him so willingly, so *eagerly*—he could admit to himself that he had always had these feelings for her. As he exposed her nakedness to his hungry eyes, he felt somehow deceitful...and yet, somewhere in his mind, he knew that he had crossed some invisible plane of conventional morality into an amoral darkness where existed no right or wrong, no good or bad—only pleasure, only the feeling, only the moment, only what he could have while he could have it...

END PART TWO

PART THREE

On a moonless night in Dallas, the Bradley mansion was a glittering oasis of light as Carter Bradley's social affair to raise money for the Texas Republican Party was getting into full swing. Inside the house, movers and shakers from all over the State mixed and mingled as Mary Lynn Bradley flitted from room to room, doing her best to be a gracious hostess. Noticing that another elegant couple was just arriving, she fluttered through the crowd to meet them in the foyer. "Oh, hello, hello, hello!" she said in her typically effusive style. "It's so good to see you! George...you just keep getting more handsome every time I see you. And Betty Lou—just look at you! You look absolutely *ravishing* tonight! You'd better stay close to her, George—somebody's liable to try to steal her away from you tonight."

Exchanging hugs and kisses with the new arrivals, she escorted them into the house and started introducing the couple to others nearby. Once she was assured that her new guests were successfully integrated into the festivities, Mary Lynn excused herself and went to the study, where her husband was talking to Claude Loomis, his personal attorney. She knocked lightly and then poked her head through the door. "Carter, can't all this business talk wait till later? We have all sorts of guests who are waiting to see you."

"I'll be there in just a few more minutes, I promise."

"Well, do hurry, please. There's just not enough of me to go around. And a lot of people are wantin' your attention."

"Give me five minutes," he said.

"Hurry," she urged in a whisper.

Once Mary Lynn closed the door, the lawyer sitting in front of the desk resumed the conversation that had been interrupted by Mary Lynn's intrusion. "So you're absolutely certain you want to go through with it?"

"Well, you're the lawyer, Claude. You said the prenuptial agreement was ironclad, didn't you?"

"As best we can tell. I've had everybody in the office look at it, and that's the consensus—ironclad. If you divorce her because of adultery, and it's proved in court, she gets a hundred and fifty thousand, her personal effects, and her car—that's it." He qualified his statement with a shrug. "Of course, she can fight it in court."

"It won't do her any good. I own the entire court system in Dallas County."

"So you want me to start proceedings, first thing in the morning?"

Bradley nodded his head. "Definitely. She's flying to L.A. to see her mother for a few days. By the time she returns, all the locks and codes will be changed, all of her things will be in a rented storeroom, and she'll be barred from the property. I'll have full-time security on the premises to guarantee it. And to back it up, I want you to file a restraining order against her."

"I would advise you to cancel all her credit cards and empty out any joint bank accounts the two of you may have," the lawyer said.

"I've already told my assistant to do that tomorrow, once she's safely in the air. We don't have any joint bank accounts. She lives on plastic. She has her own little checking account, but I doubt there's more than twenty-thousand dollars in it."

Claude leaned back in the chair. "Did you find out any more about that cowboy?"

"No. He remains a mystery, but I still believe there's some kind of connection to Billy Braddock. I know you probably think he's my personal version of Professor Moriarty; but I just feel, deep down in my bones, Braddock's got something to do with all of this."

"Well, from my vantage point, it does seem a little far-fetched to me, Carter."

"Even so, I have to satisfy myself Braddock's not involved. That's why I invited Walter Drake to the party tonight. I'm going to put a little bug in his ear, and see if I can't enlist the power of the press to flush Billy Braddock out of hiding."

"What about the cowboy? Did you locate his whereabouts?"

"No. The last time anybody saw him was at a rodeo, down near Houston. I've had that little pervert detective Edgar Gross trying to locate Braddock *and* the cowboy, and they've both disappeared."

"Do you think Mary Lynn might know where he is?"

"No, I don't. And I think it's driving her crazy. She's been moody for days, moping around and acting distraught. My guess is that she's so upset because she's lost her playmate."

The attorney gave him a sympathetic look. "Well, I want you to know...I truly feel bad for you, Carter. She's such a pretty girl, and for awhile there I

189

actually believed you'd found true love at last. It's a shame it had to come down to this."

The old man could barely suppress the pained expression on his face. "Well, I'm not too happy about it, but...that's the way it is. I feel like a fool." He paused, then added with an ironic grin, "And, to make it worse, an *old* fool...of which they say there is no fool like."

"If it's any consolation, Carter, she's the one who's gonna be feelin' like a fool when she finds out her hot little ass has got her tit in a wringer."

Bradley was thoughtful. "She's definitely going to feel *something*, I'm sure—poor, if nothing else. Which, for her, might be the worst punishment of all. She really loves to spend money. But...enough of this for now. Let's go out and join the party."

Leaving the study, the two men went their separate ways as they were absorbed into the crowd. Carter Bradley roamed around, shaking hands and making perfunctory greetings, until he noticed Walter Drake, a well-known reporter whose specialty was reporting on the lifestyles of the rich and famous—particularly the rich and famous of Texas. Bradley made a beeline across the room to talk to the writer. Extending a welcoming hand, he said, "Walter! So glad you could make it!"

"Well, thank you, Carter. Quite frankly, I was very surprised when I received your invitation. To what, or whom, do I owe the honor of the occasion? Are you trying to get a little column-space for that beautiful little wife of yours?"

Bradley took the reporter by the arm and started gently directing him toward the French doors that led to the terrace. "Oh, no, no—nothing like that. I just thought it might be a good PR move to invite the press to join the party, for a change. Maybe the next time you turn your poison pen on me, you'll dilute the venom just a little, once you've actually seen me in my element on a social occasion. You've been pretty rough on me a couple of times in the past."

The reporter gave him an apologetic look. "It's nothing personal, Carter. You know that."

"I do, and I respect that. You do your job, and you do it well." As they moved across the room, Bradley said, "Let's step out onto the terrace just a moment, shall we?" Once they were outside, away from the crowd, the oilman continued, "I do have a question I'd like to ask you, Walt."

"Ah...now the ulterior motive appears."

Holding up a hand in a gesture of protest, Bradley said, "Now, just give me a chance here." He paused to formulate his thought, then continued, "My company is trying to acquire a small oil company in North Texas, but we're in competition with Braddock Oil, and negotiations are going nowhere. In the end, whether we acquire the company, or whether Braddock Oil makes the acquisition, it will take years to recoup the investment—even at today's high price per barrel. I'm trying to figure out a way to reach an amicable solution, but management at Braddock Oil is being totally unreasonable. It's all-or-nothing with them—that's the way they do business. But if I could talk to Billy Braddock, I believe we could come to terms, man-to-man. I've known Billy ever since our days as undergrads at SMU."

Anticipating where the conversation was going, Drake asked, "Are you wantin' me to get in touch with Braddock for you?"

Bradley gave a sarcastic chuckle. "Good luck with that. He's disappeared. Nobody seems to know where he is. I know you keep your finger on the pulse of life at the top, and I was just wondering if you might know where he is, or how I could get in touch with him."

"I didn't even know he was missing."

"Well, I hired a private detective to locate him, and he came up empty. I just spoke with my personal attorney, Claude Loomis, and he hasn't been able to find out anything, either." He gave a baffled shrug. "Seems like Billy Braddock is nowhere to be found."

"Hmm—that's kinda peculiar...even by Billy Braddock's standards."

"If anybody knows where he is, nobody's telling. The only thing my man could find out was that he had a heart attack and went somewhere to recuperate. My greatest fear is that he's dead, and nobody's willing to admit it for whatever reasons—in which case, I'll have to hold a séance to talk to him. If Braddock's dead and there's no way for me to settle this matter with him personally, this acquisition fight with the management at Braddock Oil will turn into a financial bloodbath. They don't do business any other way. Never have. Those guys only play to win—at any cost."

"You know—that's very interesting, Carter. I'm definitely gonna look into that."

"Well, if you hear anything, or can find out anything, will you please let me know? I'd consider it a personal favor, Walt."

Drake nodded. "I'll let you know if anything turns up."

"I'll take your word on that." Having achieved what he had intended, Carter Bradley gave the writer a pat on the back. "Let's get back to the party. I've got dozens of people I haven't had a chance to greet. You just make yourself at home, eat and drink all you want, and try not to start any fist-fights, okay?"

"I'll try," Drake promised with a sardonic smile.

Carter Bradley walked away, grinning like the proverbial cat who ate the canary. Noticing Claude Loomis giving him a questioning look across the room, Bradley nodded and gave a thumbs-up gesture to show that his mission was accomplished.

Returning the gesture, Loomis smiled broadly and raised a champagne glass to toast Bradley's success at getting the press involved in the hunt for Billy Braddock.

Upon receiving the news that Shooter Dobbins had been arrested by the Pasadena Police Department, Chief John Wilkins had immediately flown to Houston to question him. In preparation for the interview with Shooter, Wilkins was sitting in the office of Detective Ray Pyle, about to watch a video the police made in the interrogation room the night Dobbins was arrested. Pyle was offering a preliminary explanation of the events that led up to Shooter's arrest:

... "and our officer was driving down Shaver Street, when this big biker jumps out of the bushes, beat all to hell, and runs out in the street, wavin' his arms and screamin' bloody murder. So the patrolman stopped to help and ran a routine check on Dobbins, and found out pretty quick he had warrants out on 'im, at which point the officer arrested Dobbins on the spot and brought 'im to the station for questioning. I just happened to be here that night, so I was the one who talked to 'im first." He paused, and adjusted the machine. "And with all that said, this here's what happened at that interview" ... Pyle started the video, showing him with Shooter Dobbins in the interrogation room:

"So, Stanley"—

"Hey, man—don't call me Stanley. Everybody calls me Shooter."

"Okay, Shooter...I'm Detective Ray Pyle. I'm here to help you."

"Man, I need to see a doctor."

"Don't worry. We're gonna get you to a doctor. But before we do that, I just wanta clarify a few things with you, okay?"

"Yeah, whatever. Just get on with it."

"Okay...just bear with me a minute. Now, you were telling the officers 'they' were gonna kill you. Who are 'they'?"

"The Bandidos. Braddock. All of 'em. Any of 'em. I'm a dead man if I stay in this town. They'll kill me outta disgust. They hate me."

"Did you do something to make the Bandidos mad at you?"

"Naw! I mean...yeah, in a way. See...they think I'm a worthless punk 'cause I pulled my pants down so Braddock could fuck me in the butt. But you gotta understand—I couldn't take any more of the beatin', man...I just couldn't! That animal was about to kill me!" Dobbins started to cry, and the detective gave him a handful of tissues.

"Who was beatin' you—the Bandidos?"

Shooter sniffled. "No, Billy Braddock was beatin' me. The Bandidos were standin' around, watchin' and laughin'."

"Is Braddock one of the Bandidos?"

"Naw—he's this old sonofabitch of a preacher I slapped around awhile back 'cause he was interferin' with me and my old lady. The bastard must be a hundred years old."

"Wait—I need to be sure I got this down: The Bandidos wanna kill you 'cause they think you're a punk 'cause you pulled your pants down so a hundred-year-old preacher who beat you up could fuck you in the butt? Am I gettin' this right, so far?"

Wilkins and Pyle laughed at this summary of the story Dobbins was telling, and Shooter resumed his tale. "Yeah, except the preacher wasn't old any more. He was young—like...twenty-two...real strong...I *never saw anybody so strong. I know it sounds crazy, but it was him. I know it was him. I tell you, he's a criminal...stone criminal. There's no tellin' what he'd-a done, if there hadn't been any witnesses around. I'm tellin' you, he's a menace to society!"*

"I gotta admit—anybody who'd wanta have anal sex with you *definitely sounds dangerous to me. I need to warn all the ranchers in the area to lock up the livestock."*

"Hey, you shouldn't be jokin' about this, man. This is serious. God, I'm hurtin' all over! He beat me so bad...you just can't imagine. I need to go to the hospital, man. I'm all busted up inside."

"We're gonna get you over there. I'm just tryin' to get a little more information so we can go after the man who assaulted you."

"He didn't just assault me—he tried to kill me. Plus—he knocked out my teeth, he robbed me, he shot my bike, he took my old lady...he made me stick out my chin and say 'cheese'"— Shooter started to cry again. "Oh, God...I can't believe I did that!"

"Now, get yourself together, Shooter," Detective Pyle said in a soothing voice. "Did you say he made you say 'cheese'?"

"Yeah—just before he knocked me out cold."

"Why'd he do that?"

"He was makin' a fool out of me. I'm standin' there helpless, with my pants down around my ankles, and he makes me stick my chin out, like I'm posin' for a picture, while he measures the punch. And then he tells me, 'Say cheese,' so I do it...and BLAM!— that's all I remember. The next thing I knew, I was layin' on the ground behind that bar, with fire ants all over my ass."

"Can you give me a description of your assailant?"

"It's like I told you—he looks like that damn old preacher Billy Braddock, except he's young. I don't

195

know how he did it, but he did it. He came back young and got revenge on me. He even said, 'Here come da judge,' just like I said to him when I knocked the shit out of 'im. It's him—I know it's him, except he's real big and muscular and dressed like a cowboy" ...

Pyle stopped the video. "This is pretty much all I got out of 'im. It was just a bunch o' rantin' and ravin'. We can watch the whole thing, if you want to."

"No, that's enough for now," John Wilkins said. "Didn't you say you found a couple of ounces of pot in his saddlebags?"

"Yeah. That—and an unregistered pistol. We're gonna prosecute 'im to the full extent of the law, so we can keep 'im locked up as long as possible. Maybe that'll give you time to locate your witnesses, so we can hang another coupla cases on 'im."

"I appreciate that, Ray. He made a confession right at the start of that video when he said he slapped Billy Braddock around. I didn't hear you read 'im his rights, so I don't know if the confession would hold up in court, but he partially corroborated what Billy Braddock told the doctor. And if Billy dies from what Dobbins did to 'im, I guarantee we're gonna charge 'im with murder. That's another reason I wanta hold off—for all I know Billy Braddock might already be dead. I've gotta talk to Jenny Dobbins." He leaned back in the chair. "So whadda you make out of that crazy story about Braddock beatin' 'im up? Is he settin' up an insanity plea, just in case?"

"I don't know," Pyle said. "He doesn't seem smart enough to be planning ahead like that." He paused, then added, "You can't really tell it on the video, but if you'd-a seen 'im up close, you'd realize that big cowboy, whoever he was, did a big-time number on ol' Shooter. I went to see 'im in the hospital a couple days later, and his head looked like a big black basketball with hair growin' on it. He was some kinda messed up, I do mean to tell you. I think that night we arrested 'im, when I was askin' 'im questions, he was just out of 'is gourd—and the doctor said he did have a very severe concussion." He paused. "Oh—and the regular doctor had a psychiatrist talk to 'im when he got where he could talk fairly sensibly, and the shrink said he was suffering from some sort of paranoid delusion about Billy Braddock."

"Maybe it's just a guilty conscience, comin' back to haunt 'im," Wilkins said. Then he asked, "Did you get anything out of the Bandidos?"

Ray Pyle gave him a sarcastic look. "Yeah—just what you'd expect. Nobody saw anything, or heard anything, or knows anything, or suspects anything. They said it musta happened after hours."

"Do you believe 'em?"

"Hell, no. I think they saw the whole thing, whatever it was that happened." Pyle shrugged. "But...what're you gonna do? I can't prove otherwise."

"Well, I'm gonna be honest with you, Ray—I'd be hopin' you never do catch that cowboy, if there wasn't a possibility that Jenny Dobbins ran off with 'im. I need Jenny as a corroborating witness. But as far as that cowboy goes...he did what I've been wantin' to do for a long time. And as far as Shooter goes...it couldn't-a happened to a sorrier sonofabitch. God bless that cowboy, whoever he was."

Ray Pyle said, "Well, since you're bein' so honest with me—I'm gonna be honest with you, Chief—if I do catch 'im, and he's not some kind of oil-burnin' criminal himself, I suspect I'm not gonna be able to find probable cause to arrest 'im. As far as I'm concerned, he did a public service."

Wilkins gave an approving grin. "Amen, brother."

Pyle continued, "I'm from the Wyatt Earp School of Law—it's only a crime if I consider it to be a crime."

"I knew there was some reason I liked you—you remind me of myself." The two men exchanged grins, and Wilkins said, "Let me go pay my respects to Shooter, and then I'll be headin' out. I flew in special on a Braddock Oil Company corporate jet, and they're waitin' at the airport to take me back."

"Okay, then—I'll drive you over to the county jail."

As Buck drove along a small road that ran parallel to the shoreline of the Gulf of Mexico, Jenny looked out the window, enjoying the majesty of the restless sea as it gently roiled to land, then ebbed away to begin the endless cycle anew. Jenny gave Buck a curious glance. "Are you gonna tell me what we're doin' out here? I mean, I like it, but I wish you'd tell me what all the mystery is about."

"I'm fixin' to do that," he said with a smile. "It's just right down here, a few more houses." In just a few seconds, Rodgers pulled up in the driveway of a quaint little beach house. "Get out," he told her. "See what you think."

The two of them got out of the pickup, walked onto the spacious covered porch, and went in through the open door. The house was fully furnished in tasteful, if not elegant style, the décor chosen to suggest a tropical motif that was harmonious to the idea of life on the beach. Buck followed Jenny as she went from room to room, expressing her approval at everything she saw. When she had finished the tour of the house, they stopped in the master bedroom and she gave him a questioning look.

"Does this place belong to a friend of yours, or something?"

"It's a timeshare place. I rented it for a coupla months. I figure with all you been through, a little time at the beach might do you good."

"Oh, Buck! You didn't! This must have cost a fortune!" She gave him an enthusiastic hug and kissed him appreciatively.

He shrugged. "I won my last rodeo. Had a little extra cash. Besides, I know you've been cooped up in that motel room for the past three weeks while I was out and about. I wanted to do this for you. In fact, this is part of what I was doin' while I was runnin' around town—I was tryin' to find us a little place to get away for awhile."

"Oh, my God! I never dreamed" ...

"Oh!" He held up a forefinger and paused. "Before we go back up front, I wanta show you a little something." He opened the closet and showed her a rack of new dresses, skirts and blouses with the tags still on them. "I hope you don't mind. I took the liberty. While you were sleeping, I got your clothes-sizes, then I went to the mall and found a salesgirl who was just about the exact size you are. I showed her your picture and asked her to help me pick out a few things for you, and this is what we ended up with."

Jenny stood speechless, staring at the beautiful clothes. Then, almost as if she were afraid she would ruin the dresses, she gently thumbed through the rack, touching each garment with loving care. Suddenly she put her hands over her face and started to cry, her body trembling uncontrollably as she quietly wept. Rodgers came over and put his arms around her, nestling her to his chest.

"Hey, it's okay, don't cry," he said, gently patting her on the back. "If you don't like 'em, we'll take 'em all back and you can get somethin' else. I've still got the receipts."

Through her tears, she started to laugh. "Buck, I love the clothes. They're beautiful!"

Buck looked confused. "Then why are you cryin'?"

"I'm crying because nobody's ever done anything like that for me in my whole life. That's why I'm crying. I don't deserve anyone as nice as you."

"Now, that's silly," he said. Rodgers gently led her toward the door. "You can try the clothes on later. I got somethin' else I wanna show you." He took her to the kitchen and stopped in front of a door that opened to the garage. "Now, dry your eyes and get yourself together." He paused, then said, "No, on second thought I don't think I'm gonna show you my other surprise. After the way you acted when I showed you the clothes, I'm scared you'll try to commit suicide when I show you this."

"Oh, c'mon, Buck—don't torment me!" she pleaded.

"Well, okay" ... Buck opened the door of the garage. "You told me you'd never had a car of your own, so I bought you this little Corvette convertible to give you a way to get back and forth around town."

"Oh, my God! Did you really do this?"

Her tears started to flow again, and Buck grabbed her and clutched her tightly. "Now don't get all bent out of shape again till I tell you...it's a used car—four years old, I think. I thought it would make a good starter car for you. It looks new because it was owned by a little old lady in Pasadena who only drove it on weekends at the drag races." He pulled a set of keys out of his shirt pocket. "I put it in my name so I could go ahead and get it 'cause I wanted to surprise you with it. We'll go down and transfer the title this week, and she'll be all yours."

She stood looking up at him, an expression of wonderment on her face. "Why in the name of God are you so nice to me?"

"C'mere, girl." Buck scooped her up in his arms and took her to the living room, where he sat down on the couch with her in his lap. "I'm so nice to you because I care about you more than you would ever suspect. I know you've had a hard life, and never had a chance to know anything better. The way I see it, for as long as we have each other, I'd like to be the one to make your life better." He kissed her lightly on the lips. "I wish I could kiss away all the pain you've ever known."

"I can't believe you have any feelings at all for me after what I told you about that night with Shooter and Bubba."

"Try not to think about that ever again. That wasn't your fault, and I don't hold anything against you. I know a lot more about who you really are than you think I do." He paused, and a dark look crossed his face. "One day soon, when I get a few things in order, I'm gonna have you tell me all you know about Bubba and how to find him. I think he needs a little dose of 'is own medicine...you know—eye-for-eye therapy. Who knows? It might even do 'im some good."

"He's not worth you gettin' in trouble."

"I won't get in any trouble. He's gonna know *what* hit 'im...but he'll never have a clue *who* was behind it. And I doubt very seriously the cops are gonna put his assailant on a high priority list, as long as it's just a terrible ass-whoopin' that gets inflicted on 'im."

"Really, Buck" —

"No," he interjected. "No argument. It's somethin' I gotta do for myself, as much as for you. It's like the

Bible says: '*Sow the wind, reap the whirlwind.*' Bubba don't know it yet, but he done sowed the wind. And I'm the avenging angel who's gonna see to it that the other half of that prophecy is fulfilled upon his *ass.*"

Jenny laughed at Buck's joke, then looked at him with a thoughtful gaze. "You know somethin', Buck? I feel like I've known you for a very long time. I don't know why...just something about you."

"I'm an easy guy to get to know," he said.

"And that day after you beat the hell out of Shooter, and I told you I wanted to stay with you forever" ...

"Yeah," he said in an expectant tone.

"Well, when I said that, it was partly—mostly—out of gratitude for you gettin' me away from Shooter. But I also said it because—for some strange reason—I felt comfortable around you, like us bein' together was as natural as honey and bees together."

"So what are you tellin' me?" he asked.

"I mean...I never felt like that before. And I just want you to know that I'm not the kinda girl who goes with anybody who wants her," she said.

"I never thought you were."

"Yeah," she said, "but I know it kinda looked that way, and I want you to know that's not how it is."

He nodded. "I believe you—really."

"Well, what I'm tryin' to say is—and it's not because of the dresses, or the car, or the beach vacation—I'm tryin' to tell you I think I'm fallin' for you in a big, big way. I mean...if you walked out of my life today, I'd never get over it for as long as I live."

She leaned over and kissed him with exquisite tenderness, her lips expressing some deep emotion that was more than mere passion. Buck returned the kiss as if he understood the unspoken message, and reciprocated with his own lips every expression of feeling she was conveying to him. Neither of them uttered the word *love*, but both of them could feel the love flowing between them as they lingered in the sweet embrace.

When at last they broke away from each other, Buck looked at her with a mischievous gleam in his eye. "Let's go fuck."

Laughing, she slapped him on the shoulder. "Oh, you dog! Just like a damn man—always thinkin' with the other head. Just let me go!"

He held onto her, refusing to let her out of his lap. "Hey, I was just kiddin'! Stop hittin' me! I wanna make a suggestion, seriously."

She stopped slapping his shoulder to hear what he had to say. "Okay, what?"

"Let's go fuck, really."

"Oh, you nasty thing! Turn me loose...turn me loose right now!"

Buck refused to let her go. "No, now—gimme a break, will you?" He held onto her long enough to calm her down, and then said, "I'm just teasin' you. My real suggestion was that you take a quick look at those clothes and we'll go over to the mall and you can pick out some purses and shoes to go with 'em. Maybe a little jewelry, too." He paused a moment, then added, "And then after that, we'll come back here and fuck like hell. Whadda ya say?"

Jenny couldn't help laughing at his silliness, even as she practically melted into his arms. "Oh, baby...you've done too much already."

"No, you need some other stuff to go with those clothes. Plus, I didn't pick out any casual stuff for you to wear when we're knockin' around the beach. You've gotta go with me, 'cause I don't know what to pick out for you. Besides, I'm kinda wantin' a burger, or something. Whadda ya say? We'll take the Corvette, so you can get a feel for your new car."

"You know what, Cowboy?" She didn't give him time to answer. "I have this terrible feelin' I'm gonna fall madly in love with you, and you're gonna break my heart into a million tiny pieces."

"Don't even talk like that," he scolded. He stood up and set her on her feet. "C'mon. Let's go do what we gotta do, and then we'll spend the evenin' relaxin' in our new beach house."

When Jenny had looked at the clothes and made a few decisions about what accessories she might buy, they left the house and went toward the mall. As they came to a fast food restaurant, Buck instructed her to pull in. The drive-through window was backed up, so Buck told her just to wait for him while he went inside. As he was approaching the door, he saw a newsstand and decided to buy a copy of the Houston *Chronicle* to read later. Standing in line to order the burgers, he skimmed the headlines on the front page. On the bottom half of the page, his eyes were drawn to a small headline:

Mystery Surrounds Disappearance Of Texas Oilman

The accompanying article began with a few ominous words:

> *"Rumors continue to swirl concerning the whereabouts of eccentric oil billionaire Billy Braddock, who vanished several months ago and has not been seen by anyone since. Fears are growing that Braddock has died as the result of a recent heart attack, or that he has gone into hiding because he is either physically or mentally incapable of overseeing operations at the Braddock Corporation, the multi-billion-dollar conglomerate"* ...

Buck Rodgers tucked the newspaper under his arm, unwilling to read any further. The carefree expression that had been on his face a moment before had turned serious, but he continued doing what he was doing, determined not to allow anything to ruin what until that moment been a wonderful afternoon. Once he had retrieved the food, he put on his happiest face and returned to the car, where he directed Jenny to proceed full speed ahead toward the mall.

Steve Jackson and Bobby Pardo arrived early at Docu-Tex, expecting that Artie Davis was going to send them on a new assignment. When they went into Artie's office, they saw him watching some recently-edited video related to the Billy Braddock documentary. As they came through the door, Artie stopped the machine and invited them to sit down. Once greetings were exchanged all around, Davis got right to the point:

"Look, guys, I know you were probably thinkin' I was going to send you out on the Braddock assignment today, but I've got enough footage to finish it now."

"What?" Jackson asked, his voice filled with disappointment.

Davis gestured for silence. "No, now...this ain't a debate, Steve. This is how it's gonna be. This Braddock disappearance thing is startin' to heat up, and I have a feeling it's gonna get hotter before it gets cooler. So far, it's pretty much a Texas story, bein' fueled by the big papers in Houston, Dallas and San Antonio. But this isn't gonna stay regional much longer. And for the first time in my life, I'm ahead of the curve."

"Yeah, but, Artie"—

Again Davis interrupted Jackson's attempt to argue. "Just listen, Steve. As I said, I'm ahead of the curve. But I won't be for long because the drums are pounding in the distance and the hoofbeats are thundering behind. It won't be long before the posse is on our tail—and they're ridin' big horses."

"Is this a Western?" Bobby Pardo joked.

"Yeah," Artie said, "it's a Western—and I'm the outlaw hero. People are about to know who we are. We're gonna edit what we've got and take it to market. I've got several people who are extremely interested in our little project—and they're talkin' big, big money if we can deliver a commercial product. With every passing day, the more this publicity about Braddock continues, our product becomes more valuable. This could lead to other things for all of us that we haven't dared to dream of before now. Thanks to you guys and the rest of the people on the staff who have worked so hard on this thing, I think we've captured lightning in a bottle. This thing could put DocuTex on a whole new level, if it makes the money I think it can. And with all the news copy that's being generated around the State...unless Braddock comes out of the woodwork pretty soon, it's just a matter of time until the story goes national—even global. For me, this is that proverbial tide in the affairs of men that leads on to fame and fortune. I mean to catch that tide at the flood, and you're comin' with me, like it or not. We don't have any more time to wait."

"Yeah, but we've still got a lot more people to interview," Steve said.

"I know that," Davis agreed. "And a few more topless bars to visit, I'm sure. But I've reviewed the interviews you have in the can, and they paint more than a reasonably good portrait of the man, both good and bad. Those interviews you guys didn't like—where people talked about how he helped the poor and comforted the sick? To me, they were more than people sayin' what they thought Braddock might want them to say. I saw the same interviews, and I thought the people were sincere. Those interviews tell about a man who was trying to do some good in this world. You guys didn't like those segments because they weren't as interesting to those perverted minds of yours as the stories about the fightin', drinkin' and womanizin'. But I think we've captured the essence of the man, if not the man himself. I'd like to have more, but I've got enough to go with."

"So...that's it, then," Jackson said, in a tone of gloomy resignation.

"That's it," Artie said with a firm nod. "I do want you to do one last thing, though—I want you and Bobby to film yourselves, talking about your impressions of the man you met the day before he disappeared. Give me something good, and I think I might include that in the film. You guys can do that in one of the offices around here, or go out in the back yard—but I want you to do that this morning. And as far as the legwork goes, that's the end of the assignment. Steve, I want you to start working on the script when you and Bobby finish describing your impressions of the man you met that day. And, Bobby, you'll get with the boys in the back and start working with them on the edit. And me—I'll be all over the place, makin' sure it's all done right. Okay, gentlemen?"

"Well, one thing, Artie—if something major happens before we finish, you will let us get more footage, won't you?" Jackson asked.

"Oh, yeah, definitely—*if* something major happens."

Jackson and Pardo exchanged looks. Steve said, "Well, let's go out back and interview ourselves, Bobby."

They rose to leave, and Artie said, "I just want you both to know, you did a really good job on this project. This is the first time I've ever seen you two so involved with a subject. That's what makes me so sure I'm on the right track here. If this Braddock guy can get a coupla jaundiced veterans like you interested in his life-story, it's bound to play big in Peoria, where people are actually real." Davis dismissed them with a wave of his hand. "Now, get to work. I've got things to do."

Wearing a stern look on his face, Chief John Wilkins walked into the police station and saw Rufus Johnson sitting in the lobby. He walked over to the desk sergeant and said, "Hold all my calls until further notice. And tell Jess to come to my office now." The officer nodded his assent, and Wilkins turned to the young taxi driver. "You—come with me," he said, motioning with his finger toward Rufus. The two men went into Wilkins' private office, and the Chief instructed Johnson to sit down. The taxi driver obeyed, and Wilkins propped himself on the corner of the desk. "Okay, Rufus"—

"Man, I done told you—don't be callin' me that. My name's Kareem Lumumba."

"Have you had your name legally changed, like *I* done told *you*?"

"That's my God-given name. I don't *need* to get it legally changed."

"Well, I'll tell you what, Rufus...you need to tell God that He needs to go to the courthouse and fill out the application for a name change, and then He needs to go before a judge and make it all official, so the rest of the world can appreciate what He done did for you. But until He does that, us unenlightened sinners livin' in the secular world are gonna continue to call you Rufus Johnson. You got that?"

Rufus threw up his hands in frustration. "Ma-an" ...

About that time, Police Captain Jesse Torres entered the room. "Chief," he said with a nod. Then he looked at Johnson. "Hello, Rufus. Glad you could stop by."

"My boss at the taxi company said I had to do it, or I was gonna lose my job. It sho' wasn't 'cause I wanted to see you."

Chief Wilkins took a seat behind his desk. "Rufus," he began, "we called you in here today because we're tired of you bullshittin' us. There's time missing from your day, that mornin' you picked up Billy Braddock at the hospital, and we're gonna get to the bottom of it, once and for all."

"Man, I done told you everything I know, five times. This ain't nothin' but police harassment."

"Oh, no...if we decide to harass you, you're gonna think you done died and went to hell," Wilkins said. "All we're tryin' to do is get the truth out of you—and we're gonna get it by any means necessary." The Chief looked at Torres. "Jess, go ahead and tell Rufus what you been doin' lately."

Torres smiled in a way that held a veiled threat behind the toothy façade. "I been followin' you, Rufus. I followed you to Jethro's Menswear a few months ago. You bought four-thousand dollars' worth of fancy clothes and paid in cash—new one-hundred-dollar bills with consecutive serial numbers. Two weeks after that, you spent approximately two thousand dollars at Cohen's Jewelers...paid cash—new one-hundred-dollar bills with consecutive serial numbers. When you traded up to get that fancy used Cadillac at Main Street Motors, you paid the difference in cash—thirty-five brand new one-hundred-dollar bills with consecutive serial numbers. I think I see a pattern emergin'—you seem to have a bunch o' one-hundred-dollar bills with consecutive serial numbers. That's kinda weird, don't you think?"

"Ain't nothin' weird about it to me."

"You also been stylin' around town, squirin' the ladies, and generally livin' mighty large for the money you make as a taxi driver. And everywhere you go, you been payin' the tab with brand-new one-hundred-dollar bills. Looks kinda funny to me. Your boss tells me you take home about two hundred and fifty bucks on a good week, not countin' whatever tips you pick up. So where'd you get that money, Rufus?"

"Did you ever stop and think maybe I'm just a damn good driver?" Rufus defiantly retorted. "Make a lotta tips 'cause I serve my customers well?"

"Hey, I been followin' you, Rufus. I know how you drive. You'd have to *pay me* to ride with you. You are one shitty driver, Rufus. Which brings us back to the question—where'd you get that money?"

"I earned it," Rufus said, folding his arms across his chest. "That's all I got to say. I earned it."

John Wilkins leaned his elbows atop the desk. "Okay, gangsta-man—if you wanna play hardball, that's what we'll have to do. First thing I want you to know is, I'm gonna ask the IRS to stop by and see you real soon. I think they'd like to get more details on how you earned your money, and what taxes you paid on it. But since we have reason to think you been doin' somethin' illegal *besides* not payin' your taxes, I'm gonna ask the judge to issue a warrant for us to search your house, so we can look for evidence of wrongdoin'. No tellin' what we might find in that place while we're tryin' to figure out where that money came from. Hell, we might run across some marijuana, maybe a little dope—crack, meth...who knows? I know a player like you is bound t' have some good shit stashed somewhere, in case a party breaks out."

"Now, wait a minute, man" ...

"And you know," Torres added, "when we search, we have to really be thorough. We have to bust open TV's and tear up stereos, look all inside 'em...bust lamps, rip out walls, cut clothes all to pieces—and the good part about it is, we don't have to pay for a goddamn thing we tear up, 'cause we're on police business, protectin' the interests of the law-abidin' public. That's pretty cool, ain't it?"

Rufus was flustered and scared. "Man...man...I can't *believe* this shit."

Wilkins said, "All you have to do is tell the truth, Rufus, and you can spare yourself a lot of heartache. I got reporters from all over the State callin' my little police station here in Braddock, tryin' to find out what I know about the disappearance of Billy Braddock. And every call that comes to this office, somebody in this department has to answer. And every time we get a call from another reporter...that takes away from the time we're s'posed to be usin' to conduct police business in our little town here. It's a waste of the taxpayers' hard-earned money, and that's who pays our salaries. That's *your* money, Rufus—no, wait...I guess not. I forgot—*you* don't pay *your* taxes. But you'll wish you did when the IRS gets through with your ass." Wilkins leaned back in his chair. "And the sad part about all this is...it could all be avoided, if we could just get a little cooperation from you."

Holding up his hands in surrender, Rufus finally cracked. "Okay, man—I'll tell you." The two officers waited in silent expectation. "I took the guy back to his house, just like I told you. He was in a big hurry. When we got there, he told me to wait. He went inside the house and was gone awhile. When he came back, he had a coupla bags, a cowboy hat and a gun."

"He had a gun?"

"Yeah...a .44-magnum. He was carryin' it in a shoulder holster."

"So then what happened?"

"So then he told me to drive his car over to that new neighborhood they built awhile back...I think the street was Lancelot Lane, or Court...somethin' like that. I could show you the house."

"Did he tell you why he wanted you to go there?" Wilkins asked.

"He said he was sick and we was gonna see this science guy about some kinda medicine that would keep 'im alive. He showed me this big pistol and told me not to freak out if he pulled it on the guy, 'cause he really wasn't gonna shoot 'im. He said he was just gonna scare the guy, so he'd give 'im the medicine. So we went to the house, where he picked up this little bald, nerdy-lookin' dude, and I followed 'em to that research place out there on the edge o' town. I waited in the garage for awhile, then the preacher and the other guy came back down to the garage. They talked a little bit and shook hands, and I drove the preacher back home. That's it. The only other thing I could tell you is that when the preacher got back in the car, he looked all messed up."

"Messed up, how?" Wilkins probed.

"Messed up, like...his face was red as fire, and his hair and his clothes were all wet, like he'd been sweatin' real bad. He said that science dude gave 'im some medicine."

"What kind of medicine?" Wilkins asked.

"I don't know—just...*medicine*. That's all I know."

The two policemen exchanged meaningful glances, and then Torres asked, "And then what happened?"

"And then what happened is, he told me the police might get involved if I said anything about what went down that mornin', and I should keep my mouth shut, if I knew what was good for me. And he gave me two packs of money—twenty-thousand dollars. And that's the last time I saw him. That's what I was doin' durin' that time I was missin'. That's all I know. I ain't never seen 'im since."

"Do you remember the name of the man Braddock went to see?"

"No. I don't even know if he ever told me the guy's name. I didn't care. I just wanted the money, that's all I had to do with any of it. I mean...somebody tries to give you twenty-thousand dollars for drivin' 'im a few miles up and down the road, and you ain't gonna take it?" Rufus shrugged. "He made me a offer I couldn't refuse."

"Why didn't you just tell us all this to start with?" Wilkins asked, hints of anger showing in his face.

Rufus pleadingly explained, "Man...I woulda told you right off the bat what happened, but like I say...that preacher said I better keep quiet about the whole thing, or I might get the cops on my ass. So I kept quiet—and now I got the cops on my ass, anyway. So now I'm tellin' you what happened, 'cause I don't want you tearin' up my house and throwin' me in jail. I ain't done *nothin'*, man. I just gave the man a ride, is all I did."

Wilkins and Torres exchanged looks. Wilkins said, "You know something, Rufus? This is the first time since we started talkin' that I can say I actually believe you're tellin' the truth. We already know the money ain't counterfeit, and it ain't dirty from some kinda bank-robbery. So the only way I could see you havin' that much clean money is if Billy Braddock gave it to you."

"He *did*, man. I'm tellin' you, he *did*."

The police chief considered for a moment. "I still think I oughta charge you with obstructin' justice, but I'm gonna let you slide for right now. You go ahead and go about your business...but I want you to know that we may have to ask you some further questions...maybe even have you make a positive identification of the man Braddock went to see that day. And I *by God* want the truth outta you the next time I talk to you, or I guarantee you I *will* charge you with obstructin' justice. In fact, I'll throw the whole goddamn book at you. You got that, Rufus?"

"Sho' do."

"Okay," the police chief nodded. "For now, at least, you're free to go."

The taxi driver stood up, mumbling to himself, and shuffled out of the office without another word. Torres gave the Chief a questioning glance. "Did he go see Dr. Keeler that morning?"

Wilkins nodded. "Sounds like. The description fits. I think maybe I better drop by the Braddock Institute and have a little talk with him."

Buck Rodgers stood in the locker room at the Houston Texans practice facility, suited up in full uniform. The assistant coach who had arranged the unofficial tryout eyed him up and down. "Well, at least you *look* like a football player. But there's a lotta difference between *lookin'* like one, and *bein'* one."

"Hey, coach—I just appreciate you doin' this for me," Rodgers said.

"If you hadn't paid me that five thousand dollars to put you through your paces—not to mention what we're all gettin' paid to hold this tryout—we wouldn't be doin' this right now. But I will admit I did see some stuff that made me wanta take a closer look. You're big, you're fast, and you can catch a football. I can say that about ten million other guys in this country, but I can only name a few guys who are doin' it for a livin' in the NFL. And I just want you to know that I'm doin' this for the team, not for you. I got a few players out there who came out here on their own time today, at my recommendation, to do it for the good of the team, too. So you better play as good a game as you talk, is all I can say, or you're really liable to get hurt. And I'll give you one last chance— it's not too late to back out."

"No way," Rodgers said. "I been waitin' to do this for a long time."

"Well, I guess it's time for you to go to the dance. I'm either an idiot or a genius—but either way, I'm sick o' losin' games we coulda won. Same with those guys out there—they only came down here 'cause I told 'em you might be a real prospect. You better bring it. I don't wanna be lookin' like no fool in front o' my players. And if you get hurt out there...hey, I never saw you before in my life."

"I'll take my chances."

The coach nodded, approving of the young man's confident attitude. "Let's go, then."

The two men trotted out to the field, where a group of football players in full gear were waiting for them, tossing the ball around and loosening up their muscles. The coach led Rodgers over to meet the group, who gathered together to greet the newcomer. "Boys, I want you to meet the great white hope of the Houston Texans, a nobody from nowhere named Buck Rodgers."

The players immediately started to hoot in derision. "Buck Rodgers! You gotta be *kiddin'* me!"

"You're goin' to the moon, Buck!"

"Houston, I think we have a problem!"

"You shoulda stayed on the farm, Bubba! You playin' with the big boys now!"

Rodgers took the kidding all in stride. "It's nice t' meet you fellas, too."

This started another round of derisive laughter, and then the coach blew his whistle and said, "Okay, quit with the bullshit. Let's see what the kid's got." He turned to Rodgers and explained, "These guys aren't the first-teamers, but they're plenty good. Every one of 'em was a star somewhere before he came here, so don't underestimate their talent." He turned to the assembled group. "We're just gonna do a few simple handoffs, maybe a couple of lateral passes to see what he can do with 'em once he gets 'is hands on the ball...nothin' fancy. You offensive guys, I want you to really block for 'im...give 'im a chance to show what he's got. Defense—I want you to knock 'im on 'is ass every chance you get...make 'im pay for 'is sins. And that's it. We'll prob'ly know after two plays if we wasted our time." The coach clapped his hands together. "Let's play ball!"

The offense huddled up and the quarterback said, "Okay, I'm just gonna say hut—hut—hut...we'll center the ball, and I'll hand off to you on the right side. Hit the line between the guard and the tackle on the right side. You linemen just use a standard blockin' scheme to open a hole for him. Is that simple enough?"

Rodgers nodded. "Yeah, I think so."

The offense moved up to the line and the quarterback set the play in motion. The timing on the handoff exchange was awkward and Rodgers dropped the ball. As he scrambled to recover the fumble, the defensive tackle slammed into Rodgers full-force from the blind side and knocked Buck flat on his back. The tackle stood over him triumphantly, beating his chest and screaming like Tarzan. That started all the players hooting and hollering again. The coach shook his head and muttered, "I shoulda known this shit was gonna happen."

Jumping up from the embarrassing position the big tackle had put him in, Rodgers said to the tackle, "Nice play, man." He hurried back to the huddle and gave the quarterback an apologetic look. "My fault," he said. "I was a little off on the timing."

"Okay—we'll try that same play...to the left this time," the quarterback said.

"No—to the right. I wanna go to the right. I owe that tackle another shot at me. He didn't hit me hard enough the first time."

The quarterback looked at Buck as if to question whether that last blow had knocked him senseless. "Are you sure?"

"I'm sure," Buck said.

The quarterback gave a shrug. "Okay," he said, his voice doubtful. "Same play, to the right. You guys block for 'im, okay?"

The play again went into motion, but this time Rodgers took the handoff smoothly and held onto the ball. He hit the line with an amazing burst of speed and saw that the defensive tackle who had stopped him before was fighting off his block. Realizing that it was payback time, Rodgers resisted the impulse to finesse his way past the defenders and instead slammed headfirst into the big man. The force of the blow sent the tackle reeling backwards. As the big man fell to the ground, Buck blew past him into the open field, where there was nothing but green grass between him and the goal line. He went a few yards further, then stopped running and came back toward the line of scrimmage. This time, the players were hooting and hollering at the tackle, who was picking himself up off the ground. On the sideline, the coach was saying, "God-damn!" He clapped his hands together. "All right! Good play, farm-boy!"

Back in the huddle again, the quarterback called the same play to the other side, but Buck protested, saying, "No, why don't you just give me a little lateral pass to the left and let me see if I can slick my way through the line?"

Again, the quarterback looked at him as if he were crazy. "Hey, listen, cowboy—you ain't got no distractions, no interference—*nothin'* to keep those guys off your ass. You're the only one out here, and they're all layin' in the cut for you. How you gonna slick your way through the line?"

"Hey, I got blockers up front. That's all I need. Just give 'em a little push. I'll do the rest myself."

"Okay," the quarterback said to the other players in the huddle. "We'll do a short lateral pass to the left and cowboy's gonna pick 'is hole. On hut-three."

Rodgers caught the pass four yards behind the line of scrimmage. No large holes opened up in the line, but he saw a slim opening between the center and the guard and Rodgers headed for that little sliver of light in the defensive line. Seeing the direction the runner was taking, the linebacker stepped to the side and closed the gap. It appeared that Rodgers was about to be stopped in his tracks. Suddenly, he made a little juke-move that caused the linebacker to shift his weight just slightly off balance—just enough for Rodgers to make contact with him and then spin out of his grasp into the open field, where—again—the only thing between him and the goal line was green grass. Buck ran a few steps further to show that the play would have gained big yardage, then returned to the huddle.

The coach clapped his hands together and yelled, "C'mon, defense—show me somethin'! It's no damn wonder the team's losin'. Any clodhopper off the street can get past you! Let's see some defense!"

The informal tryout ran for over an hour. Rodgers ran short inside pass routes against the linebackers and consistently beat them to the ball. He showed that he was sure-handed when the ball was thrown his way and that he could run with it after the catch. His speed, power and pure raw toughness were apparent to everybody who witnessed the tryout. By the time the session was over, he had earned the grudging respect of all the pros who had participated in the scrimmage. The coach told everybody to hit the showers, and all the players shook Rodgers' hand, wishing him well in his quest to join the team. Once everybody but Buck and the coach had showered and left the facility, the coach invited him into the office.

"I tell you what, cowboy—that was some damn good runnin' you did out there today. You sure you ain't never played football before?"

"Well, you know...I played a little sandlot here and there."

"That wasn't no sandlot moves you were makin' out there. That was some good shit. You sure you didn't get a concussion somewhere along the line and forgot you played somewhere before?"

"You can check around. Maybe I got amnesia and don't know it."

"You ever been in jail?"

"No. You can check that, too. My record's clean as a whistle."

The coach shook his head in disbelief. "I don't know...you're mighty damn good for a guy from nowhere who ain't supposed to know shit from shinola."

Buck gave a shrug. "Maybe I'm just a natural."

The coach gave him a probing look. "Maybe you are." He leaned back in his chair and propped his feet up on the desk. "I tell you what—I'm gonna talk to the head coach about you and see if he'll give you a look. If we get to do this again, we'll have a full team on both sides of the ball, and then we'll *really* find out what you can do. But I'll tell you—I was surprised by what you showed me out there today. I've seen first-round picks who didn't do that well their first time out. Gimme a few days to see if I can work things out with the team, and I'll check back with you when I have something definite, okay?"

"Will do," Buck said. He stood up, preparing to leave. "I just wanta thank you again for takin' the time."

"Hey—if it ends up helpin' the team, it's time well spent. And, if nothin' more ever comes out of it, me and the guys made a few extra bucks apiece for a couple hours' work today. Plus, nobody got hurt. *And*, to top it all off...I think we mighta found a pretty good prospect who can help the team. So, all in all, it's been a damn good day for all of us."

Buck smiled. "Well, I'll be goin', then."

As Buck started for the door, the coach called after him, "Be sure and stay in shape, okay?"

"Always," Buck said, giving the coach a cheerful wave of the hand. He continued down the corridor, smiling to himself, as he made his way out of the building and back to his pickup.

As soon as Rodgers was out of sight, the coach picked up the phone and made a call. "Hey, Coach— this is Wilson, assistant offensive coach?"

On the other end of the line, the head coach asked, "Yeah, Wilson—what do you need?"

"I'm sorry to bother you at home, Coach—well, kinda sorry, but not completely sorry" ...

The head coach interrupted. "Just say what you wanta say, Wilson, and get it over with. I'm havin' an outdoor barbecue with friends right now, and I don't wanta talk business while I'm relaxin'."

"I understand, sir, but I really need to talk to you the first time you get a chance. It's about a guy who could really help the team—I mean, *really help the team.* I swear—this could be big, really big."

"What *big?*"

Immediately, with the least amount of encouragement, Wilson warmed up to his task. "Listen, Coach—you're not gonna believe this, but I think I've stumbled onto the most helluva prospect from outta nowhere you've ever seen in your life" ...

As he stood ringing the doorbell on the front porch of the Braddock mansion, Joe Lindsey had a worried look on his face. Time and time again he rang, his manner growing more agitated with every passing moment that nobody came to the door. At length, he saw Maggie through the window, moving unsteadily toward the front of the house. She opened the door wearing an old housecoat, her appearance worn and haggard. She offered Lindsey an unenthusiastic greeting.

"Oh—Joe...whadda ya want?"

Lindsey knew immediately that Billy Braddock's housekeeper had been drinking. He stepped across the threshold and closed the door behind him. "Maggie, are you all right?"

"I s'pose."

"Well...can we talk?"

Maggie nodded. "Sure, why not? Let's go sit in the kitchen. It's my favorite room in the whole damn place."

Lindsey followed Maggie as she staggered uncertainly to the back of the house. Once they were in the kitchen, Maggie poured herself a large glass of wine from a bottle that was sitting on the counter, not bothering to offer Joe anything by way of hospitality, the way she normally would have done. The two of them sat down at the small dining table. "Maggie," he began, "my wife and I have been worried to death about you. Are you sick?"

"No, I'm not sick," she said. Then she added, "Sick at heart, maybe—but physically sick? No, I'm not sick."

"Well, you missed church last Sunday, and you haven't been answering the phone" ...

"There's an answerin' machine," she interrupted. "I've got your messages. I just haven't felt like talking to anybody."

Not knowing how to approach the subject diplomatically, Lindsey asked a direct question: "Maggie—have you been drinking a lot lately?" When Maggie didn't answer, Lindsey's face became a living portrait of solicitous interest. "Is there anything Mary or I can do to help you?"

"Can you find Billy and bring him back?" she asked with a humorless smile.

"Is that it? Is that why you're not yourself—you're worried about Billy?"

"I'm worried sick about 'im," Maggie answered. "I guess I've worried myself into a state of total depression."

Giving her a sympathetic look, Joe said, "Listen, Maggie—we're all worried. We all want Billy back."

Maggie gave him a look that openly mocked his words. "Joe...you have no idea what you're talking about. Where Billy Braddock's concerned, you can't compare my feelings with yours, and it's ridiculous for you to even try."

"Well, of course, Maggie...I know that," Lindsey diplomatically replied.

"No, you *don't* know that," she emphatically disagreed. "You don't even *begin* to know that."

He looked confused. "I don't think I understand, Maggie."

"That's right—you don't."

"Well, could you help me to understand?"

Maggie thought about it for a moment, then said, "Well, Billy's prob'ly never coming back, anyway, so I guess it doesn't matter." She took a large swig of wine. "Do you remember when I told you I met Billy in the first grade?"

"Yes, I do."

She paused, then continued, "I loved that boy the first moment I ever saw 'im. He was so cute. He'd lost one of his baby teeth in front, and he had this big gap where the tooth was missing...and when he smiled, it made him look so comical...but in a way that was absolutely endearing to everyone who saw that silly little smile. He was such a handsome little fella—even at that age."

"I'm sure he was," Lindsey commented, noticing that Maggie's countenance had brightened considerably as she spoke about Billy Braddock.

"And another charming thing about him was...I don't think he had any sense of personal vanity at all. He smiled all the time, missing tooth or not, and he didn't care who was laughing at him. At that age, he always seemed to have a sense of humor about himself. I actually think he had fun with the imperfections that drive most kids that age completely crazy. But he was...so...cute."

"I can almost picture it in my mind," Lindsey said with a smile. "I remember when I had front teeth missing in first grade. I didn't smile for several months."

"Well, Billy did—and I loved him for it. The only problem about Billy was...all the other girls liked him, too. And that was a problem for me, 'cause I didn't wanta be part of the crowd. So, while all the other girls were goin' crazy over 'im...I never let 'im know how I felt about 'im. I just stood back and watched all the other girls make fools of themselves, but I stayed to myself. It went on like that for years...I never let on how much I cared. And every year that passed, I wanted him more and more, but I just wouldn't let on. By the time we were in the ninth grade, he just had too many irons in the fire for me to even think about gettin' together with 'im. I was determined I wasn't gonna be another fire for him to put his iron in."

Maggie paused for a moment to take another long drink of wine, and Lindsey asked, "So what happened? How did the two of you end up being so close?"

"How'd that happen? I guess it started in third grade, when his mother died. She was the one who got Billy interested in the Bible."

"I've always wondered how that all began."

"Oh, yeah—Billy's mother. She was a good woman—nothin' at all like his crazy daddy. His daddy was a wild man. But when Billy's mama died all of a sudden, it hurt Billy so much. She really was the glue that held his whole world together. He tried to hide the pain, but I could tell he was really hurtin' inside. And one day out on the playground, I told him how bad I felt for him and that he could call me any time he needed to, if he just wanted someone to talk to. That's the only time I ever saw Billy cry. He thanked me for caring...and, after that—I don't know...I could just tell he saw me differently from the way he saw the other girls."

"So that's how a lifelong friendship started," Lindsey said. "I always wondered what the story behind your relationship with Billy was."

"It's more than that. When we got in high-school our Sophomore year, I was elected to the cheerleadin' squad. By my Junior year, I was head cheerleader. To look at me now, you'd never know it...but I was once a beautiful girl, a long time ago, really beautiful."

"I believe you," Joe nodded.

"And Billy—he wasn't just beautiful...he was the star football player of the Braddock Broncos from the day he made the team. He was so good...just *so good*, like some kinda ragin' fury in motion when he got the ball. It was incredible to watch 'im run. You would've had to see it the way I saw it to realize how good he was. And, because I was a cheerleader, I saw every game he played. And every time I saw him play, I loved him more. And the bad part is...I also saw him—well, I didn't actually *see* him—but I knew he was sleepin' with every pretty girl in school—whoever he wanted, whenever he wanted—everybody but me. That was my sweet, crazy Billy."

"Kinda like Hugh Hefner, without the financial incentives?" Joe suggested.

Maggie gave a harsh, drunken laugh. "Exactly. The girls just wanted *him*...Billy Braddock. It wasn't about his daddy's money. It wasn't about the football team. It was about *him*...this Greek god of Youth and Beauty who had been sent from Mount Olympus to dwell amongst us lowly mortals. That's how I'll always remember him—like a Greek statue, come to life. And I didn't blame any of those girls for what they did. They were all doin' the same thing I wanted to do, but my pride wouldn't let me. I don't know the percentage of the girls he slept with, but I'd guess he prob'ly slept with at least thirty percent of all the girls who were in school durin' the time we were there."

Stating the obvious, Joe said. "Ladies' man."

"No, no, no—you're wrong there," she contradicted him, recklessly waving the big glass of wine over the table. "*Man's* man—that's what Billy was—a man among men. But I will admit he sure did love the ladies—or at least, a certain few parts of their anatomy that gave him pleasure. As far as

225

actually *lovin'* any of the girls he slept with...that didn't happen with Billy—not ever. He was just havin' fun."

"Billy's told me a number of times he wasn't exactly the walking epitome of what a moral human being should be," Lindsey said.

"To say the least," she agreed, with a smile that implied an understanding beyond anything the simple pastor could ever comprehend. Then she continued: "But, where Billy was concerned, I took the moral high-ground—not because I was so moral, but because I didn't wanta be just another one of his easy conquests."

"Well, at least you had a sense of self-respect."

"I was stupid, is what it was. Because of the way I'd acted toward him all those years, Billy thought I didn't like 'im—except as a friend. I coulda lost every chance I ever had with 'im. But I really think that made him start wantin' me all the more. Somewhere along the line, I think it started drivin' him crazy that I was the only girl in school who'd never thrown herself at him. And then, in our Junior year, when time for the prom came around—I still don't know what made him do it—Billy caught me alone in the school parking lot, and...in the cutest, shyest way you could ever imagine...asked me out to the prom."

"Love at last," Lindsey said.

"It was *always* love, as far as I was concerned. But on the night of the prom, everything changed. All those years I had waited...I don't know...I just couldn't wait any more. He didn't seduce *me*—I seduced *him*. I practically tore 'is clothes off, tryin' to get to 'im. I changed from Goody Two-Shoes to the Whore of Babylon, all in one night, and I didn't care. I wanted it. And as far as I was concerned, that night made the feelings I had always had for him just totally everlasting. It was like eatin' the forbidden fruit—once you taste it, there ain't no goin' back."

"Yeah, Billy has said that many a time in his sermons," Lindsey agreed.

"And it's true," she said. "If Billy and I hadn't had that night together, I woulda prob'ly gone off to college and met some nice normal guy with nice normal ambitions to go to work for a nice normal company, and we woulda gotten married and had a coupla nice normal kids, and I woulda forgotten all about Billy Braddock." She paused, took a swig of wine, then added, "Well, not forgotten—there's just some people you never forget. But I would've remembered him as a former classmate who happened to be a football hero when I was a cheerleader. It wouldn't have been any more than that. You know what I mean, Joe?"

"I do," Joe Lindsey said.

"Anyway, the night of the prom, we made love all night, over and over again, until the sun came up. It was my first time to do somethin' like that, and it really hurt...but—oh, I tell you, Joe—it hurt *so good.* It was worth all the pain. It tore up my kootchy-koo so bad, I could barely walk for a week after that." She laughed, remembering. "But once we practiced for awhile, making love to Billy was like nothing I've ever known with anyone since. It was wonderful" ... As she said this, hints of sadness started to creep back into her eyes.

"Why didn't you and Billy get married?" Joe asked.

"I don't know. It just didn't work out. We were lovers for awhile, but" ...

She set down the wine glass and suddenly started to cry very quietly, covering her face with her hands. Lindsey got up from the chair and came over to put his arm around her. "It's okay, Maggie. Don't cry. It's all right."

"You say you know how I feel?" she said, wiping her eyes with a napkin she took from a napkin-holder on the table. "You *don't* know. You don't."

"I realize that now," Lindsey said. "I'm sorry, Maggie."

She continued, "We never got married, but after my husband died, and Billy came back to town and started the church, he asked me to come run his house for him. I didn't have any children...no close kin...I didn't have anybody—not until Billy asked me to take care of his house for him."

"Well, thank God for that."

"I suppose so," she said, with an agnostic tone in her voice. "Taking care of Billy's needs became my whole reason for living. That's all I did—I ran the household. Billy had turned preacher, and he stuck to his principles...he never asked me to go to bed with him, even though I used to pray to God every night he would come to me. But...no—he never did. After our high-school days, we never made love again. I've stayed in this house with him for the last twenty years, taking care of him...seeing to his every need...and loving him the whole time—loving him with all my heart and soul. I never got over him—I *never will* get over him. And these years we've been together, I've seen what life with Billy might have been if things had worked out differently. For the past twenty years, I've been all but a wife to him...and he's been a kind, generous wonderful man to me. And now he's gone, and I don't think I'll ever see him again. And it's killing me" ...

This time, Maggie began to weep openly, unable to restrain the anguish that was boiling inside her. Lindsey again made an attempt to comfort her, but all to no avail. Eventually, when Maggie had regained control of herself, Joe asked, "Maggie, would you like Mary to come over and stay with you for a few days? Maybe some of the other ladies from the church?"

She shook her head. "No. With Billy gone, it feels like a death in the family. Just let me grieve in my own way. I wanta be alone."

"Maggie" ...

"I mean, it Joe—leave me in peace...or torment, or whatever it is I'm going through. I don't want a bunch of old biddies fawning over me. I wanta be alone."

Realizing that further pleading would get him nowhere, Joe asked, "Well, can I at least check in with you every couple of days—at least that? I'm the one in charge of Billy's congregation in his absence—surely you wouldn't deny me the opportunity to watch over one of his most precious people in the world, would you, Maggie?"

Maggie took another gulp of wine. "You can stop by, just to see if I'm still alive, if you want to. Just don't make a pest of yourself."

"Thank you, Maggie," he said, giving her a hug.

"Now, really—I want you to go away, Joe. I love you, and I appreciate your kindness, but I want to be alone."

Lindsey gave a humble nod of the head. "Certainly, Maggie. I'll check back with you in the next day or so."

"Be sure it's 'or so'—I don't want you back here botherin' me again tomorrow."

"As you wish," Lindsey agreed. "I'll pray for you, Maggie—and for Billy."

"Goodbye, Joe."

As he walked out of the kitchen, Joe Lindsey glanced back at Maggie. She looked pitiful, sitting at the table with the tumbler of wine in her hand and the ravaged look on her face. The thought occurred to him that Maggie would not live much longer if Billy Braddock didn't return home soon.

Jenny stepped into the garage of the beach house and found Buck lying down on his weight-bench, pushing a huge barbell into the air, every muscle of his powerful body straining. She stopped and watched, unable to believe that a man could actually push that much weight up and down the way he did, over and over again. Buck made one last mighty effort, his muscles quivering, as he got the barbell over his head and back onto the rack. He sat up and glanced at her, the strain of the workout showing on his face.

"Whoo-ee! Almost didn't make it." He squeezed his arm with the other hand. "I don't understand it. Two months ago, I could do thirty reps at this weight without breakin' a sweat. I just barely made it that time. Damn! It oughta be gettin' easier, not harder." He continued to squeeze his huge arms in an exploratory manner, as if trying to figure out whether the muscles were losing their tone. "I just don't get it."

Looking at the powerful form sitting on the weight-bench, Jenny was unconcerned. "You've been workin' out a lot, since you had that tryout with the Texans. Maybe you're just overdoin' it, honey."

Buck considered the idea. "Yeah, maybe you're right. I *have* been hammerin' on it pretty hard. I'm just tryin' to get ready for the big day when they call back to say the head coach wants to take a gander at me."

"That would be so great," Jenny said, coming over to sit beside him on the bench. She kissed his cheek. "Can you imagine? My baby, playin' in the NFL—wouldn't that be somethin'?"

"Yeah, it would," he said. "Sure pays better than the rodeo."

"Listen, sweetie," she said, "I'm fixin' t' start supper. Do you have any special requests?"

"Naw...just whatever you wanta fix is good with me."

"Well, why don't you jump in the shower while I'm doin' that—I mean, if you're through workin' out for awhile."

"Yeah, I think I'm gonna give my body a rest. These muscles need a day or so to repair themselves." He stood up and pulled her up by the hand. "Jenny, I just want you to know" ...

"What?"

He checked the thought. "Oh, nothin', really. I just wanted to tell you how much you've brightened my life since you came into it."

She hugged his sweaty form. "I feel the same way, honey."

He let her go, turned her around, and gave her a little spank on the rear end. "Go in there and get supper started. I'm gonna hop in the shower."

While Jenny prepared supper, Buck showered and dressed, slipping on a pair of blue jeans and a tee shirt. The radio in the kitchen was blaring as Jenny busied herself with her chores, and Buck sat down on the couch and turned on the television. He had missed part of the evening network broadcast of the national news, but he watched idly, wondering if much in the world had changed since the last time he had attempted to keep up with events. There were refugees in Africa, polar ice-caps melting, rain forests burning...the usual world crises were still on display. When the network took a commercial break, Buck went into the kitchen to grab a beer from the refrigerator.

"How's it comin', babe?" he asked.

"Oh," she said as she turned over the pork chops in the frying pan, "maybe another...thirty minutes? Somethin' like that."

"Well, if you need any help, just let me know," he offered.

She gave him a smile. "Everything's under control. You just sit down and relax. You've worked hard enough for one day."

Returning to the living room, Rodgers sat back down on the couch just as the commercial break was over. The next story on the news got his full attention:

> *"Turning now to news around the nation...tonight in Texas, influential lawmakers and business leaders around the State are calling for the Texas Attorney General to launch an investigation into the mysterious disappearance of billionaire oil tycoon Billy Braddock. The former star athlete-turned-preacher left his home several months ago, and nobody has seen him since. Rumors abound that Braddock, who controls a global business empire with assets estimated to be worth hundreds of billions of dollars"* ...

Buck immediately muted the volume, afraid that Jenny would walk in and see the images being shown onscreen. To his horror, he saw that they were showing pictures of the young Billy Braddock in his football uniform when he was playing at SMU...Braddock appearing on the *Ed Sullivan Show* with the All-America football team in New York City...Bronco Billy standing beside Johnny Unitas in a Baltimore Colts uniform during their rookie year.

He was amazed to see how exactly like his old self he was now. But, as much as he was amazed, he was afraid that Jenny would put the puzzle together sooner or later if this kind of publicity continued. There was no way she could see those old likenesses of Billy Braddock and not eventually realize that he and Buck Rodgers were one and the same. He knew he had to do something immediately. Going to the bedroom, he donned a pair of sweat socks and athletic sneakers, and then he went into the kitchen.

"Listen honey...somethin's come up. I have to go out for a few minutes. I'll be back soon."

Jenny gave him a look of disappointment. "Ohhh...it's almost ready."

"I'll be back pretty quick."

"Well, Buck" ...she said in a tone of protest.

"Just keep it warm. I'll try to hurry."

He gave her a reassuring kiss on the forehead and went out to his truck. Inside the vehicle, he searched through his wallet and pulled out a list of phone numbers. Tucking the list in his shirt pocket, he drove down the highway toward Houston. Along the road, he saw a small beer-joint and decided to stop there. Inside the building, he walked directly to the bar and sat down. The barmaid came over to greet him.

"Well, hello, handsome—what can I get for you?"

"Do you guys have a pay-phone?"

"No, honey," she answered. "All we have is a house phone."

"Would you mind if I borrow it for just a minute?"

"I have to ask you two questions: The first one is, are you drinkin'?"

He hesitated, "Uh...yeah. Gimme a beer...best in the house."

"Okay, Mr. High Roller," she said with a grin. The barmaid opened the beer and set it on the bar. "And the second question is—is the call local?"

"Yeah."

She motioned for him to come around. "You need to come over to this side of the bar, and I'll have to dial the number for you."

Buck did as she said. "I kinda need to huddle back here against the wall because the juke box is so loud."

"Sure...whatever. I'll turn it down a little."

"No, that's okay." He showed her the paper. "It's that number, right there." The barmaid dialed the number and handed the list of phone numbers back to him. The phone rang, and a voice on the other end of the line answered almost immediately.

"Levesky residence. May I help you?"

"I need to speak to George Levesky," Buck said.

"May I say who is calling?"

"You may. Tell 'im it's his boss, Billy Braddock. And tell 'im I want 'im on the phone immediately."

"Oh, Mr. Braddock! Yes, sir. Just give me one moment."

There was a brief pause, and then a man answered the phone. "This is George Levesky."

"George, this is Billy."

"Billy! Where in the name of God have you been?"

"That's not important. What *is* important is that I want all this publicity about my so-called 'mysterious disappearance' to stop. I can't pick up a paper or turn on a TV that I don't see somethin' about myself. You know how I hate that high-profile publicity. You need to put a screechin' halt to it, George."

"Billy, this thing has just mushroomed. It's out of our control."

"Well, you need to get it under your control, George."

"I don't know how to, Billy," Levesky protested. "The press has gone crazy over this, and it just keeps gettin' worse, every day."

"I tell you what, George—you call a meeting of the board for nine a.m., two days from now—that'll be Friday. Tell all of 'em I said to get off their overpaid asses and have those big butts parked in the chairs of the corporate boardroom—on time—or they're finished at Braddock Corporation. I also want you to have my housekeeper Maggie Carlyle flown to Houston for the meeting. I'm gonna wanta talk to her on a secure line in a room by herself. When I say to Maggie what I have to say, there won't be any further questions as to whether the real Billy Braddock is alive and well and livin' wherever he damn well pleases."

"Billy, my caller ID says you're somewhere in town right now."

"Right. And I want you to know that it's a short hop downtown for me to show up and fire a bunch o' worthless bastards, if I have to. I'm gonna tell *you*, and I want *them* to know...if you don't handle this publicity crisis and get my name out o' the headlines, I will fire every one of your sorry asses and start all over from scratch. Am I making myself clear, George?"

"Indubitably, Mr. Braddock."

"All right. You'd better start tonight. Get everybody together...includin' Maggie...and I'll be callin' the boardroom at nine a.m., the day after tomorrow."

"I'll get right on it."

"And, George...if you are stupid enough to try to trace this phone call in an effort to track me down— no force in heaven or earth shall spare you from my wrath."

"I understand completely, Mr. Braddock. You need say no more."

"Okay. You better get started right now. You got a lot to do before Friday mornin'."

"I'll begin immediately, sir."

235

Buck hung up and handed the phone back to the barmaid. ""Damn, handsome," she said, "sounds like somebody made you mad."

"Somebody did," he said with a steely-eyed look. Taking a twenty-dollar bill out of his pocket, he put it on the bar. "Keep the change. And thanks for lettin' me use the phone."

"You haven't even touched your beer," she protested.

"Next time," he said with a wave.

Buck hurried back to the beach house, where Jenny was waiting for him on the front porch. She stood up as he came toward her, and then ran to meet him, throwing her arms around his waist, as if he had been gone for days. "Oh, honey, I'm so glad you came back! I was so worried!"

"What were you worried about?" he asked.

"That look on your face when you left—you looked like you were ready to kill somebody. I've never seen you looking so mad. What happened?"

"It's nothin' to worry about. I just remembered somethin' I forgot to do."

She caressed his cheek. "Do you wanta talk about it?"

"No. It's taken care of. Let's have supper."

They went to the kitchen, where Buck sat down at the table as Jenny prepared the plates for them. She set the food on the table, and asked, "You want a beer, or would you rather have milk?"

"Milk sounds good, baby."

Once everything was in place, they sat down to eat. "Buck, have you decided where we're goin' when the lease expires on the beach house?"

"Not really," Buck said. "I guess it all depends on whether the Texans call me back for a real tryout. That's the main thing right now."

"What if they don't?" she asked.

"If they don't? I dunno...have you ever been to the Rockies?"

Jenny laughed. "I've hardly ever even been outta Braddock. This here is the farthest I've ever been away from that sorry little town."

"Well, if you like the mountains, and beautiful crystal-clear streams just brimmin' over with hungry trout who are hopin' you'll catch 'em and eat 'em, you'll love the Rockies. It's great up there."

"That sounds like fun."

"If that's where we end up goin', you'll be hooked on the place, I promise. They don't call it God's country for nothin'." Buck bit into a piece of pork chop and suddenly grimaced in pain. "Oh, damn!" He stuck a finger in his mouth and pulled out a small piece of bone.

Concerned, Jenny asked, "What happened?"

"I just bit down on this little piece o' bone, and...God, that hurt!" Buck stuck his finger back in his mouth and felt around the lower molars. "Damn," he said. "I think I've got a loose tooth. I shouldn't be havin' any" ... He suddenly stopped talking and sat silently at the table, a stricken look on his face.

"Honey? Are you sick?" Jenny asked.

"No. No." Buck got up from the table. "I don't feel hungry right now. I think I'm gonna go walk on the beach for a little while."

Jenny pushed her plate away and came to him. "Buck? Will you tell me what's wrong? What is it?"

"I just wanta go walkin' alone for a little while," he said. "Lemme grab a beer to take with me. Might help me relax."

"I'll get it," Jenny said. She got a beer out of the refrigerator and handed it to him. "Baby, what's goin' on this evening? I mean, everything was all okay, and all of a sudden you're actin' all strange. If you're sick, I want you to tell me."

"Just finish your supper. I...I'll be back soon."

237

Jenny followed him to the front door and stepped out on the porch, watching as Buck slowly walked away along the shoreline in the evening twilight. The distraught look on her face told the story of her inner turmoil as she watched him go. "Please don't leave me, Buck," she whispered, as the careless ocean wind played through her hair. "I love you" ...

The Friday morning call to the Braddock Coporation's Board of Directors came promptly at nine o'clock. "George?"

"Right here, Mr. Braddock."

"Did everyone show up?"

"The entire Board is present, Mr. Braddock."

"Good. Now, here's why we're doin' this: I do not now like, and never have liked, to have my name and face plastered all over everywhere. I ain't Josef Stalin, I ain't Chairman Mao, and I ain't Donald Trump. And this crap that's been going on lately has got to stop right now. I wanted you all to be present this morning because we're gonna clear up any questions anybody may have about my so-called 'mysterious disappearance.' I haven't disappeared, gentlemen. I'm lookin' at myself right now, and I can see my hands and arms and legs and feet very clearly. I can't see my face right now, 'cause I'm not anywhere near a mirror, so I can't swear to a certainty that my face hasn't disappeared. Otherwise, though, the rest of me is plainly visible to the naked eye. So there's no mystery, 'cause I haven't disappeared."

One of the men at the table spoke up. "Billy, this is Ed Sumner. I have a question."

"Ed...how are Nancy and the kids?"

"Everybody's just fine, Billy."

"Is your son still goin' to that Ivy League school...Harvard, was it? Or was it Yale? I never can keep those two sissy-boy schools straight in my mind."

"Yale, Billy. And, yes, he's got one more year to go. But he's doing very well."

"So what's your question, Ed?"

"Well, the press is going to ask us how we can be certain we talked to the real Billy Braddock, so I thought I'd ask a question only the real Billy Braddock would know. Is that okay with you?"

"Definitely. That's why we're doin' this. Ask away."

"Well, at our last meeting, we discussed an acquisition we're trying to make, but we've run into some problems. We talked about it for several minutes. Can you tell me what it was we were talking about?"

"We talked about our attempt to acquire the Yucca Oil Company up in the Texas Panhandle. Carter Bradley has turned what shoulda been a simple business proposition into an ugly bidding war. I told you to go for the jugular on this. Under no circumstances is Carter Bradley to acquire Yucca Oil, I don't care if we end up havin' to hock grandma's jewelry to keep 'im from getting it. That's what we talked about."

The men assembled around the table exchanged looks and nods all around. Then another of them spoke. "Billy, this is Webb Richards."

"Webb. Glad you could make it. You still shootin' a seven-handicap?"

"I do on the days I don't start the round at the nineteenth hole first. On those days, my handicap goes up to forty-one."

"And that's just on the first hole, as I recall," Braddock said. There was a round of chuckles from the group of executives, and Braddock continued, "That Jack-and-Coke's gonna get you yet, Webb."

"I usually manage to hold it down to a low roar, Billy."

"That's true. You've always been one of those drinkers who knows how to pace himself. I've known you for years, and I've yet to see you drunk. So, what's your question for me today?"

"Just one question: Where did we go eat after the last Board meeting you attended?"

"I got no idea. I left right after we concluded our business."

George Levesky interrupted the proceedings. "Billy, excuse me, I just want to ask the board members a question."

"Go ahead."

Levesky looked around the room. "Is there anybody here who doesn't believe, based on the voice, the speech patterns, and the knowledge of company business that only he would have—is there anybody here who doesn't believe this is the real Billy Braddock?" The men around the table took no time at all to agree that this was the man himself. George Levesky said, "Billy, we could drag this out, but we all know for a fact that you're Billy Braddock. It's indisputable."

"Do any of you have any doubt that I'm in my right mind and capable of making sound business decisions?"

Again the group came to a unanimous conclusion. "You sound better than ever, Billy. There's no question in anyone's mind that you are the genuine article, that you're fully competent, and that this media circus is spun from whole cloth."

"Do you know who's behind it?"

"We've traced the original rumors back to that society leech who calls himself a journalist...you might know him—Walter Drake?"

"I know who he is. I want you to talk to legal and see what options we might have to stuff a dirty sock in his mouth."

"Well, you know how it is, Billy...freedom of the press, and all."

"Talk to 'em, anyway. I don't mind tellin' you boys...this whole thing has pissed me off like I haven't been pissed off in awhile."

"We understand, Billy," George Levesky agreed. "All of us know how you've done your best to keep a low profile over the years."

"Is Maggie Carlyle there?"

"We've got her waiting in a private office just down the hall."

"Okay, then. The Scriptures say that out of the mouths of two or three witnesses, a matter is established. Now, I've convinced you guys that I'm really me. Maggie's the one person who knows me better than anyone else in the world. I've known her since I was in the first grade. She's been my housekeeper for the past twenty years, ever since her husband died. There's something that only Maggie and I know...no other living human being has this information. There'll be no question in Maggie's mind as to who I am when we get through talking. After that, I want you to call a press conference, and I want the whole lot of you get in front of the cameras and tell those idiots in the press to get off my ass."

"We'll do that, Billy."

"And one other thing: You tell the legal department to tell that foolass Attorney General to keep his nose out of my business. I saw where he's s'posed to be considerin' launchin' an investigation into my whereabouts to find out if I'm dead or alive...or whatever the hell his purported reasons might be. I don't want that damn politician tryin' to use me to get some face time on the boob-tube. You tell him if he doesn't keep his nose out of my business and attend to his constitutional responsibilities to the citizens of this State, he's liable to find *himself* under investigation. I'll spare no expense to make his life miserable if he doesn't drop the whole idea like a hot potato."

"We'll see that he gets the message, Billy."

"I appreciate that, George. Any further questions, gentlemen?"

"I have one, Billy."

"This sounds like Erwin Easley. Is that you, Erwin?"

"It's me, Billy."

"Long time, no see, my friend. How you doin' this mornin'?"

"Just fine, Billy. Just fine."

"And for the record, just so you'll know I know who you are, I'll ask you how your diet's goin'. You still doin' Weight Watchers?"

"No, I quit that. I'm on a diet of soup and bananas right now."

"Well, good luck. From what I saw of you last time, you're gonna need it." The men around the table laughed at Billy's joke, then he continued. "Just kidding, Erwin. Keep up the work. I know you'll eventually win the fight."

"Thanks for the encouragement," Easley replied.

"Now, what's your question for me, Erwin?"

"Well, Billy...they're gonna ask us why you did what you did—what are we supposed to tell 'em?"

"You tell 'em the truth. Tell 'em I did have a heart attack, and on the advice of my doctor, I decided to take a little vacation away from all the stresses of runnin' the church and keepin' track of my various business enterprises around the world. Tell 'em I felt free to do that because I know full well both my church and my business are being handled by my personally handpicked surrogates, who I am confident are fully capable of keeping the ship on an even keel."

"We appreciate your vote of confidence," Erwin said. "Is there any time frame when we might expect you back?"

"I'll be back when I get back. If I need to talk to you, I'll call you. Until then, you guys just do your jobs." He paused, then said, "Connect me to Maggie."

"Gimme just a second, Billy." George Levesky left the boardroom and walked down the hall, where Maggie waited patiently beside the phone. He stuck his head through the door. "Maggie, we're about to transfer the call over here. When that first button lights up, just pick up the phone."

"This button here?" she asked.

"Yeah. Just watch that button." Levesky went back down the hall to the boardroom. "Billy, I'm transferring the call now. I just want you to know, on behalf of all the board members, that we do appreciate your checking in with us. We've been under siege around here for the past few days. I know I feel better, and I'm sure all the rest of our company does, too. And we'll do our best to scotch these rumors, once and for all, starting today."

"You do that, George. And all you other fellows—thanks for coming. We'll talk again in the future."

The button lit up on the phone in the office where Maggie was waiting. She picked up the phone immediately. "Billy?"

"Hi, Maggie. How have you been?"

"Oh, Billy...I've been so worried about you." She started to cry.

"Now, get yourself together, sweetie. There's no need for that."

"Billy, you just don't know what you've put me through."

"Well that's one reason I asked 'em to bring you to Houston. I wanted to reassure you I'm alive and well and doin' just fine. Also, I know how you have a tendency to start drinkin' when you get really upset, and I didn't want you doin' that to yourself. You haven't slipped off into the bottle, have you, Maggie?"

"I did. I'm sorry."

"Well, stop doin' it, Maggie. You're talkin' to *me* now, and there's no need for you to be all depressed and drinkin' all the time."

"I won't do it any more, Billy. I promise."

"Good. I don't wanta lose you." He paused, then continued, "I guess you heard about all that stupidity that's been goin' on about my disappearance."

"It's all over the news lately," she said.

"Right. That's why I'm havin' to prove beyond any doubt that I'm me."

"I know it's you, Billy."

"I know you do, Maggie. But I'm gonna bring up somethin' that only you and I are alive to tell about. It's our secret that we haven't discussed since we were in high-school."

"I know what it is."

"Don't say anything. Let *me* tell *you*. That way there can't be any possible doubt that I'm who I say I am."

"Okay, Billy—you tell me."

"You got pregnant in our Senior year of high-school."

"Yes."

"I was the father of the child."

"You were."

"And when my daddy found about it, he went crazy. Told me I was gonna ruin my whole future if I married you, and he wasn't havin' any part of it. So he went to your daddy, and they worked out a deal where Wild Bill would pay your daddy to keep 'is mouth shut and make you get an abortion."

Tears were streaming down Maggie's face. "That's what happened."

"The abortion got rid of the kid, but somethin' went wrong. You got an infection and they had to remove your uterus to save your life. After that, any hope of you ever havin' any children of your own was gone forever."

"Yes, yes, that's true," she sobbed.

"I always felt bad about that, Maggie. I never forgave my old man for what he did. Or myself, either, for lettin' him pressure me into goin' against what my heart and soul wanted to do. I loved you, Maggie."

"I know."

"And when you married Mike Carlyle, I made certain that he got on at the refinery and I put him on the fast track to promotion, 'cause I wanted him to be able to provide well for you."

"You did that?" she asked in surprise.

"Mike wasn't the brightest bulb on the Christmas tree, Maggie. You know that."

She laughed through her tears. "Yes, I do. He was a good man, but he sure wasn't a genius."

"But he went to work every day, and showed up on time. And, as time went by, he got fairly good at his job. I always kept track of you, 'cause I wanted you to have as good a life as possible, considerin' the circumstances."

"I always had this feelin' in the back of my mind that you were my guardian angel, Billy." She paused briefly, then asked him, "Since we're talkin' about this, I just wanta know—do you still have any feelings for me, Billy?"

"For the longest...longest...time, you were the only woman I ever loved. I still have feelings, but" ...

"But what, Billy?"

"That's all I wanta say...I still have feelings for you."

"I never stopped loving you, Billy."

"I know that." There was an awkward pause. "Have you ever told anybody what we just talked about?"

"No, no one."

"Neither have I. And the only other people who knew about you gettin' pregnant and havin' an abortion are all dead now. Only the real Billy Braddock would know about this. So, do you believe it's really me?"

"I believed it as soon as I heard your voice."

"Well, you and the board of directors are all gonna have to go out in front of the TV cameras and tell 'em you are certain, beyond any doubt, that you talked to the real Billy Braddock. Do I sound to you like I'm in my right mind?"

"Of course you do," she emphatically responded.

"You tell 'em that, too, if they ask."

"When are you comin' home, Billy?"

"I'm not sure yet. But you keep yourself together until I return. I don't wanta be havin' to send you to alcoholic rehab."

"I promised you, Billy, and I'll keep my word."

"All right, Maggie. Just be assured of my love for you."

"I love you, too, Billy."

"Okay, then. I'll just say goodbye. You take care of yourself."

"Goodbye, darlin'."

Maggie set the receiver down and started to cry, covering her face with her hands. In the boardroom, seeing that the call had disconnected, George Levesky went back to the office where he had left Maggie. When he saw that she was crying, he immediately went over to offer comfort, getting her some tissue, and patting her gently on the back to try to calm her down. Once Maggie had regained her composure, Levesky asked her, "Are you satisfied the man you just spoke with is Billy Braddock?"

"It couldn't be anybody else. It was him."

"We're gonna hold a press conference in about an hour. Are you up to speaking before the cameras?"

"Yes."

"Fine. Why don't you let me escort you down to our cafeteria, and we'll have a cup of coffee?"

"That would be nice," Maggie said, as she allowed Levesky to help her out of the chair. "I'm so very tired, but I feel so much better, knowing Billy's all right."

At the beach house, Jenny was finishing her morning chores when the phone rang. She went to answer the phone, and a voice on the other end of the line said, "Yes...is Buck Rodgers in? This is Coach Wilson of the Houston Texans."

"Oh, yes, Coach Wilson! We've been wonderin' if you were gonna call back." She paused a moment. "Buck's gone out for awhile this mornin' to take care of some business, but I expect him back soon."

"Well, if you wouldn't mind, would you ask him to give me a call the first time he gets a chance?"

"Oh, sure. I've got a pad and pencil right here." She jotted Coach Wilson's number down on the pad, and Jenny read the number back to him to be sure she had it right. "I'll give this to him as soon as he comes in."

"I appreciate it very much. You have a nice day."

"You, too, Coach Wilson. Nice talkin' to you." Jenny put the phone down and jumped in the air with glee. "Oh, Buck! You're gonna be so happy! My baby's gonna play in the NFL!"

Going back to the bedroom, she hurriedly made the bed and went into the living room, where she turned on the television. One of the local channels was broadcasting a live news conference from the front steps of the Braddock Corporation's headquarters in downtown Houston. The company spokesman was George Levesky.

... *"the entire board of directors was present for the conversation, and I can tell you unequivocally that Billy Braddock is alive and well and in possession of all his mental faculties. We recorded the conversation, and we will give the press a redacted version of the call, so as to eliminate any doubt that it was the real Billy Braddock."*

A reporter shouted, *"Why has he been in hiding?"*

"It is as I told you before. Billy did have a heart attack, and he's been recuperating. He wanted and needed to get away from the day-to-day stresses of a very demanding life. In addition to conducting oversight of all his business enterprises, I'm sure you all know he is the pastor of a large non-denominational church in Braddock, Texas. That would be a lot for anyone to do, and all of you should be able to understand why it was advisable for him to reduce his workload in order to properly recover from his heart attack."

"Mr. Levesky"—another reporter shouted, but the company executive cut him off before he could ask the question.

"Before we get into a bunch of other questions, I want to introduce you to Maggie Carlyle. She's been a personal friend of Billy Braddock's for well over half a century, and she knows Billy better than anybody else in the world. Maggie also spoke with Billy in a private conversation, and she wants to tell you her

impressions." George motioned her toward the microphone. *"Maggie, won't you come over?"*

"Ohh, sweet little Maggie," Jenny said aloud.

Maggie came to the microphone, looking uncomfortable in the glare of all the public exposure. *"Thank you. I'm Maggie Carlyle. I talked to Billy, and what we talked about was stuff that only Billy could possibly know. I've known him since we were in the first grade, I've run his household for the past twenty years, and I've seen him almost every day during that time. Nobody trying to impersonate Billy could fool me. It was definitely Billy Braddock."*

"Maggie! How did he sound?" a reporter yelled.

"What? How did he sound? He sounded like Billy Braddock. He's the same as he always was. He just told me not to worry, and he'd be back when he's rested up."

Jenny watched until the press conference was over, and then she turned the TV off. She sat, remembering that day beside the highway, when Shooter had beaten Billy Braddock so badly. Tears started to fall from her eyes. "Lord," she said aloud, "please forgive me for causin' Reverend Braddock to get hurt. I'm so sorry, Lord" ...

The dentist was showing Buck Rodgers the panoramic X-ray of his teeth. Pointing toward the molars on both sides, he was saying, "You can see right here all the bone-loss around the back teeth on both sides. See how the jawbone is eaten away?"

"Yeah, I see it," Buck said.

"You can probably get by a little longer without pulling that very back molar on the left side, but it's gonna keep giving you trouble. There's just too much bone-loss around the tooth. The tooth itself is perfect."

"Well, whadda ya think's causin' this?" Buck inquired, an expression of serious concern on his face.

"Truthfully, I don't know," the dentist said. "Your gums appear to be in good shape, your teeth are in perfect condition...they look like brand new teeth, I swear—perfect. There's no plaque buildup, no obvious gum disease...I have no idea what could cause something like this. My best guess would be that maybe you've somehow managed to get a staph infection around the bone, and it's been eating away for awhile. I can't remember seeing anything this bad in someone who didn't have periodontal disease or some other apparent condition that would present an obvious cause. It doesn't really make sense to me. But there's no question that something's going on. This much bone loss in someone as young as you are, with the overall good oral condition that you appear to have, is certainly not normal—at least, not in my experience. I'll have to look in the textbooks to find an explanation for this."

"And there's nothing you can do?" Buck asked.

The dentist shook his head. "I can refer you to a specialist. Maybe he can find out what's causing the problem. But I don't think anyone can save these back molars. There's just too much damage. Those teeth will have to come out, sooner or later—sooner, most likely."

Rodgers sighed. "Well...let me call you back. I need to talk to another doctor before I take this dental work to the next level."

"Just a minute. I'll be right back." The dentist left the examination room and went to his private office. When he returned, he handed Rodgers a business card. "This is an associate of mine, Dan Harris. He specializes in treating periodontal disease. If you decide that you want to go the extra step, give his office a call and tell them I conducted the initial examination and referred you to them."

"I'll do that. Thank you, doctor."

As soon as he got down to the parking lot, Rodgers took out his cell phone and called the Braddock Institute. When the receptionist answered, he asked to speak to Dr. Keeler. "Tell 'im it's Billy Braddock calling."

"Oh, Mr. Braddock. Please stay on the line. I'll page him immediately." In less than two minutes, Charles Keeler was on the line.

"Billy? Is that you?"

"It's me," he said.

"Billy, I'm so glad to hear from you," he said, the relief in his voice apparent, even over the telephone. "How are you doing, Billy? Is your health holding up?"

"Charles, I think I may have a problem. I wanted to talk to you about it."

"Absolutely. What's going on?"

"Charles, I...I don't know how to explain this so you'll understand, but I've noticed lately that when I work out with weights, it's been getting harder to do what I could do with no problem at all just...oh, say—a month or so ago. And I've been on a strict training regimen like I never did back when I was in college. But with all that, I seem to be gettin' weaker every day."

"Anything else?"

"I just left the dentist's office...five minutes ago. He showed me an X-ray, and those new teeth I grew a few months back are startin' t' fall out. The bone around the teeth is bein' eaten away."

"Is there anything else going on?"

"No, nothin' else really specific. But those two things are obvious as hell."

There was a pause as Keeler formulated his words. "Billy, I have to tell you the truth, as much as I hate to have to do it. And I can promise you're not gonna like what I have to say."

"I gotta know the truth, Charles. Ever since I bit down on a little pork bone the other day and my tooth felt like someone stuck an ice-pick in my gum, I've been rememberin' you tellin' me the monkey was startin' t' fall apart. Is that what's happenin' to me?"

"I'm afraid it is, Billy. The serum does miraculous things, but it doesn't last. Since the last time I saw you, Kimba's gone way downhill. We're at the point now with him that it's not much more than a death-watch. I don't know how much more time he's got, but I doubt he'll live much more than a year longer—if that."

"So there's no hope."

Keeler sighed audibly. "I have no reason to believe that there is, no."

"Can you give me a time frame?"

"I don't know, Billy. You're the first human subject who's tried the serum. I would guess, based on what happened to Kimba...within six or eight months—maybe less, maybe more—you'll be physically middle-aged. Then, likely within three or four more months—maybe somewhat longer—you'll become an old man again. There's no way to pinpoint a timeline, but it's definitely going to happen. Based on everything we know about the serum, the deterioration process is very rapid, and it gains speed as it progresses. You...you may be an exception, considering the fact that you're a human being. Maybe the serum will last longer in your case. But it won't last forever, I'm sure of that. I don't want to extend any false hope. I doubt the results in your case will be much better than they have been in Kimba's case. I'm sorry, Billy."

"What about another dose?"

"We've tried that. It's killed every subject we've ever tried it on. A second dose means certain death. That's the one thing I'm absolutely sure of." There was a long silence. "Billy? Are you still there, Billy?"

"I gotta go, Charles. Thanks for the information."

"Billy, don't hang up. I need to tell you that the taxi driver who drove you to my house that morning told John Wilkins you came to see me, and Wilkins came over here and questioned me."

"What did you tell 'im?"

"I told him you just came to find out if we had developed anything to repair heart-damage."

"Did he believe you?"

"I don't know."

"Well, I'm not gonna worry about it. He can't prove anything."

"Billy, why don't you come home? Maybe we can find some way to help you."

"If you find some way to help Kimba, I just might do that. If not...I'm runnin' outta time, and I've got things to do before the end comes. Goodbye, Charles."

"I'll pray for you, Billy."

Once the call was concluded, Buck Rodgers returned to his pickup and sat down in the vehicle. He stared straight ahead for a long time, watching the traffic on the street pass in front of him, his face expressionless. Finally, he put the keys in the ignition and drove back to the beach house where Jenny eagerly awaited his return. As soon as he came through the door, she came running from the kitchen to greet him. "I've got a surprise for you, honey—but first you have to give me a kiss."

"What surprise?"

"Kiss first," she said with a coy little smile as she puckered her lips. Buck kissed Jenny's soft lips, savoring the sweetness as he had never done before.

She had to push him away. "Oh, stop that! You're gonna cause my panties to fall off!"

He held her close to him, loving the inexpressibly wonderful feeling of her body against his, unwilling to let her go. "What surprise do you have?"

Her eyes were sparkling with delight. "Do you know a Coach Wilson who works for the Houston Texans?"

"Did he call back?"

"He sure did. His number's right over there by the phone." He let her go, and to her surprise, the look she saw on his face was not joyful, as she had anticipated. Instead, there was a kind of sadness in his eyes. "Aren't you happy to hear that, honey?"

Buck sat down on the couch. "Would you grab me a beer, honey?"

"Well...sure." She went to the kitchen, retrieved a beer, and set it on the coffee table. "What's wrong, baby? I thought you'd be all crazy-happy to hear that."

"I wanta ask you a question."

She sat down beside him on the couch and took his hand. "Okay, ask me."

"If you could live anywhere in the world, where would you wanta live?'

She thought about it. "Oh, I don't know. I guess right here, in our happy little home beside the sea."

"I mean...if I wasn't with you...where would you wanta live?"

"Are you leavin' me, Buck? Is that what this is?"

"No, honey—I'm askin' you...where would you be happy, with or without me?"

"I wouldn't be happy anywhere in the world without you."

Unable to get a direct answer out of her, he asked, "But you really do like this little place near the ocean, don't you?"

"I love it. When I was a girl, livin' out in the West Texas desert, I always dreamed of havin' a place on the beach, with the wind and the waves, and...you know—just look out the window. See how beautiful it is? That's what I used to dream about."

"I'm gonna talk to the guy I rented this place from and see if I can't make 'im an offer he can't refuse. I'm gonna get this place for you...if you're sure that's what you want."

"Well...it is, but...baby, there's somethin' goin' on here that makes me think you're about to say goodbye. Have I done somethin' wrong?"

"No, of course not. I've only been in love two times in my life. And you're the second love to ever come along in my life. Everybody else was just...you know...people I met along the way to the place where I found you."

"Who was your first love?"

"Just a girl I knew, a long time ago."

"Buck...honey...I...I just feel kinda weird. You just seem so sad, and I thought you'd be happy. I don't understand. Aren't you gonna call Coach Wilson?"

"I'll do that later. Right now, I need to go back to town and see a few people. I got some important business I need to take care of." He gave her a lingering kiss. "I love you, Jenny. I honestly do really, truly love you."

"Honey, I love you, too—with all my heart and soul."

"Well, I'm gonna go for awhile. I'll be back. Don't fix supper tonight. If we decide to eat a full-blown meal, we'll go out for dinner."

"Okay, honey." He got up from the couch and kissed her goodbye, then turned toward the door. "Do you know how long you're gonna be?"

"I'm not sure. But I *will* be back."

Jenny followed him out to the porch, watched as he backed the pickup out of the driveway, and followed his progress down the road until he was out of sight. She sat down on the front-porch swing and stared out toward the ocean, watching the gentle waves as they rolled in and broke along the shore. She wasn't sure why, but she felt like crying, and suddenly tears spilled out of her eyes and began to run down her cheeks...

... "and all the arrangements have been made, per my explicit instructions, is that correct, Fred?"

"To the very letter, Mr. Braddock."

"So if Buck Rodgers goes into the bank and draws cashier's checks worth millions of dollars out of the account, there won't be any hassle?"

"The president of the bank will take care of him personally. And all the necessary paperwork will be completed, and the appropriate amounts taken out, so that all the taxes will be prepaid. The amount on the checks will be the full dollar value, tax-free to the recipients. Notarized documentation that all taxes have been paid will come with the checks, in case the IRS wants to ask any questions about it."

"You know, Fred...you've done a very good job for me over the years, and I want you to know I truly appreciate all you've done. You've shown me you're more than capable at helping people to manage their money."

"You're too kind, Mr. Braddock."

"No, actually, I'm not kind when it comes to business. Business is dog-eat-dog. Religion is kindness, pure and simple. That's where a lot of preachers go wrong—they get their religion and their business mixed up, and pretty soon it's all about business, and religion is just a way to get more money to fuel their business interests."

"I've heard you say words to that effect in the past, Mr. Braddock, and I heartily agree."

"Fred, the cashier's checks are for the benefit of some people I don't want to go begging in this world. I want 'em to be properly taken care of. I'm gonna give every one of 'em your office number, and I want you to see to their very best interests as if you were seeing to mine."

"I will, sir."

"Just remember—to the extent that you did it for the least of these, you did it for me. Are we clear on this subject?"

"Absolutely. I will do everything in my power to serve their best interests."

"And you're a hundred-percent certain the recipients of these cashier's checks are in no danger of incurring any upfront tax-liabilities, is that correct?"

"None whatsoever."

"Okay, I think that's all I have for you now. I'm gonna tell Buck Rodgers to go over to the bank and get the cashier's checks right away."

"Please remind him to bring the proper identification, Mr. Braddock. We're talking millions of dollars here, and the bank won't do anything if he can't prove who he is."

"I'll tell 'im."

"I just want to say, Mr. Braddock, that I hope your recuperation period goes well. I look forward to the day when you'll be back up to speed."

"Thank you, Fred. Goodbye."

Hanging up the phone, Billy Braddock stepped out of the phone booth in the hotel and walked the three blocks to the bank, where they were expecting the arrival of Buck Rodgers. Once he was inside the lobby, Rodgers walked over to one of the desks where a bank official was sitting and said, "I'm here to see the bank president? Mr. Weissman, I believe it is?"

"Mr. Weissman? Is he expecting you?"

"He should be. I was sent by Billy Braddock...of the Braddock Corporation."

"May I ask your name?"

"Buck Rodgers."

The bank official called the bank president. "Mr. Weissman? There's a young man named Buck Rodgers here to see you. He says he was sent by Billy Braddock, of the Braddock Corporation. Yes, sir. I certainly will." The man looked at Rodgers. "He said for you to go right in. It's that office on the other side of the lobby. His name is on the door."

"Thanks," Buck said.

Rodgers entered the office of Mr. Weissman, who came from behind the desk to offer a warm greeting. "Mr. Rodgers! So glad to meet you. I'm Harold Weissman."

"Buck Rodgers. Nice t' meet you, too, Mr. Weissman."

"Fred Covington has already briefed me on what we have to do today, so all I need to find out from you is what checks you want to draw, in what amounts, and to whom these checks are to be given. We'll figure out the taxes to be paid, and get that done, and then you'll be all ready to go in no time" ...

After having dinner at a French restaurant on Memorial Drive, Buck and Jenny took the freeway down to Clear Lake, where they found a quiet establishment situated on the waterfront. They ordered Margaritas and went out on the veranda. In the quiet evening, with the breeze blowing off the water, they sat side by side, watching the moon sparkle off the waves.

"It's so beautiful here," Jenny said.

"It is that," Buck agreed. "Nights like this make it possible to imagine what forever must be—eternal moon, eternal stars, eternal sea" ... He gave her an unmistakable look. "Eternal love" ...

"Do you love me, Buck? Really?"

He gently kissed her lips. "I do, baby. I really do. More than you could ever know."

"Honey, I know somethin's been on your mind lately. Do you wanta talk to me about it?"

"Not just yet."

"Well, baby...I been feelin' like I'm walkin' on pins and needles lately. Somethin's goin' on. I don't know what it is, but I can feel it. And I keep havin' this terrible...I don't know—*dread*—that you're gonna walk out on me any day now."

Buck kissed her again. "Don't be morbid, darlin'. Let's just enjoy the evenin'. If I ever leave you, it won't be because I *want* to. It'll be because I *have* to."

"Why would you ever have to?"

Buck shrugged his big shoulders. "Things happen in this life we just have no control over. People have car wrecks, get killed in random violence, get sick...there's all sorts of things that can happen. The only guarantee of anything in this life is this very moment we live, right now, this second. That's all. Everything else is a pure gamble. I might die of a heart attack ten seconds from now, I don't know. Nobody knows. *'The race is not to the swift, nor the battle to the strong, but time and chance befall them all.'* That's Ecclesiastes, Chapter Nine, if you wanta look it up."

"I didn't know you knew the Bible, Buck."

"I know a little bit. Not as much as I'd like to know."

There was a long silence, as Buck stared contemplatively toward the water and Jenny wondered what she could say that would put him in a more festive mood. After thinking about it, she finally decided that nothing she could do or say would change the dark mood that seemed to dominate the evening, in spite of all the splendor around them. She lightly touched his arm. "Buck, could we call it a night? I'd like to go back to the house."

"Sure, baby," he readily agreed. "I ain't on top of my game tonight, either."

They drove back to the beach house and went inside. Buck took a beer out of the refrigerator and turned on the television. Jenny went to the bedroom and got out of her clothes, then changed into a sexy negligee she had bought the day before. She freshened her makeup, sprayed just a hint of new perfume, and went into the living room. Buck didn't see her until she walked right in front of him. Seeing this vision of beauty standing before him, he said, "Whoa, baby! Don't you look like *somethin'*!"

"Come into the bedroom. I wanta talk to you."

Buck eyed her up and down, and then pretended to be uninterested. "Nah...I'll be in later. There's a rerun of *I Love Lucy* comin' on."

She took the remote control out of his hand and turned off the television. "Get your ass in that bedroom right now."

"Well, if you insist" ...Buck said, with a feigned expression of disappointment on his face. He stood up from the couch. "I never get t' watch my favorite shows. It's just sex, sex, sex, all the time."

"Right now, big boy," she ordered. "Stop whining, and get your ass back there. And hurry up about it," she added, giving him a little shove to propel him forward. Once they were in the bedroom, Jenny started to undress him. "I want you to get that big, strong, beautiful body out here and let me have my way with you. I'm gonna make love to you like you've never been loved before" ...

When Jenny awoke the next morning, Buck was gone. It didn't even occur to her to worry about that fact, because Buck always got up early to run on the beach, or lift weights, or take care of whatever business it was he was always doing in Houston. Lying naked in the bed, remembering the wondrous night of love they had shared, she stretched her muscles and said aloud, "Oh, Buck—I love you, I love you, *I love you*—you big, handsome, wonderful, beautiful man! I love you!" She lay there a few minutes, luxuriating in the joyous serenity of loving and being loved, and then—reluctantly—she made herself get out of bed. Putting on a housecoat, she went into the kitchen, where she noticed an envelope lying on the table. On the front of the envelope was a single handwritten word—*Jenny*. Her heart jumped, fearing the worst. Inside the envelope, she found two business cards tucked inside a typewritten letter; and, in the letter, all her worst fears were realized. The letter began...

My darling Jenny,
Words can never convey what you have meant to me during the time we have been together. You have added a sense of fulfillment to my life that, not so long ago, I could never have hoped to experience. I'm sorry that I was not as truthful with you as you were with me, but I hope in time you will understand. I never meant to be cruel. I truly

am sorry that I wasn't honest with you from the very beginning, but I didn't know how to be. I ran into you by accident that night in Pasadena, and things just took off from there. From that beginning, when I beat the dog out of your no-good husband, I could never see a jumping-off point where I could actually tell you the truth about who I was. I was caught up in the moment, trapped in desire, a fool in love. I couldn't help myself. That is my error, and it is a human error, and I apologize for that. I was afraid if I told you the truth about who I was, I would lose you—and that was a chance I was not willing to take. That's the only excuse I have.

If you look in the closet in the bedroom, you will find my leather suitcase. Inside the suitcase, you will find roughly eight-hundred-thousand dollars in cash. That money is yours to keep. If you haven't found them yet, there are a couple of business cards enclosed with this letter. Hang on to those cards. Fred Covington is a man here in Houston I want you to contact. He will show you how to use this money to your best advantage. Fred also has the deed to the beach house. I've already signed the place over to you, and all you need to do is go over there and put your signature on the document to make it all official. For your own best interests, I want you to call Fred today and get started toward establishing the good life you have been too long denied. The cash in the suitcase is only a token amount, compared to what you will have in the not-distant future. That money is more than enough to keep you going for now. What other things I have in store for you are contingent on your filing for divorce from

Shooter Dobbins as soon as possible. The other business card is a business card for Bert Duffy, my personal attorney. I've already told him to expect your call. Let Bert handle your divorce. He knows every judge in town, and he will expedite the process to the full extent the law allows. You need to get Shooter Dobbins out of your life, once and for all, as quickly as possible.

There is one other contingency: You must never, never, ever, ever tell anyone what I'm about to reveal. If you do, you will lose every long-term benefit I'm offering you. I beg you, if you ever loved me—or if you ever loved yourself—do not do that. Everything I'm doing for you has been arranged by Buck Rodgers. That's the name you always use when you are talking about these matters to anybody— Buck Rodgers. Buck is my surrogate representative for the good I'm trying to do for you. That's the only name you should ever reveal. I cannot stress that enough, Jenny. Do not forfeit your legacy by telling people that Buck Rodgers and Billy Braddock are one and the same.

Finally, sometime this morning, you will receive an overnight special-delivery package from the Braddock Corporation at this address. In the package is a video of a recent segment of the "CBS Evening News." Watch the video, and pay close attention to the pictures they show of Billy Braddock as a young man. You will recognize the face, but the news report won't be about the man you know as Buck Rodgers. That person in the video is actually me...Billy Braddock. The man who has loved you all these months—Buck Rodgers—is also Billy

Braddock. Both people are the same person. I truly hope you understand this. I can't tell you how it happened—I still hardly believe it myself. Just accept that it did happen. For all practical purposes, I—Billy Braddock— came back from the living death that old age is, and I was resurrected as Buck Rodgers, the young man I used to be. Unfortunately, it was only temporary—an old man's Indian Summer, as it were—one last opportunity to be young, and wild, and crazy, and madly in love—one last chance to revel in the joy of living.

But now...now I have to return to the place whence I came. The Scriptures tell us, 'The wages of sin is death.' There's no way of getting around it. The Word of God is true. But in these beautiful days of sunlight and stars and youth and beauty and love I have known with you, I have learned like I never knew before what a precious gift God gave us when He gave us life. I have learned what a precious gift you are. You are a wonderful woman, Jenny, and I hope you never forget that for as long as you exist. I don't have much time to live, but I want you to know that you have made the last days of my life some of the best days of my life. I loved you the first time I ever saw you at the women's shelter in Braddock, I love you now, and I will always love you—
Forever and ever,
Billy Braddock

Jenny puzzled over the letter, trying to comprehend the meaning of the words Buck had written. Was he trying to tell her that he was Billy Braddock? That just couldn't be true. Then, slowly, the realization of something else—something much worse—began to sink in. Buck was gone. He wasn't coming back.

Numb, she got up from the table and went to the bedroom as if she were sleepwalking through a nightmare. Opening the closet door, she found Buck's suitcase. She put the bag on the bed and opened it. The sight of the contents inside left her breathless: Reams of hundred-dollar bills, more money than she had ever seen in her life. She sat down on the bed and looked at the money. But her reaction was not one of particular delight. She hardly seemed to comprehend what she was seeing. All she could think about was the fact that Buck had gone away.

She had sat on the bed for a very long time, not moving, when she heard a knock at the front door. Going to the door, she saw a delivery man with a package. "I have a delivery for Jenny Dobbins."

"I'm Jenny."

"Just sign here, please."

Signing for the package, Jenny opened it and found a video disk inside. As Buck had told her there would be, she saw that it was a recording of a recent network news broadcast. The story was about the disappearance of Billy Braddock. When the pictures of Braddock as a young man began to flash on the screen, she suddenly understood the full import of what Buck had said in the letter—Buck and Billy really were the same person. Suddenly, she started to cry.

"You didn't have to go. I would have loved you, no matter who you were" ...

Having ridden his bull for the full eight seconds, the little cowboy clambered over the fence surrounding the rodeo arena and came walking toward Clete Justus. "Hey, Clete! Did you get a load o' that? Looks like I'm gonna be takin' top money tonight, don't it?"

"You talk big shit when you're ridin' a milk-cow, don't you, Shorty?" Justus retorted. "The rodeo ain't over yet."

"Might as well be. You know you can't ride Widowmaker. How many times has that sucker thrown you clear outta the money? Five? Six?"

"Like I say...it ain't over till it's over, you sawed-off little runt."

The little cowboy gave a derisive snort and walked away. From behind the starting gates a voice called out, "Justus! You're up next!"

Widowmaker was in the chute, looking meaner than ever. He seemed to recognize Justus as soon as he started climbing the fence to mount up. When Clete sat down, the big bull snorted his disapproval and started struggling to throw the cowboy off his back before they could even open the gate.

Justus held on tight and said to the bull, "We ain't gonna dance till they start the music, you sorry sack o' shit."

The announcer said, "And now, comin' outta chute number three, it's Clete Justus, ridin' Widowmaker!"

The gate flew back, and Widowmaker roared forward—twisting, turning, snapping side to side— and Clete Justus sat atop the big bull, being thrown around like a rag doll. It seemed like an eternity before Widowmaker finally made the move that sent Clete flying off his back, but the actual time involved was only four seconds. Clete knew he was out of the money before he hit the ground. He also knew that he didn't have any time to lie in the dirt and calculate his losses, because Widowmaker was the worst bull on the circuit to try to attack the rider after the ride. Jumping up as quickly as possible, Clete ran for the fence and got over the top rung just ahead of a big horn aimed straight for his hind end. Once he was safely on the other side of the fence, Justus brushed the dirt off his clothes, his face a picture of frustration.

"Sonofabitch! I hate that goddamn bull!" Clete growled.

"Mr. Justus? Cletis Ray Justus?"

Clete turned to see an odd little man in a business suit and a derby hat, carrying a briefcase. "Yeah, that's me."

"Mr. Justus, I've been sent here by a Mr. Buck Rodgers."

"Buck?" Justus grinned. "How the hell is he?"

"I wouldn't know, sir. I've never met the man." The little man extended his hand. "My name is Wilfrid Leeds. I work for Covington and Associates in Houston." Mister Leeds took a manila envelope out of his briefcase. "I have this for you from Mr. Rodgers. You might want to open it now."

Clete opened the package and pulled out some paperwork and a small envelope. Fastened to the paperwork was a cashier's check. Clete looked at the check. "Five hundred thousand"—

"That's five million, sir. Five million dollars. Tax-free."

Justus eyed the little man suspiciously. "Is this a joke?"

"No, sir, it is not," Leeds said with a serious look. "It's a tax-free gift to you from Mr. Rodgers. Perhaps the letter he enclosed will explain the matter further." Clete opened the letter and read it. After reading what Buck had written, Justus looked at Leeds with a puzzled expression. "I don't get it. It says here he's givin' me this money 'cause I was a friend when he needed one." He shook his head and looked again at Leeds. "You sure this ain't some kinda joke?"

"Please believe me—it's completely true." Mr. Leeds took a business card out of his pocket and handed it to Justus. "I hope you'll hang onto this card. Mr. Rodgers has requested that you go see my employer, Fred Covington. Mr. Covington is a world-class business advisor, and he can help you set up a way to manage your money, so as to get the most benefit possible from the gift Mr. Rodgers has given you. I can't urge you strongly enough to take full advantage of Mr. Covington's expertise. If I were you, I'd call the office tomorrow."

"What's all this other stuff here?"

"It's just a copy of the paperwork we have on file in Mr. Covington's office, showing that all the taxes on this money have been prepaid."

Shaking his head, trying to comprehend the magnitude of what was happening, Clete said, "Man, this is...this is unreal."

"I urge you to put this check in a safe place until you see Mr. Covington. If you will call him tomorrow, he will find time to see you, at the behest of Mr. Rodgers."

"Yeah...yeah, I'll do that," Clete said in a tone of bewilderment.

Leeds extended his hand. "So...congratulations on your good fortune, Mr. Justus. I do hope you will use the money wisely."

"Thanks." Clete put everything but Buck's personal letter back in the envelope. He read the last few lines again:

> *"You once told me you were thinking about going into the business end of the rodeo, and if that's really what you want to do, this is your grubstake to*

that end. You also said something about starting a cattle ranch, and this money should get you headed a good piece down the road in that direction, too. Whatever you do with the money, I hope it serves you well. This is the end of the trail, compadre. We won't meet again in this lifetime. But I will always remember you and the hand of friendship you extended to a raw rookie when I really did need a friend. God be with you—Buck."

Justus removed his cowboy hat and scratched his head. "I don't get it. Where'd that kid get all that money?"

"You've really done it up good, this time," the middle-aged woman was saying to her daughter as she looked at the legal summons that had just been delivered to the house. "You never did have a lick of sense, Mary Lynn."

"Mama, please—don't harp on it. I know I messed up."

"You coulda had millions...*millions*! All you had to do was keep your panties on for another few years, and you coulda screwed anybody you wanted to—and been rich doin' it. Now look what you got—nothing! You don't even have that piece of worthless trash you went so damn crazy over!" She threw the legal papers down on the table and looked hopelessly toward the ceiling. "Where did I go so wrong?"

"Oh, God, Mama—I can't take much more of this. It's not bad enough Carter's lawyers are filing every kind of writ known to man on me—I have to listen to this crap from you? Can't you be on my side for once?"

There was a knock at the front door. Mary Lynn left the room to get away from her mother as much as to answer the door. She found a little man standing on the front porch. "Are you Mary Lynn Bradley?"

"Not for long. Are you another process-server?"

"No, ma'am. My name is Wilfrid Leeds. I work for Covington and Associates, a company based in Houston, Texas. Buck Rodgers sent me."

"Buck?" her eyes lit up. "Where *is* he?"

"I don't know, Mrs. Bradley. Mr. Rodgers asked me to bring you a tax-free gift of three million dollars."

"Three million dollars!"

"Yes. It's in the form of a cashier's check." Leeds handed her a large envelope. "He told me to tell you that he feels partly responsible for the current state of affairs in which you find yourself, and he hopes this money will help you to get your affairs back in some semblance of order. All the necessary documents are in this envelope. If you decide to go back to Texas, my employer hopes that you will come see him."

"Buck? Buck wants me to come see him?"

"No, ma'am. I mean my boss, Fred Covington. He's a business advisor to many wealthy people, including Mr. Rodgers, and he would be honored to be of service to you in any way he can." Leeds handed a business card to Mary Lynn. "Do you have any questions?"

"I have one."

"Yes?"

"Am I dreaming?"

On a cloudy afternoon in Houston, Bubba and Kitty came speeding down Telephone Road and pulled up in front of Bill's Icehouse. The two dismounted Bubba's chopped-down Harley and went into the open-air bar to have a beer. Finding a table in the corner, they sat down to talk.

"Okay, Kitty," Bubba said, "I'm gonna leave you here for awhile."

"Do you know how long?"

Well, it shouldn't be too long. They know I'm comin'. The deal's all set."

"I don't know, Bubba...it just seems strange to me, the Bandidos callin' you outta the clear blue sky to set up a dope deal with you."

"What—you don't think I'm in the same class as the Bandidos, or something?"

"No, it just seems weird they'd have you come all the way down here from New Mexico to do a drug deal with 'em in Houston. I mean, it's not like they don't have plenty of clients right here locally."

"I told you...they said they're doin' this 'cause Shooter recommended me to 'em. There's a pretty good market in New Mexico. Maybe they're openin' up a new territory."

"Well, how come Shooter didn't call you and talk to you about this himself?"

"Well...*duh*," Bubba sarcastically remarked. "Could it be because he's still on the lam? I imagine the cops still ain't caught 'im for beatin' up that preacher."

Kitty shook her head doubtfully. "I don't know. It just seems kinda strange" ...

Bubba waved his hand impatiently. "Look, bitch—just let *me* do the thinkin', and *you* sell the pussy, okay? Which brings me to why we're here. While I'm gone, I want you to get out there on the street and see if you can't catch a few tricks. You can kinda help defray the expenses for this trip if you put your talent to good use."

"Okay, Bubba. Whatever you say."

"And try t' stay within three or four blocks of this place here, so I can find you pretty quick when I come back. If the deal goes down, and everything's cool, I'll need to go back to the room and pick up the money."

"Okay," Kitty agreed.

"And if the heat starts hasslin' the workin' gals, don't take any chances. Just head on back to the motel and wait for me there."

"I'll do it," Kitty agreed.

Bubba drained the can at a gulp. "Okay. I'll be back soon."

"And where's this place you're goin' again?"

"It's kinda out in the country, the other side of Pasadena. It's not too far from here."

"Okay...well, hurry every chance you get."

"You just keep that hot little pussy busy. It'll make the time pass faster."

Bubba left the icehouse and headed out of town toward Pasadena. Following the directions he was given, he came to a dilapidated house that was situated in a rural section of the county about a mile off the main road. Seeing several bikers congregated in the front yard, all wearing the colors of the Bandidos, he was sure that he had found the right location. He pulled up in front of the house, parked his bike and dismounted. A very large biker with long hair, full beard, and skull-and-crossbones tattoos on both forearms sauntered casually toward him.

"You Bubba?" the biker asked.

"Yeah, I'm Bubba. You Red Dog?"

The biker looked around. "Red Dog? I don't know no Red Dog." He looked around at the other bikers. "Anybody here know a Red Dog?" The other bikers all said they didn't know anybody by that name. "Sorry, Bubba. We don't know no Red Dog."

"Well, ain't this the Bandidos Clubhouse?"

"This dump?" the big biker said with a laugh. "Nah. This is just a nice, quiet place where we come to whoop a motherfucker's ass every now and then."

Immediately sensing that something was terribly wrong, Bubba became wary of the menacing assemblage. "I guess somebody made a mistake." He backed away as if to get back on his motorcycle. "I better go call Red Dog and make sure I got my directions straight."

"Well, wait a minute," the big biker said. "Didn't you say you're Bubba?"

"Yeah."

"You comin' here outta New Mexico?"

"That's me."

The Bandido turned and grinned at his companions. "Naw, there ain't no mistake. We been expectin' you."

Bubba began to act visibly nervous. "Now listen...I was told by this guy Red Dog to come here about a dope deal that was set up by Shooter Dobbins."

"Shooter Dobbins?" The biker looked around in puzzlement. "Any of you know Shooter Dobbins?" The other bikers answered in the negative and then started slowly to encircle Bubba. "Nope. We don't know no Shooter Dobbins, neither. But now that you mention it, we *were* told to come out here...not for a *dope deal*, but to do a *deal* on a *dope*."

"Now, wait a minute," Bubba said, an unmistakable expression of fear creeping into his face, "I think" ...

"And I believe...yeah, the name *Dobbins* did come up in the conversation," the biker said, nodding his head with certainty. "But it wasn't no *Shooter* Dobbins. It was a woman's name." He turned to look at his companions. "Anybody remember that woman's name?"

"I believe it was *Jenny* Dobbins," one of them said.

"Yeah, that's what it was—Jenny Dobbins."

"What's that bitch got to do with this?" Bubba asked.

"I don't know, man. I just know we're s'posed to do a deal on a dope, because of somethin' involvin' a woman named Jenny Dobbins, and you're the dope who showed up for the deal." The big Bandido assumed an aggressive posture, meant to intimidate his quarry. "Oh, yeah...and we were told to give you a message before we do the deal."

"What message?" Bubba asked.

The burly biker took a note out of his shirt pocket and read it to Bubba. "The message was: *The sins you do, two by two, you pay for one by one.*"

"Now, please, guys...that bitch asked for everything she got" ...

"Hey, man," the biker said. "I don't know nothin' about nothin', or who did what to who, or how, or why—and I don't care one way or the other, neither. All I know is what I've been told to do. And what I'm here to do is a dope deal. And you're the dope. And here's the deal: You're fixin' t' take a serious ass-whoopin'."

"Listen, man...I don't want no trouble," Bubba said in a pleading tone. "I've got big money back at the motel where I'm staying" ...

"We'll talk about that later," the biker said. "We'll get the money soon enough. You're gonna give us *all* your money before we're through, and anything else you got that's of any value." He paused long enough to give Bubba an evil grin. "But don't worry man. We was told to fuck you up real bad, but not to kill you. So you'll be in the hospital for awhile, but you'll prob'ly live." Suddenly, as if by magic, the bikers produced a variety of chains, pipes, clubs and brass knuckles. "Well, would you look at this?" the big biker said in mock surprise as he looked around at all the weaponry. "It looks like we're gonna have a rock concert, and *you're* gonna be the *drum.*" He motioned to the others. "Okay, boys...let's start the music! *Get 'im!*"

It was ten o'clock in the morning, and Jenny Dobbins was still lying in bed, unable to force herself to get up and face another day without Buck...or Billy...or whoever that handsome cowboy really was. Her life with Shooter had been an empty life, but she had never felt as empty when she was with Shooter as she did now. She had a suitcase full of money in the closet, a beach house that had been purchased for her as a gift, a nice sports car in the garage—and, as far as she was concerned, no discernible reason to go on living. As she lay there, staring at the ceiling, a knock came at the front door. Covering her ears with the pillow, she started to ignore the summons; but, despite the pillow, she could hear the muffled voice of a woman calling her name.

"Hello? Is anyone home? Jenny? Jenny Dobbins?"

Wondering who might be calling, curiosity got the best of her. Jenny got out of bed and went to the door. Standing on the porch was a classy-looking woman in her mid-thirties, smiling in a practiced manner that looked confidently professional. Jenny opened the door. "Yes?"

"You must be Jenny. You're just the way Mr. Rodgers described you. I'm Alicia Miles. I was hired by Mr. Rodgers to help you get off to a good start as you begin your new life."

"New life?"

"May I come in, Jenny?"

"Oh, sure. I'm sorry. I didn't mean to be rude."

"You don't need to apologize, honey. I understand how it is when you're trying to set your life back in order during and after a divorce—especially when you're moving to a new town and beginning a whole new life from the ground up."

"Maybe I'm not quite awake yet, Miss"—

"Alicia. Just call me Alicia. I hope you'll think of me as a friend. Why don't we sit down here on the couch a moment? We've got some things to discuss, and not much time to do it."

Jenny acquiesced to the request. "Alicia," she said, repeating the name so she would remember it. Jenny then continued, "I'm not sure I understand what you're talking about. You said you had talked to Buck"—

"Yes, he called me early yesterday morning. He was referred to me by George Levesky, of the Braddock Corporation. Buck told me that he was afraid it might be very difficult for a young girl all alone in a big city like Houston to find her way to the better life I know he wants you to have. So I'm being paid very well to take you by the hand and help you along until we get your feet firmly on the ground. And Mr. Rodgers was very specific about what he wanted."

"Did he say anything about me?"

Alicia Miles touched Jenny's hand in a reassuring manner. "He didn't give me any specifics about the exact relationship between you and him,

276

but it was more than obvious that you are someone who is very, very important to him. That's really all I know. I won't ask any questions about your relationship. It's my job to be your mentor, friend and companion until we get you on the fast track to success."

"I can't live without him," Jenny mournfully declared. "I don't care about being on the fast track to anything."

Giving Jenny an empathetic look, Alicia replied, "Honey, I've been through this before myself. I felt the same way. Once I got through the transition—and I'll tell you, it took two full years before I got there—things got much, much better. Now I look back on it, and I still have a few regrets, but I no longer agonize about it. When a relationship is over, you go through a grieving period, the same way you do when a loved one in the family dies. And then, eventually, you begin to heal. Things get better over time, and life begins anew. It's just the way we human beings are made. My own experiences have taught me that we're a lot more resilient than we think we are. Just give it some time—you'll see what I mean."

"What exactly are you supposed to do for me?"

"Mr. Rodgers gave me an agenda for today. We're to go to Covington and Associates to talk to Fred Covington about a large sum of money Mr. Rodgers left here with you. I think there's a deed to be signed, and other arrangements for your financial future to be made."

"I remember Buck saying somethin' about that in his letter."

"That's partly why he asked me to come see you. He was afraid you might not realize the importance of seeing Mr. Covington, and maybe you wouldn't do it. But I assure you, Jenny—we must do this. Doing the things that Mr. Rodgers has outlined for me to help you with will change your life in ways you never dreamed."

"I just want Buck back," Jenny said.

Alicia gave her a penetrating look. "Just trust me, Jenny. This is what Buck wants for you. I assume he's doing this because he loves you, or cares about you very much. This is a once-in-a-lifetime opportunity. If someone offered me a chance like this, a swampful of alligators and the Chinese Army couldn't stop me from following up on it." She laughed lightly at her own hyperbole. "And later today, we have to stop by the office of Bert Duffy— they call him 'Bulldog Duffy' around the courthouse 'cause he's so mean in court. Mr. Rodgers wants Mr. Duffy to represent you in a divorce from your estranged husband."

"Yes. Gettin' rid of Shooter would be a good thing, no matter what else I do, or don't do."

"Well, those two things alone are going to take up the whole day, so we'd better get started. I should tell you that once we get the foundation of your new life securely laid, we'll then start building the rest of the structure that will be your future. I'm going to help you do whatever you need to do to get into a college program, and we'll start you on a career path of your choice." She touched Jenny's knee in a confidential gesture. "Jenny, once we get these things taken care of, the world is yours to own. You can literally do anything in the world you want to do. You wouldn't have to work at all, but neither Mr. Rodgers nor I think that would be good for you. If we can get you into some gainful employment that you enjoy, you'll find that being engaged with constructive activity will be a protection against the dissipation and debauchery you see in so many of the idle rich. Mr. Rodgers doesn't want that for you, and you wouldn't want that for yourself."

"Do I have to get all dressed up for this?" Jenny asked.

"Oh, no. We're running late now. Just throw on a pair of blue jeans and a blouse, and we'll take care of this essential business. Later on, if you think you'd like to do it, I'll enroll you in the school of charm and etiquette that I attended, and they'll teach you how to do all the things you need to know to fit in with what they call 'polite society.' It's fun. But for now, let's get you dressed. Oh, and we don't want to forget that large sum of cash we have to take to Mr. Covington, and also" ...

The Church of the Living God was filled to capacity. Word had spread around town that Pastor Joe Lindsey was going to deliver a message from Reverend Braddock to the congregation, and everybody in attendance waited in eager anticipation. As was the custom, the church choir, accompanied by the faithful in attendance, sang a hymn to begin the services, and then Pastor Lindsey came to the pulpit. He smiled at the audience and began his opening statement:

"I'm glad that everybody could be here today. It seems to be an unusually large crowd on this particular occasion. I see some sinners who haven't been here in quite a while." He singled out one of the men in the audience. "Willie, where you been hidin'? It's been so long since I saw you, I was afraid you'd died."

The crowd laughed, and Willie shouted, "Well, since the football preseason started, I been home prayin' for the Dallas Cowboys!"

"Well, what about before the preseason started? Where were you then?"

"I was home prayin' for the Astros!"

Again the crowd was amused by the comment, and when the laughter died, Joe answered with a smile, "Well, I'm sure the Lord is proud of you for your conscientious devotion to prayer, Willie." He paused, and then his look turned serious. "I know why we have such an unusually large crowd today, and I won't prolong the agony by making you wait through a long sermon to find out what Reverend Braddock's message to our congregation is. I know we've all been concerned about him, and so I'll just go ahead and read the letter he sent to me. The letter begins, as follows:"

My dear Brothers and Sisters in Christ,

As of today, I am resigning my position as the Chief Pastor of the Church of the Living God. In my stead I am appointing Pastor Joe Lindsey to the position, subject to the final approval of the Church Board. I strongly recommend Joe to the position on a permanent basis, because I know him to be an honest, sincere man who loves the Lord and who loves the work he does in the service of God and his fellow man. He is a faithful husband and a devoted father to his children. As one who has served this congregation for the past twenty years, I cannot recommend Joe highly enough, and I hope the congregation will offer him your full support and assistance in order to make his transition to the position as easy as it can possibly be.

You may be thinking that this resignation was prompted by old age and sickness, but I want you to know that such is not the case. I am resigning because I no longer consider myself to be morally fit to be leading a congregation of God-fearing Christians. Recent events during my absence from the pulpit have convinced me that I never changed from being the same old sinner I was in my youth. The repentance I thought I had attained, the renunciation of sin I thought I had accomplished—it is clear to me now that none of that actually happened.

I realize now that by the time I started this church, I hadn't quit sin—sin had quit me. I had grown too old to chase the pretty girls, scuffle in the barrooms with the tough guys, and drink all night long with the boys. By the time I changed my evil ways, the girls didn't want me, most of the men could whip me, and the drinking made me so sick that I could hardly get out of bed the next day. That's not repenting of your sins. That's simply a matter of getting too old to sin any more.

Of course, I didn't know this at the time. I truly believed that I had repented of my former conduct and attained God's grace, and I set out to do good works as a way of atoning for my evil past. But as I say, recent events that I will not discuss here have proven to me that the man I was before I started this church never died. He's always been there, alive and well, trapped in a prison of aging flesh, and waiting—like the proverbial genie in the bottle—just waiting for a chance to escape. All I have to say further about this subject is that the genie escaped, and forced me to re-evaluate everything I thought I knew about myself and my relationship with Almighty God.

The ultimate result of these recent occurrences to which I refer is that I have learned I still have a long way to go in my quest for salvation—and, to that end, I begin my journey in that direction today. We all know that Jesus warned 'Judge not, lest ye be judged.' Usually we think of that as making condemnatory judgments against others. But a lot of people, especially religious people who ought to know better, tend to judge themselves righteous, without actually consulting God as to how He might feel about their gracious judgment of themselves. But God is no respecter of persons, and He most assuredly does not hold as high an opinion of any of us as we all tend to have of ourselves. Remember the admonition of Jesus at Matthew 7:22, 23: "Many will say to me in that day, 'Lord, Lord, did we not prophecy in your name, and expel demons in your name, and perform many powerful works in your name?' And yet then I will confess to them: I never knew you! Get away from me, you workers of iniquity." *I truly have tried to do good works, brothers and sisters. But I truly do not believe that I am the man God would have me be, if I ever hope to attain the gift of everlasting life.*

And so I go. God is waiting for me to do what I thought I had done twenty years ago. I hope you'll pray for me in my quest. But I go, secure in the knowledge that I leave the congregation in capable hands, and I hope you will continue to assemble together for fellowship in the Lord, all the more, as you behold the day drawing near. And again I ask that you offer your full support to my friend Joe Lindsey. He will be a good shepherd to the flock for the Lord Jesus Christ. I have enjoyed the time I spent with you, and I hope you will remember me kindly, in spite of the error of my ways.

May God bless and keep you every one—

Billy Braddock

Setting the letter down on the pulpit, Joe Lindsey looked at the congregation. "You now know everything I know about Reverend Braddock's reasons for resigning. Brother Braddock left no further information as to why he was taking this action at this time. From what I got out of this letter, he apparently seems to believe that he has somehow fallen short in the eyes of God, but I could only guess what might have caused him to draw this conclusion. I will pray for him, and I hope you will also pray for him...that God may send His Holy Spirit to alleviate whatever inner torment and doubt Brother Braddock may be experiencing. For now, we will discuss this matter no further, although I will return to the subject very briefly at the end of our regular Sunday service. And without further preliminaries, we will begin our regular service. Today's topic for our sermon is: *Learning to Forgive, That We Might Be Forgiven*" ...

High in the Colorado Rockies, an elderly couple was fishing in a crystal-blue lake on a glorious mountain morning. Their legs dangled off the edge of a pier that was situated near a boathouse that served the tiny valley resort nearby. A young couple came walking down the dirt road that led to the pier and approached the older man and woman.

As they drew near, the young man said, "Good mornin', folks! Are the fish bitin' today?"

"Not so's you'd notice," the elderly man on the pier replied. "I've caught one fish in about an hour. 'Course, I'm just doin' this to be doin' somethin'. If you're really wantin' t' catch some fish, I believe you'd do better if you'd follow the road around the bend there. There's dozens of shallow streams over there, and I know there's fish in 'em, 'cause you can look downstream and actually see 'em. All you need to do is kinda drop your fly out a ways ahead of you so the fish can't see you, and you're just about bound to catch somethin'. Around the streams, the bugs are out, and the fish are jumpin' out o' the water to catch 'em. Here in the lake, around the pier...I don't know...we're not doin' much good. But, then again, we're just doin' this to be doin' somethin', anyway."

The young man looked in the direction the elderly fisherman had indicated. "Around the bend. We'll try that. Thanks for the advice." He held out a handshake. "I'm Les Thornton. This is my fiancée, Renee Davis. This is our first trip up here."

The old man extended a big paw. "I'm Billy. This here's my wife, Maggie."

"We're on our honeymoon," Maggie said. "Just got married two days ago. I've known Billy since the first grade, and he finally got around to marryin' me."

"Oh, that's wonderful!" Renee exclaimed.

"Congratulations," Les said at almost the same time.

"Thank you," Maggie answered with a gracious smile. "It's been a long time comin'."

"Yeah, we went out to Vegas to do a little gamblin' and she caught me in a moment of weakness."

"Billy, don't say that!" Maggie said, gently slapping his thigh.

Billy ran on. "Yeah, she'd lost all 'er money in the slot machine, and I started feelin' sorry for her, tried to comfort her, and the next thing you know— BINGO! I was roped, throwed, hog-tied and branded before I knew what hit me. I tell you, son—you better stay outta that town, if you know what's good for you. It's an evil, evil place. A man goes there single, with money in 'is pocket, and wakes up one morning, married and broke. Keep that in mind if you ever head out that way."

Laughing, Maggie gave him an affectionate shove. "Don't be tellin' them that. They might believe you."

"It's the truth," Billy said, looking at the young couple with a wry grin. "It happened to me, just like that."

Les and Renee laughed at the interplay between the newlyweds, and Les asked, "Are you folks gonna be up here for a few days?"

"Oh, prob'ly another week or so," Billy answered.

"Well, why don't we get together one evening this week and have a fish-fry together? I've got a fancy propane cooker, and I bought all the fixin's over at the general store. The only thing I haven't got is the fish."

Billy smiled. "It's mighty nice of you to ask. Let's just do that. Are you folks stayin' in the cabins over there?"

"Yeah," Les said. "We're in number twelve."

"We're right across the courtyard in number twenty-two. Let's plan on it."

"Sounds good. I'll get back with you, as soon as I land a few fish. It's my first time to try my hand at fly fishin', in addition to bein' my first time up here in the Rockies."

"Well, you folks try those streams around the bend. If you don't do any good on your own today, I'll meet you in the mornin' and show you some of the tricks of the trade."

"We'd sure appreciate that," Les said. "And thanks for the tip."

The couples exchanged their goodbyes, and Les and Renee continued their trek down the road toward the streams Billy had pointed out. Once they were out of earshot, Renee said, "Weren't they the most precious couple in the world? Did you see how she put her arm around him, right after we walked away? That was so sweet. You could tell they were really in love."

"Yeah, they seemed really happy together," Les agreed.

"Do you think when we're that old, we'll still have fun together and love each other like that?"

Les shook his head uncertainly. "Oh...I don't know. When you're that age, you'll prob'ly be too ugly for me."

Renee slapped him on the shoulder. "Oh, you mean thing! You're the one who's gonna be too ugly"
...

The world premiere of *Bronco Man*, the first-ever theatrical release by DocuTex Films, was held in Braddock, Texas, in front of a packed house who had come to the Ritz Theater to see a movie about Braddock's most prominent native son. As the film wound to its conclusion, a video montage showed Billy Braddock at various times and places in his life. He was shown as a young man riding Brahma bulls, and as an old man serving food at a soup kitchen. In a few compressed seconds the scope of his life as an athlete, party boy, businessman, and preacher appeared on the screen. As the final seconds played out, the voice of Steve Jackson could be heard over the final fading images:

> *"In the wake of the media frenzy surrounding his purported disappearance, Billy Braddock resigned his ministry and*

retired from an active role in running the Braddock business empire. Today he lives quietly in an undisclosed location, far away from public scrutiny—just the way he always wanted."

As the credits rolled, the audience rose as one and gave the film, and the men who had made it, a standing ovation. A few minutes later, outside the theater, a group of reporters waited to interview the filmmakers. Artie Davis was the first to step out on the red carpet and face the waiting journalists. In the glare of floodlights, an interviewer asked, "Artie, now that your first full-length film has officially been released, how did you gauge the audience reaction?"

"Well, I heard people laughing out loud in parts where it was intended to be funny. I noticed people crying in places where I thought it was sad. They listened with rapt attention where we intended the film to be serious and substantive. My best estimate is that they were totally caught up in the story. I've seen big-budget movies that didn't engage an audience the way this film did. My personal feeling is that this movie is going to do remarkably well, both nationally and globally. It's just a helluva story, any way you look at it."

"Thank you, Artie, and—oh, wait! Here's Steve Jackson, who did a lot of the field reporting and also added the voice-over narrative to the film! Steve! Steve! Could we talk to you for just a moment?"

Blinking in the glare of the lights, Steve said, "How ya doin'?"

"Steve, can you give us any insights as to how you felt about the audience reaction tonight?"

"It was fantastic," Jackson said. "More than I could ever have hoped for."

"How about the man who was the subject of the movie? After all the interviews you did, what was your take on Billy Braddock?"

"Let me say first of all, without a larger-than-life character like Billy Braddock, we wouldn't even have had a movie—he's the key to the whole thing. I mean, here's a guy who's been everything from a fornicator to a philanthropist, a saint to a sinner...you know—just about everything, both good and bad. In his youth, he was known for his ability to hurt people physically. But in his old age, he was known for his dedication to trying to heal people spiritually."

"Do you feel this film captures the essence of the real Billy Braddock?"

Steve shook his head doubtfully. "I don't know, really. We learned a lot about him through the course of all the interviews we did, and I think everybody who saw this film tonight will agree that he was a man of extremes. But somewhere between all the extremes in his life lies the real man. And I'll be honest with you: For all I know about Billy Braddock, I still can't say I actually know who the man himself really is. But then again...I don't know...does anybody really know who anybody is? I can't say. I guess people out there who wanta know the real Billy Braddock just have to come see the movie and judge for themselves."

"Well, thank you, Steve. And before Mayor Rusty Stubbs presents you fellows with the Key to the City, let me just ask you" ...

Finally, two hours later, when the crowd had dispersed, all the autographs had been signed, and the hubbub had died down, Artie, Steve and Bobby stood talking to Police Chief John Wilkins and Mayor Rusty Stubbs beneath the theater marquee. Stubbs was saying, "I just wanta thank you for all the publicity you've brought to our little town here. We don't get a lotta strangers here, unless they're here to do some business with Braddock Oil, or something over at the Medical Research Center. But this might change things a lot. We might even get us a little bit of a tourist industry goin' out here in the middle of the desert. Lord knows we could use the extra tax revenues."

"Well, Mayor, if our little film ends up helpin' along those lines, we'll be really glad it worked out like that," Artie said.

The police chief looked at Steve and Bobby, "You know, boys, the first day I met you out in front o' the church, I didn't think you'd ever amount to a hill o' beans. You looked like a coupla bums to me. But this is one time in my life I'm glad to be wrong. I just want all of you guys to know I'm real happy for you. You made a hell of a movie."

"Well, thanks, Chief," Steve said.

"So what do you boys have next on your agenda?" Mayor Stubbs asked.

"I don't know," Artie said. "There's a lot of options open to us now, because of this movie. I feel, in my heart of hearts, this film you just saw is going to succeed beyond our wildest expectations. If I can keep this staff and crew together, we can take the money we make from this film and use it to turn the spotlight on another likely subject...I don't know—next time out, we might come up with a full-blown blockbuster."

"Yeah, *blockbuster!*" Bobby yelled, giving Steve a high-five handshake.

"*Blockbuster! Blockbuster!*" Steve and Artie chimed in, and the three men exchanged high-fives all around.

Once their impromptu celebration was over, Artie looked at the mayor and the police chief apologetically. "Sorry 'bout that, fellas. We're just a little hyped-up tonight. It's been a big night for us."

"*They're* hyped-up. I'm *souped* up!" Bobby grinned, waving a whisky bottle.

"Oh, hey...we understand," Stubbs said. "I'd be the same way if I'd done what you guys have done."

"Well, I guess we'll be goin' on," Artie said. "I just want to express our appreciation for all the hospitality you folks have shown us."

"Anytime," Stubbs said. "Anytime."

They exchanged their farewells, and the three filmmakers walked away down Main Street. Bemused, the mayor and the police chief quietly observed their departure until the men turned the corner at the end of the block and disappeared into the night.

The sudden silence all around them seemed profound in the still desert night. Stubbs said, "Well, John...I guess that's all the excitement for awhile."

Wilkins nodded. "I guess it is. Sure was fun while it lasted, though, wasn't it?"

"Yeah, it was," the mayor agreed. "Makes it harder to go back to the same old grind."

The two men started walking toward their cars, and Wilkins said, "So I guess I'll see you tomorrow."

"Oh, yeah, for sure. Meet me at City Hall bright and early."

"Bright and early? Any particular reason?" Wilkins asked.

"Yeah. I've figured out a way to get those pay raises for me and the City Council without havin' to increase property taxes."

Wilkins gave him a look of mild disbelief. "*Another* raise for you and the council?"

"Hey, we deserve it. We do a fantastic job for this town."

"No shit?" Wilkins said with a sarcastic grin.

"Don't crack wise, John."

"I guess I'm gonna have to buy me a microscope so I can see all that fantastic shit you guys do," the Chief replied.

"Very funny," the Mayor said, with a frown.

"So how do you plan to conjure up this magic wage increase without having to increase the property tax?"

"I'll fill you in on the details tomorrow, but here's the general idea: If we were to increase the fines and quotas on traffic tickets and court costs and cut back on the amount of money we're spendin' on non-essential services—things like parks maintenance, new books for the public library, social services for the poor" ...

"Are you shittin' me?" Wilkins said with a look of angry disbelief. "Do you know what Billy Braddock would do to you if he was still in town, and you came up with some bullshit plan like that?"

The mayor gave a shrug. "Yeah, well...that's just it, John—Billy ain't here no more. I'm runnin' the show now. You gotta get used to that idea, my friend. Things are gonna be different around here, now that Billy Braddock's gone" ...

-THE END-